TAILGATES & FIRST DATES

LOCALS #3

HALEY RHOADES

This is a work of fiction. Names, characters, businesses, places, events, and incidents are either the products of the author's imagination or used in a fictitious manner. Any resemblance to actual persons, living or dead, or actual events is purely coincidental.

Any trademarks, service marks, product names, or named features are assumed to be the property of their respective owners and are used only for reference. There is no implied endorsement.

Tailgates & First Dates, The Locals #3
Copyright © 2019 Haley Rhoades
All rights reserved.

Cover Design by Germancreative on Fiverr

eBook ISBN: 978-1-959199-02-1
Paperback ISBN-13: 978-0-9989590-7-8

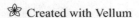 Created with Vellum

ENHANCE YOUR READING

To Enhance Your Reading of Tailgates & First Dates
read the Trivia Page near the end of the book
prior to opening chapter #1.

No Spoilers-I promise

Check out my Pinterest Boards
for insights into
The Locals Series & characters.

DEDICATION

To all my high school classmates that remain in our hometown. Years and parenthood led me to see what you always knew.

CHAPTER 1

Hamilton

I glance at my phone one more time—she texted again.

Madison: I want to be a fly on the wall of bullpen 2nite
Madison: World Series (Baseball emoji)
Madison: Have fun! (heart emoji) u

I glance around the locker room to ensure no one's watching. I don't want the guys to have fodder for teasing.

Me: wish u were here

Me: (heart emoji) u

I'm beginning to worry. If I'm this nervous for game one, how nervous will I be when I am the starter in games four and seven? I turn my cell phone off then tuck it into my suit jacket in my locker. I kiss my index finger and press it to my favorite picture of Madison. In profile, she's looking at me and laughing on the tailgate of my truck near the start of our senior year.

I miss her laughter, and I miss her attending all of my games. I miss her.

"Time to go," Stan yells through the locker room. "That means you, too." He swats my ass with his ball glove.

Side-by-side we walk, the last two to leave the locker room. "You ready for this?" I ask the centerfielder.

"Waited for this my whole life." Stan states the obvious.

I wish my dad were here. I scan the crowd, noticing many fathers with sons in the stands. There's an empty seat somewhere that my dad should be sitting in. I wish he were alive to see me pitch in the World Series. I like to think he's on my shoulder. I miss our long talks—I could use his advice. In my heart, I know what he'd tell me, "First the World Series, then focus on making Madison mine."

Madison

It's really happening–tonight the Chicago Cubs play the New York Yankees in the first game of the World Series. Alma and I plan to order pizza again—we must keep our post-season tradition alive. In the afternoon, I take Liberty and McGee to the park for a couple hours in hopes of wearing them out.

Hamilton will pitch in the fourth and possibly seventh games in the series. My stomach flip-flops every time I remember that Memphis and I have tickets to game four in Chicago. Last night, Alma's daughter, Taylor, called to brag that they have tickets to games three and four. I wish we could find a ticket for Alma, but I'm glad she'll care for Liberty while I attend the game.

As if I'm not nervous enough, my phone buzzes non-stop for an hour. My high school friend in Athens is first.

Adrian: I'm so nervous
Adrian: I can't sit still
Adrian: I've cleaned entire house
Adrian: Y isn't Ham pitching tonight?
Me: He's slated for game 4
Adrian: bummer (sad emoji)
Adrian: I'll still watch

Next, I hear from Alma's oldest daughter, the heart surgeon in Chicago.

Taylor: hosting 6 couples
Taylor: for 2night's game
Taylor: can't wait for game 3&4
Taylor: Wrigley will be rockin'
Me: 6 couples?
Me: you're crazy (sticking tongue out emoji)
Taylor: potluck
Taylor: easy Peasy
Me: r u off tomorrow?
Taylor: no, I can't be off the day after all 7 games
Taylor: my elective surgeries rescheduled
Taylor: Cubs fans, lol
Me: that's good
Me: lighter week then?
Taylor: Yes!
Taylor: gtg
Me: Go Cubs! (fingers crossed & baseball emoji)

Two other friends in Athens, Bethany and Salem, text that they are watching tonight's game at Winston and Adrian's house. The last texts are from my only single friend in Athens.

Savannah: watching game @ Adrian's
Savannah: may not last long
Savannah: can't be myself
Savannah: with little ones nearby
Savannah: will go home yell & cuss
Savannah: hard to censor myself
Me: I understand
Me: I yell @ the TV
Me: Good Luck! (4 leaf clover emoji)

With each new text conversation, my nerves grow exponentially. I turn the volume up on the TV as the pregame show begins. Alma bakes cookies in the kitchen, claiming it helps calm her nerves.

"Liberty," I call toward my daughter as she plays with blocks on the carpet. "Let's go help Alma in the kitchen."

She wastes no time standing to follow me into the kitchen. I scoop her up and buckle her safely in her highchair near the table. With one pan already in the oven, the kitchen smells divine. Nothing compares to the smell of fresh baked chocolate chip cookies.

"Wow!" I stare at the large mixing bowl of dough resting on the counter near Alma. "That's not one batch is it?"

"It's three batches," Alma admits. "I needed to fill two hours until game time." She shrugs as she places balls of dough on two more cookie sheets.

I chuckle. "That should keep you busy until game time." I

open the refrigerator door, scanning for a snack. "When should I order dinner?"

When Alma shrugs again, I decide to go ahead and order the pizza on my phone, "All done. You keep on baking. The pizza will be here in an hour."

CHAPTER 2

Madison

"Want anything from the kitchen?" Alma asks with our empty paper plates in her hands.

"I could go for some of your cookies."

Liberty toddles behind Alma and McGee brings up the rear as the group enters the kitchen. During the commercial break, I quickly make a trip to the restroom. While I wash my hands, my cellphone vibrates.

Savannah: I'm headed home
Savannah: Too much talking
Savannah: distracting
Me: 3 innings
Me: shocked you lasted that long

Savannah: need to yell
Savannah: someone's gotta score soon
Me: Cheer loud!
Savannah: I will

I tuck my phone in my back pocket on my way to help in the kitchen.

"Let's go," Alma instructs her two little shadows.

"Need me to carry the cookies?" I offer.

"I've got it, if you help Liberty carry her treats."

I look at my daughter's hands. One clasps her cup, the other tightly grips a bone for McGee. He walks beside her with a careful eye on the treat she carries. I love his patience with her—they truly are best friends.

We settle back into our seats for the fourth inning. The Cubs score two and the Yankees score one. Liberty finally falls asleep during the fifth inning, so I carry her to bed during a commercial break. In the bottom of the sixth, the Yankees tie it up. By the top of the seventh, I'm pacing and turn the volume up as Alma heads to the kitchen to bake the final batch of cookies. *If I'm this nervous now, how bad will I be when Hamilton pitches?*

On my path back towards the TV from the front door, I glance towards the kitchen. My stomach plummets as I watch in slow motion as Alma's feet slip out from under her. I cringe when the hard bump sounds as her head makes contact with the table before she lands on the tile floor and a loud groan escapes her mouth.

I wake from my trance, darting to her side, silently praying she'll be okay. McGee licks her flushed cheeks; I shoo him away. My role model suddenly looks old and frail on the floor. "Don't move!" I order as I roll up a kitchen towel and place it under her head. She groans weakly again as her hand clutches her right hip.

"I...can't...move," she stutters between labored breaths.

"Then don't try to move." I assume my motherly tone. My insides quiver with fear for my friend; my future hangs in the balance. I muster all the strength I can to help her through this. "You hit your head, too." I gently walk my fingertips down the back of her head until she winces. I glance down at my fingers. They're wet with fresh blood, so I am quick to pull them out of Alma's line of sight. Rising, I inform her, "I'm calling an ambulance. Don't move." I rinse my hands before returning to her side.

"9-1-1 what is your emergency?" the calm, male dispatcher greets.

"My friend fell...she bumped...bleeding." The words stream much too fast from my aching throat. "her head and is bleeding...I think she hurt her hip."

"What is your address?"

I rattle off our address and Alma's name and age and am informed an ambulance is en route. The calm, male voice instructs me to assist Alma in holding a cloth to her head wound. Moments pass as if they are hours. My heart races, and my hands tremble. He remains on the line with me even when I hear the sirens and get up to unlock the front door.

When the ambulance pulls up, I greet the EMTs on the front lawn.

I lead the way back inside as the EMTs follow with duffels on their shoulders. Nervously, I watch as they assess her vitals, press on her hip, then peek at the head wound.

"We'll need to transport her to the hospital," the older EMT states while rising to stand beside me. "She needs stitches and an X-Ray of that hip."

I nod. It's all I can do. My sinuses burn as tears threaten. I can't let them fall—if they start, I'll never get them to stop.

"You're welcome to ride with us…"

"My daughter is upstairs." I frantically look from Alma to the front room and back. I pat Alma's forearm. "Liberty and I will follow the ambulance to the hospital."

Mid-groan, Alma nods.

"This should help with the pain." I watch as the EMT injects pain meds into her IV.

One first responder stays with Alma while the other fetches the gurney. I decide to quickly gather Liberty and our bag so I'm ready to leave when they do.

I throw a few items into the diaper bag from the nursery before I lift Liberty into my arms. Back downstairs, I drop the bag at the landing before grabbing both my purse Alma's on the way into the kitchen. Alma's eyes are heavy with sedation as the two guys, now joined by a female and another male, maneuver her onto the stretcher, strap her in, then raise it up with guard rails secured.

"I'm Hale," the female states. "Can I help you to your vehicle? You have your hands full." She gestures to Liberty and my bags, but her pleasant smile does little to calm my racing thoughts. "Let me carry…"

I decide to entrust our purses rather than Liberty to her care. The weight of my daughter keeps me from spiraling out of control. *I can do this. Alma needs me to keep it together.* In the living room, I ask her to grab the diaper bag before I lock and pull the door shut behind us. Outside, neighbors gather on the sidewalk in front of the house.

I use the key fob to unlock Alma's minivan. As Hale places our bags in the passenger seat, I approach our next-door neighbor, Mr. Edwards. "Alma fell. It might be her hip. Would you be able to let McGee out before bedtime if you don't hear back from me?"

Just as I knew he would, he tells me not to worry. He will dog-sit until he hears from me tonight or tomorrow. He's done this before, and Alma trusts to leave her spare key with him. I thank him and head for the minivan as the ambulance doors close on Alma.

The ride to the hospital seems to take forever. I whisper cuss words as the ambulance barrels through a red light, and I must stop. I sit idly as only one car moves through the cross street and the light remains red. *C'mon. C'mon.* My stomach somersaults as I accelerate at the green light. I attempt to wrangle my thoughts from Alma to the road and cars around me. At the next intersection, I zoom through on yellow, not wanting to wait for another red light.

I worry for my friend. *This is exactly why her children wanted someone to live with her. Her children! Crap!* I instruct hands free to dial Taylor, but Alma's daughter does not answer her cell phone.

"Taylor," I barely recognize my quivering voice. Clearing my throat, I try again. "Alma fell. I called an ambulance. We are on the way to the hospital. I'm going to call Trenton next. If you don't hear from him, call me when you get this message."

"Call Trenton." I order. I'm anything but patient as the car speakers echo the ringing of his phone.

"Hello," his deep voice answers.

"Trenton, Alma fell. I'm following the ambulance to the hospital. She needs stitches on the back of her head, and they need to x-ray her hip." I gulp in a breath as I turn into the hospital behind the ambulance. *Crap! I can't park in the ambulance bay.* I frantically search for a nearby parking lot.

"Madison, is she okay?" Anguish is heavy in his words.

What kind of question is that? I just told him I called an ambulance. No! She is not okay!

"I mean, do you need me to book a flight? I can be there in…three hours."

"She was in a lot of pain. They gave her meds and it seemed to help. She didn't talk much, but her eyes seem to understand." I try to calm his fears while mine run out of control. *Alma means everything to me. She has to be okay.*

"I'm at the hospital now." I slide the two purses into my backpack that doubles as a diaper bag. "I left a message for Taylor. Can you call your sisters and fill them in for me? I'll be in touch as soon as I know anything."

I sense Trenton's hesitation. Since his father's death two

years ago, he's tried to step up for Alma. I'm sure he wants to be here. "Text or call with any details. No matter how small they might be. I'll call Taylor and Cameron, then I will pull up flight information in case I need to hop a plane tonight."

I open Liberty's door. Having already pulled the stroller from the back, I quickly pop it up and lock the wheels. Liberty barely stirs when I move her from the car seat to recline in the stroller. I drape a blanket from the sunshade to prevent the interior lights from disturbing her.

I almost forget to lock the van on my way to the Emergency Department entrance. The automatic doors of the hospital swoosh open, and I enter a bustling waiting area.

Careful not to roll over any toes, I slowly maneuver the stroller to the reception desk.

At my turn, I state I followed an ambulance in with Alma for stitches and possible hip injury. The staff member taps a few keys on her keyboard before excusing herself to the back hallway.

Do I stay here? Should I take a seat? I'm not sure if she's done with me. I look around the waiting area as if someone there knows what I should do. The sound of a door buzzing then unlocking startles me.

"Come on back," the staff member instructs. "She's in the second bay on the left." I follow the direction her arm points and thank her.

Alma lays in a hospital bed, her eyes closed when I peek through the drawn curtain. Her skin has a grey hue instead of the normal pinkness. Monitors beep as wires and tubes attached to her body to machines on both sides of her bed.

She looks posed instead of comfortable. Her arms are too perfectly placed at her sides, on the blanket that covers her lower body.

"Alma, I'm right here." I pat her forearm to ensure she can feel me beside her, and her eyes open a sliver. "Hey. How you feelin'?"

Alma opens her mouth. Only a moan escapes as her eyes search the room, struggling to find me.

"It's okay," I sooth. "Don't talk. Just rest. Liberty and I will be right here if you need anything."

The sharp scrape of the metal curtain hooks on the rod slice the silence as a nurse quickly moves to Alma's bedside.

"I'm Madison," I greet anxiously. "How is she?"

"Are you her relative?" The nurse doesn't pause her deliberate actions to look my direction.

I open my mouth to explain my relationship and quickly realize if I'm not family, I might be asked to leave. "I'm her daughter."

"The doctor hasn't been in yet. I'm hanging fluids and pain medications for her IV." She glances to me with a warm smile.

Good. She's not the Nurse Ratched type.

"Doc will be in here next. We'll know more then." As quickly as she came, she exits.

I slide my backpack into an empty chair just as my cell phone vibrates in my back pocket. It's an ESPN alert. The Cubs won four to three in nine innings. *Good thing Hamilton wasn't on the mound tonight.* I forgot all about the baseball game. Wanting something to do to fill the minutes while I wait, I shoot a text to him.

Me: Congrats on the win!
Me: Alma fell, we're at hospital
Me: stitches & hip x-ray, will keep you posted

I slide my phone back into my pocket as four people in scrubs step into Alma's area. The man in the white coat scrolls through screens on his tablet while barking directions to the others. One holds a stethoscope to Alma's chest while another prepares a blood pressure cuff at Alma's arm. The third person quickly jots down results on a paper chart.

My head spins with directions, numbers, and terms that I don't understand as they fly around me. I peek into the stroller; Liberty sleeps as if she's home in her own crib. I wish I were as oblivious to the situation as she is.

Two of the nurses assist in propping pillows behind Alma's shoulders. Her pain meds seem to have kicked in; she doesn't react to any movements. They tilt her head to expose her cut to the doctor. I watch as another nurse injects the numbing agent along the cut then as stitch after stitch closes her wound.

Pleased with his work, the doctor exits the room to assist the next patient. "The nurses will assist you from here," he throws over his shoulder as he walks away.

"We've stopped the bleeding," the male nurse addresses

me. "We're taking her down to x-ray. She'll probably be gone an hour or more." He nods as the other nurses wheel Alma's bed from the area. "You're welcome to stay here or out in the waiting room. Get yourself something to eat, relax, and we will bring her back as soon as she's done. If you're not here, we will look for you in the waiting room."

I smile and nod. I have no intention of leaving Alma's area. Trenton, Taylor and Cameron are counting on me. I need to update her kids—I send a group text.

Me: Alma in x-ray
Me: I'll text when hear anything
Taylor: Thank you
Taylor: Thank God you were there
Trenton: Thanks for update
Trenton: I can catch a 10:30 or 11:45 flight
Trenton: Just say the word
Cameron: Trenton, mom's okay, chill
Me: I'll text soon

I note the time is just after nine before returning my phone to my pocket and scanning my surroundings. I pull my phone out again. I need to write; I need to record my feelings. In my Notes app, I attempt to record everything I feel in this moment. My fingers fly across the keyboard of their own accord.

Lost, alone, afraid, deserted, vacant, void, childlike, unworthy, left behind yet again, destined to be alone, in a cave, a hole, as deep dark chasm, deserted island, dark, scared, weak, at war, abandoned, failure, falling, in limbo, I want to hit something, I want to scream at the top of my lungs, I want to yell "Why me?", needy, sad, devoid, bankrupt, helpless...

Unaware an hour passes, I'm still lost in my thoughts and app when Alma is returned.

"How'd she do?" My voice is weak, foreign to me.

As the two nurses scurry to return Alma's bed and IV, one shares. "She's sedated. Results should be available soon." And with that, they are gone.

The curtains form a modicum of privacy as I approach her bedside. "Alma?" I try to wake her, but she doesn't stir. I worry. *Should she be so out of it? Is she really in so much pain that they must knock her out?* "Liberty and I are still here. I've texted your kids. They're worried." I sigh deeply. *Is she hearing any of this?*

Dr. Anderson enters, startling me.

"How's she doing?" His voice cuts through the tension.

Confused, I look his way. *Why is my Ob/Gyn here?*

"How are you holding up?" He looks around the room, assessing Alma's status. "I overheard at the nurses' station that one of our own is here. There are still several of us teaching that worked with her husband for years."

"She hasn't really said much since the fall," I state,

hoping he will ease my worries. "Should she be able to carry on a conversation while on the pain meds?"

Dr. Anderson looks from me to Alma. He rubs her forearm then pats it a few times. Seeing no reaction from her, he moves closer to her head. "Alma?" He pauses. "Alma, can you hear me?"

"I know she's in pain, but why did they knock her all the way out?" I ask, voicing my concern to him.

"Everyone reacts to medications differently," he explains. "I'll check on the dosage."

I realize he hopes to make me feel better, but it does little to rest my concerns—I fear something is not right.

"How about you," he glances to the stroller. "or Liberty? Do you need something to drink or a snack from the cafeteria, a vending machine?"

I simply shake my head. My stomach roils at the thought of food.

"I'll be back in a bit." Dr. Anderson smiles, pats my shoulder, then disappears beyond the curtain.

I look to my phone again, hoping to pass the time faster. Unfortunately, 45 minutes pass, seeming like hours. The sound of the curtain opening rescues me. Two nurses move around Alma, taking vitals and making notations.

"She'll need surgery," a nurse states without looking my way. "We'll be admitting Alma, and surgery is scheduled for 11 tomorrow." Now they both sympathetically look my way. "You're welcome to stay until we settle her into her room."

I nod. I'll definitely stay.

"Visiting hours are over, but we will sneak you up with us for a few minutes." The male nurse raises his chin towards the stroller. "Your little one must be able to sleep through anything."

"Alma and I wore her out at the park today, so she'd sleep through most of the ballgame tonight." I shrug as sadness rushes over me. *Our plans for a World Series game one party completely failed tonight. Looks like I'll be watching the game alone tomorrow night.*

"Who do you root for?"

"I have a friend that plays for the Cubs." *A friend. Friend? Hamilton is still my friend. He can be more and still be my friend, right?*

"Armstrong," he states. Surprised, I nod, and he continues. "I played against him for two summers."

"What team?" I ask, repositioning myself in the uncomfortable chair. "I attended all of his games."

He played for the Moberly American Legion team. We discuss two memorable games between Athens and Moberly at Districts before he excuses himself.

Helplessly, I follow behind as they transport her upstairs. Thirty minutes later, Alma is situated in her private hospital room for the night. I say goodnight and push Liberty back towards the elevator. My feet feel heavy as I approach the van. I move Liberty carefully and fasten her safely into her car seat. Once buckled in my own seat, I connect my phone to Bluetooth and call Alma's kids.

Trenton answers first. We wait a moment for the girls to join the call.

"Alma's tucked into room 408 for the night. Hip surgery is scheduled for 11 tomorrow."

Trenton interrupts me. "Did Mom ever gain consciousness?"

"No. Dr. Anderson checked her dosages, but he didn't seem worried. He claims they are ensuring she is comfortable." I try to sound like I believe this explanation.

"I'm booking my flight now," Trenton states. "With the drive, I'll arrive about 10."

Taylor rattles off flight times. She talks out loud as she works through the timelines. "I'm flying into St. Louis. I land at 7:15."

Trenton jumps in. "I land about the same time. We can meet at baggage claim and share a rental."

I focus on the drive home through the dark, desolate Columbia streets.

"Cameron," Taylor calls to her baby sister over the phone lines. "What do your flight options look like?"

"I've got something I need to work out before I can book a flight."

Trenton and Taylor urge Cameron to book a flight and just call in to work tomorrow. Clearly, they don't understand her hesitation.

"I'm home," I butt in, ready to end this call. "I've got to get Liberty inside and let McGee out." I don't hide my exasperated sigh. "I'll talk to you in the morning."

CHAPTER 3

Hamilton

Madison: Alma has hip surgery
Madison: tomorrow at 11
Me: how are you holding up?

I dial her phone before she can respond.

"Hello." Her voice sounds so small.

"Are you home?" I ask in almost a whisper. I know she'll hear me as I speak into the mic and wear my earphones.

"Yes," she yawns. "I've been home about 30 minutes. How about you?"

"I'm on the bus back to the hotel," I explain in a hushed voice. I try not to draw the attention of the entire team.

"I'm good," Madison lies.

"Um, Madison, it's me. You don't have to appear to have it all together. Tell me the truth." I already know the truth.

"I'm scared. What if something happens during the surgery? She's acting weird on the pain meds. Things go wrong in surgery all the time, and with her age, there's more of a risk." She sucks in a shuddering breath. "What if she's not strong enough to walk after the surgery? What if she can't come back home? She looks so frail lying in the hospital bed."

"How is she acting weird?" I ask concerned.

"Since the fall, she hasn't spoken a single word," Madison releases a frustrated sigh. "She groans in pain, but she hasn't spoken. They keep her so high on pain meds, she's out of it. Her eyes search the room and never focus on any one thing." Madison pulls in a deep breath. "I worry it's her head injury. I mean, she should say something or mumble. She doesn't even try to speak."

"You want them to give her enough meds to keep her out of pain, right? Ask her kids. Maybe she reacts this way to strong pain meds. It's natural to worry. She's important to you. I know you can't just turn it off. Remember, the doctors and staff see this all the time. They know what to look for, and they are taking good care of Alma. You need to make sure you are strong for her. You need to be sure to eat, stay hydrated, and get enough sleep so you can help her on the other side of her surgery. She'll lean on you more for a while. You know?" I try to be the voice of reason when Madison's anxiety and fears threaten to engulf her.

"Yeah," she agrees.

"Yeah?" I chuckle. "Is that a 'Yes, I understand and will take care of myself'. Or is that a 'Yeah, I'm done talking on this subject'?"

"You're right. I'll focus on what needs to be done and have faith it will all be okay," she murmurs.

"We're at the hotel. I should let you go." I rise from my seat, grabbing my bag.

I want to talk to her for hours, but I have big things going on this week.

"Okay. Good luck tomorrow night. I assume I will watch the game with Alma in her hospital room," Madison sighs.

"I love you, Madison," I state.

Loud hoots and cat calls surround me. The teammates standing near me holler, "We love you, Madison!"

"So much for a private conversation." I laugh.

She giggles. "I love you, too," she states before we disconnect.

CHAPTER 4

Madison

I drop Liberty off at the Mom's Day Out program at the church at 8:30 on my way to the hospital. Oblivious to Alma's issues, Liberty quickly joins her little friends playing on the carpet of her classroom. I'm glad she hasn't picked up on my stress. She deserves to play without a care in the world.

When I walk into Alma's private room later, Dr. Anderson sits at her bedside. For a moment, I wonder how he knew to be here. My brain quickly assumes since he's on staff and formerly worked here with Alma's husband, he has many ways to know when a friend is admitted for surgery.

"Good morning," he greets, rising to offer me the chair.

"Hi. Has she spoken to you this morning?" I cringe at the sound of fear in my voice.

"No. They're keeping her sedated to avoid pain. Did you contact the kids?" Again, he gestures for me to take the seat he vacated.

"Yeah. I called them last night." I sit, pulling my knees toward my chest and wrapping my arms around them. "They should all arrive before her surgery." I squeeze Alma's hand in mine. *Is it my imagination? Did she just squeeze my hand back?* I repeat the gesture. This time I feel nothing.

"I've got rounds, but I will back before her surgery. Do you need anything?" Dr. Anderson places his large hand on my shoulder, drawing my attention from Alma toward him.

"No. I'm good. Thanks."

Alone with Alma, I rub her forearm while I speak to her. "I'm here. Liberty is at church, but she'll be here when you get back from surgery. I hope you can hear me. I want you to be strong. I need you to fight. Hip surgery can't keep the Alma I know down," I bite my lower lip, hoping she can hear me. "Liberty and I need you. Remember that and don't doubt how much we love you."

I wipe the tears from my cheeks before grasping her hand again. The rhythmic sound of the beeping heart monitor lulls me into a trance.

"Knock. Knock."

I squeal. Trenton, Taylor, and Cameron stand at the open hospital room door. I clutch my chest in an attempt to keep my racing heart from exploding.

"Sorry. We didn't mean to scare you," Taylor states, walking to her mother's bedside.

Trenton joins her while Cameron comes to my side. Wrapping her arm around my shoulders, she whispers, "How are you holding up?"

I nod as I reply, "I'm fine." I look toward Alma. Her children are calling to her, attempting to stir her consciousness. "She still hasn't been alert enough to speak."

Taylor assumes the chair I previously occupied while crooning to her mother. Trenton gently rubs Alma's cheek from the other side.

I need to give them time alone, so I make my way to the door.

"Where do you think you are going?" Cameron calls to me as she jogs to my side in the hallway.

"I need a break," I fib because I feel out of place. With Alma unwell, I fear my spot in my adopted family will fade. "I'm going to the bathroom and getting a drink."

She tucks her hand in mine. "I'll join you."

"Don't you want to visit with your mom before her surgery?" *They just got here. Shouldn't she want to spend time with Alma?*

"Like you said, she hasn't been lucid enough to talk. I'm sure my siblings will let her know I am here." She tilts her head at me while we wait for the elevator. "I'm not good in these situations. My siblings take over, and I get in trouble for everything I say or do. Besides, you've been by yourself—I'll keep you company."

We step into the elevator, and the doors slide shut.

"Where to?" Cameron asks with her finger poised to press a number for a floor.

"I'm not sure."

"I thought you needed a bathroom break and a drink," Cameron reminds me.

I shake my head. "I just needed to give them privacy."

"Uh-uh," she scolds. "They don't need privacy. You're part of this family now, and you deserve to be in the room as much as I do."

Her words do make me feel a bit better.

"Let's find the cafeteria," she suggests. "I could use a snack and a decent cup of coffee. I'm sure you could use a pop. The caffeine will do both of us good."

When the nurses enter to whisk Alma off to surgery, her room is crowded. Dr. Anderson stopped by to visit as he promised while Trenton, Taylor, Cameron, and I all stand nervously watching the clock in anticipation of the surgery. We take turns kissing Alma's cheek or patting her arm as they push her out the door.

Dr. Anderson assures us she is in excellent hands before

exiting. Unsure what to do, the four of us stand lost in the now nearly empty room.

"I need to go pick Liberty up from church," I explain, gathering up my purse. "I'm going to run by the house to let McGee out. Can I bring you anything?"

Trenton and Taylor plan to eat in the cafeteria and sit in the surgery waiting room. Cameron asks to join me on my drive.

Exhausted from her playtime at church, Liberty still sleeps in her stroller when the nurses wheel Alma back into the hospital room. The medical team scurries to situate her and record vitals. Taylor and Cameron squeeze into the room and stand by my side.

"She's getting so big," Taylor whispers, peeking into the stroller.

"I still can't believe she's one-and-a-half," Cameron states. "She's so tall and smart."

"Too smart for her own good sometimes," I agree. "She and McGee can be quite the handful when they play." I turn from Alma to face the women. "This week, we lost track of them for a split second. We followed Liberty's chatter to find them in Alma's bathroom. Liberty stood in the bathtub with both hands on the knobs to the faucet with McGee sitting nearby."

"Were they going to take a bath?" Cameron giggles.

"Well, Liberty wore only her diaper. Her clothes were strewn in the hall and on the bathroom floor. Whether it was just one or both of them, someone planned to get wet." I shake my head and turn to face Alma's direction again. "Thankfully, she can't turn the knobs yet."

"Oh, just wait." Taylor places her palm on her cheek. "The twins used an entire bottle of bubble bath in the tub once. We had bubbles everywhere. Liberty will keep you on your toes, but you won't want it any other way."

The three of us chuckle as the staff finish with Alma and Trenton enters. "The surgery went as planned. She should be waking in the next half-hour or so," The female nurse states as she adjusts the call button on top of Alma's blankets. "Press the nurse call button when she wakes or if you need anything." With that, we are once again alone with an unconscious Alma.

CHAPTER 5

Madison

Liberty and I keep Alma company in the third inning of the second World Series game. Taylor and Cameron left to get dinner for our group and let McGee out. Trenton is taking a walk to call his wife and kids with an update. The afternoon was smooth; Alma woke, said a couple of words to us, then nodded off and on. The staff claims she's progressing nicely, and they plan to assist her with walking a bit in an hour or so.

The score is one to one; the Cubs are tied with the Yankees. Liberty sits in my lap, pretending to read one of her books. Alma, alert at the moment, watches the game with me.

"Coming to the plate is the designated hitter for the Cubs, Hamilton Armstrong," the announcer states. "A bold move on the part of the coach." A second announcer explains

Hamilton is a pitcher and usually a pitcher doesn't hit in either league for another pitcher.

I stand, placing Liberty in the chair. I glance at Alma; she wears a smile. "He's hit well all season." I state the obvious and Alma agrees.

My nerves are through the roof. Hamilton isn't supposed to pitch for two more games. Now that he's active in this game, though, I have even more butterflies in my stomach than I did before.

The first pitch is a ball brushing Hamilton back from the plate. That's a dirty move. The opponent is sending a message. I wonder if they studied Hamilton's hitting from the regular season. He likes outside pitches and crowds the plate to get a better swing at them. The second pitch is a slider across the outside corner of the plate for a strike.

"C'mon, Hamilton!" Alma croaks.

I wonder if her pain meds are wearing off. I'll need to call the nurse after Hamilton hits.

Hamilton crushes the third pitch that looks like a fastball. As he sprints to first, the ball flies deep into left field. It bounces off the wall with an advantageous hop away from the leftfielder. Hamilton continues to second and the runner on third charges towards home. As Hamilton slides safely into second for a double, the ball soars toward the catcher at the same time as the runner slides across home plate. It's close.

I hold my breath as I await the call from the official. The Cubs runner returns to step on the plate as the catcher scrambles to find the baseball. He returns the ball to his glove and attempts to tag the runner. The head umpire signals safe. The Cubs now lead two to one and Hamilton gains an RBI. He beams on second base when the camera zooms in on him.

I hop up and down, trying to refrain from cheering at the top of my lungs. "Yes!"

"Da-Da!" Liberty cheers from the chair behind me.

"Yes, Daddy got a double!" I inform her as I scoop her in my arms to celebrate. We high five Alma and dance at her bedside.

Alma cringes as she coughs. I return Liberty to the chair. "Are you okay? Do you need more meds?" I've tried not to hover all day as her children are overly protective.

Alma doesn't answer. I decide to press the nurse's call button just in case. Alma coughs again. Her eyes search the room as her mouth opens.

"Alma," I call to her. "What's wrong?"

Her mouth moves as if she's trying to speak, but no sounds escape. She's in distress. I press the call button again. Something is wrong; I know it. I dart toward the hallway, not leaving the door frame.

"Help!" I scream. "We need help in here! Hurry!"

A nurse exits another patient's room, running my way. I scoop up Liberty and stand at Alma's bedside. Three nurses gather around her as I move against the wall so they can work. The head of her bed is lowered while one nurse calls to Alma, attempting to get her to answer; the others record vitals.

In the blink of an eye, a nurse pages for assistance. I'm

unable to make out the announcement as tears cloud my vision. *This can't be good.*

"Miss," a voice calls. "Miss, I need you to step into the hallway." A nurse places a firm hand on my shoulder to guide me out of the room.

"What's happening?" I wail, unable to restrain my emotions.

The nurse returns to the room without a reply. I lean against the wall, my eyes raised to heaven. "Please. Please help her," I beg God.

"Ma-Ma?" Liberty's tiny hand pats my cheek.

I attempt to pull myself together—I don't need to scare her. I kiss her cheek then pull my phone from my pocket. I open the group text from yesterday.

Me: Get back here, NOW!

I don't look for a reply; I tuck it back in my pocket. "It's okay," I sooth Liberty, rubbing her back. "The doctor and nurses are helping Alma right now. We're okay." I hope my words console her more than they do me.

A raucous at the end of the hall draws my attention. "Sir!" a female voice yells. It's Trenton. He doesn't acknowledge her. Instead, he runs towards us.

"What happened?" He gasps for breath.

"I don't know. One minute we were high-fiving Hamilton's double, the next she couldn't utter a sound and looked confused." I shake my head. "I paged the nurse but had to run in the hall to yell for help."

Trenton extends his arms for Liberty. I don't want to give her up; she anchors me in this chaos. She leans toward him, so I relinquish her. Trenton pats her back while murmuring that everything will be alright. I'm not sure if he's directing it towards Liberty, me, or himself.

"Taylor and Cameron were already on their way back when you texted," he explains still breathless. "They'll be here any minute."

Several long moments pass. I retell my account to the girls, and we all stand scared, hoping for an explanation soon. Liberty wiggles down to sit on the floor near my feet, playing with my cell phone. When it vibrates, she extends it to me. It's an ESPN alert. The score remains two to one in the top of the seventh inning. The World Series game is no longer in the forefront of my mind. I return the phone to my daughter.

After what seems like an eternity, Trenton peeks his head into Alma's room for answers. The rest of us remain frozen in the hallway, staring into space. Trenton emerges as Alma is wheeled from the room with several staff members flanking both sides of her. I refrain from reaching to her as it's clear they are in a hurry to their destination.

"They're taking her for an MRI," Trenton states.

"A stroke?" Taylor asks, and Trenton nods.

In my shock, I didn't think to ask her what might have happened, even though she is a cardiologist. She probably had a pretty good idea all this time. Sobs escape Cameron as her legs go weak, and she slides down the wall to the floor.

Liberty immediately approaches. She places her hands on Cameron's cheeks. As is her way, her dark brown eyes search Cameron's. I wish I could shield Liberty from all of this. It has to be confusing. I'm selfish; I want her with me when I should have secured a babysitter.

"O-Tay?" Liberty asks.

In her own little way, she is trying to make Cameron feel better. I gnaw on my lip. *How do I explain this to someone so young?*

Taylor states she'll fetch the food from the car and be right back. I don't offer to help her carry. I can't move. If I move, I might react. If I react, I might lose what little control I'm hanging on to.

Trenton brings two more chairs into the hospital room then urges Cameron, Liberty, and I to take a seat. *I didn't even notice him leave. I wonder where he stole the chairs from.*

As she promised, Taylor returns with food, and we eat in silence for a bit. Trenton turns on the game to find it's still two to one in the top of the ninth.

"I'd like the Cubs to score a couple here." Taylor snaps our silence.

"They can win by a run," Trenton teases, trying to ease the tension.

"I'd feel better with more of a cushion for the end of the game." I agree with Taylor. It would make the win seem safe.

I busy myself with pinching off pieces for Liberty, eating my slice, and watching the end of a game that I can't get excited about. We watch the postgame celebrations as the

Cubs secure their second win in the series. In our room, there is no cheering, only fake smiles when we make eye contact. It's clear our thoughts are with Alma.

I opt to keep Liberty in my bed tonight. I know it's selfish; I can't be alone. She sleeps peacefully next to me as I prepare to send an email update to Hamilton.

From: alwayswrite@gmail.com
To: armnhammer@gmail.com
Subject: Fly the W
    Congrats on the single, double, and two RBIs. I watched the game tonight in Alma's hospital room. It was hard not to cheer at the top of my lungs when you hit the double to steal the lead. You brought a large smile to Alma's face as we high-fived.
    Just think, the next 2 games are in Chicago. I bet Wrigley will be lit.
Alma's surgery went off without a hitch we were told. She was alert off and on all afternoon. But, halfway through tonight's game, she had a stroke.
    Trenton was calling his family somewhere for privacy, and the girls went to get us dinner. One minute, Alma was cheering, and the next thing I know, it

happened. I was so afraid, and I'm still scared to death. The doctor confirmed it was a stroke after the MRI but stated it would take some time to know how much damage it caused. As visiting hours were over, he urged us to go home and promised us more answers in the morning.

Like an idiot, I looked up strokes on the internet—now I will never sleep. It's hard enough for someone her age to recover from total hip replacement. Add a stroke to it, and it might be impossible. I know her kids are all worried about it, too.

I'm sorry to deliver such upsetting news on the eve of an awesome win for you. I feel I need to keep you posted.

I'll email you tomorrow when we hear from Alma's doctor.

Love,
Madison

CHAPTER 6

Hamilton

I close Madison's email, placing my phone back in my coat pocket. I guess I won't text to ensure she is up then call her like last night. My excitement to share tonight's game with her evaporates.

My head in my hands, I hunch forward, elbows on my knees. An acrid taste fills my mouth, and my stomach feels heavy. The overwhelming need to comfort Madison feuds with my need to celebrate with my team.

My mind races with possibilities. The team flies home tomorrow; our next game is in two days. I could hop a flight tonight and be in Columbia when she wakes up. Since I start game four, I could spend the entire day with her and fly home in time for game three.

Coach will understand when I explain what's going on, that my head isn't here with the team, as it is. I'll promise him a clearer head in time for my start in the fourth game.

Coach's voice floods my brain. "I'm counting on you to hit in any given game. Your bat is hot, and we'll use it. We may use you as the DH or a pinch hitter, so be ready."

As much as I love Madison and want to help her through this tough time, I cannot abandon my teammates. I hope she understands.

"Yo," Stan nudges my shoulder, standing in the aisle beside me.

"Sorry." I shake my head and rise from the bus seat.

"Where's your head at?" he inquires.

"Madison wrote me. The woman she lives with suffered a stroke during our game tonight."

"Dude, I'm sorry." He lowers his voice as we exit the charter bus at our hotel. "How bad is it? Did the hip surgery cause it?"

Unable to keep emotion from my voice, I open her email, passing my phone for him to read.

"You need to be there, but you have to be here," Stan states, understanding my dilemma.

At the lobby, most of the team heads to the bar to continue the celebration. Stan suggests we head up to my room.

"She's your number one fan," he reminds me. "From all you've shared, it feels like I know her. Madison wants this for you. She'd pitch a fit if you missed any part of the World Series with your team."

He's right. She'd kick my ass if I didn't enjoy every minute of this week.

"Take some time," he orders. "Text her, call her, whatever, just make sure she knows you're with her in thoughts and prayers. Then, join the team for drinks. I'll meet you down there."

Then, he's gone. I'm alone in the empty, much-too-quiet hotel room. I place my suit jacket in the closet, remove my tie, and unbutton my top button before rolling up my sleeves.

With cell phone in hand, I stare out the window. The lights sprawl out as far as the eye can see.

I choose to return her email, hoping she's already asleep. She'll need all her strength to help Alma and her family get through this.

CHAPTER 7

Madison

In the two days since Alma's surgery and subsequent stroke, Taylor and Cameron hurry home for work and to rearrange their schedules for another trip to Columbia. Trenton works via the internet and reschedules many of his appointments from Alma's hospital room. Alma's physicians informed the group that due to the severity of her stroke; she will be transferred to a long-term care nursing facility. While they expect her to make improvements, they are confident that she will not be able to return home. Once the shock wore off, Trenton and Taylor discussed some major decisions they need to consider as soon as possible. Not wanting to face the truth, I excused myself from such a discussion. Cameron wasn't far behind me. Although she claims her older siblings rarely listen to her opinions, I believe she tries to avoid these situations.

Tonight, is game three of the World Series. Taylor and her spouse have tickets. I'm supposed to attend tomorrow night's game with Memphis, and she promised to call today for an update on Alma. I'm writing on the deck, watching Liberty and McGee play in the backyard when my phone rings.

"Hello," I greet, placing my laptop to the side. Quickly, I click the save button before shutting the lid.

"How are things?" Memphis wastes no time.

"They're transferring Alma to a nursing home this afternoon." My voice conveys my anguish in this development. "Trenton is with her. I opted to stay home."

"I'm sure her kids found her the best facility, and she will have the best care available." Her words do little to ease my worries. "How are you?"

"Scared." It's true. I'm scared of everything.

"Trenton plans to fix a few things then put Alma's house on the market," I sigh dejectedly. "I need to start searching for a new place to live."

"Will you stay in the Columbia area?" I detect a hint of wistfulness in her voice. "You're done with college, and your writing career allows you to live anywhere. Have you considered leaving Columbia?"

I close my eyes for a moment. I hadn't thought of this. I've only made a list of things I need to do to move out—it didn't occur to me that I can move anywhere. This revelation makes my decision even more daunting. I need to choose a state and town before I can start apartment hunting.

"I'm sorry," Memphis interrupts my thoughts. "It's a big decision, and I just made it bigger."

"No, you're right." I sigh again. My eyes follow McGee as he chases Liberty with the ball in her hand. "It should make it easier to move, but deciding on a location is more than I can handle right now."

"You are more than welcome to stay with me in Athens while you consider where to move. I mean, I'd love for you to move back to Athens, closer to all of your friends, but I understand if you still want distance from your mother."

The thought of being close to Memphis in the absence of Alma is comforting, but I'm not sure I am ready to move back near my mother. I've liked not worrying every day about her drinking, her arriving home safely, and what she is up to. Distance did wonders to ease that anxiety that haunted my life. *Does living near Memphis and my friends outweigh living near my mother?*

"I'll have to think about it. Thanks for the offer." A real smile slides onto my face for the first time in days. "I might plan a trip up to visit when things calm a little here." I clear my throat, preparing to deliver my next news. "Memphis, I think I'm going to have to give up my ticket to tomorrow night's game. It just doesn't feel right to go with all that Alma is going through down here."

"I was actually going to ask you if you still wanted to go," she confesses.

"Of course, I want to go. I mean, it's the World Series, and Hamilton will be pitching. I don't want to miss it, but I need to be here to help Alma settle in at her new place." I roll my head and neck, seeking to release some tension. "I don't know yet when her daughters will be back, and Trenton plans to head back to Tennessee for the weekend to visit his family. I don't want Alma to be all alone in a nursing home without someone to visit her. I know I can't do much, but I can keep her company."

"I knew you'd want to be there for her."

"Do you think you can find someone to go with Amy and you on a day's notice? I'd hate for the ticket to go to waste." I hope Hamilton's sister will take someone in my place.

"I'm sure Amy's 'friend' will gladly go," she chuckles.

"She claims they are still just friends?" I try to remember if it has been a year now that Amy and her guy friend have been glued at the hip. Memphis' words not mine.

"Oh, one minute in the room with the two of them and it's clear to see he is not her friend." Humor laces her voice. "My daughter is just in denial. She won't even admit they are friends with benefits. I've made it very clear I wouldn't have a problem with it—she just prefers to be in denial."

"Well, whatever he is, I'm glad he can use my ticket."

"He played American Legion ball with Hamilton for two summers. Amy hinted last week that she wished she asked Hamilton to send him a ticket, too." Memphis clears her throat. "I'm sure he will be thrilled to attend."

"And since it's an overnight trip, maybe Amy will finally confess they are a couple," I tease.

"I didn't think about that. I wonder if she will share a room with me or him." Memphis giggles. "Oh, this could be so much fun. I'll get to watch her squirm."

"Be nice," I scold. Liberty is laying in the grass with her head on her arm. I fear my girl is in need of a nap. "Well, I need to let you go. I've got stuff to do and more to consider now."

We say our goodbyes before I whisk McGee and Liberty inside for an afternoon nap.

———

The Cubs won last night, so tonight's game could end the series if they win again. I'm sure this adds more pressure to Hamilton's appearance on the mound. I tried to talk to him last night after the win and again this morning, but the team is keeping him very busy. I did get to hear from Taylor about how exciting it was in Wrigley last night. I'm glad Memphis and Amy will be there tonight for Hamilton. I'm very jealous. Adulting sucks sometimes.

Liberty and I drive home for a few hours to relax before we return to watch tonight's game with Alma. She's in a private room, but it is very tiny. It's hard to keep Liberty entertained inside the four walls for an entire day.

I open my phone to see if I've missed anything while I move around the house, picking up and packing toys for tonight. Looking at my last text to Hamilton, I realize he hasn't texted me since yesterday morning. I purse my lips, contemplating sending him another text, when my phone vibrates.

Savanah: Got time to chat?
Me: yes, call me

I promptly answer my ringing cell phone. "Hey, girlie. It's been too long. What's up?" I fake excitement.

Savanah and I were close in high school; we bonded over our difficult situations at home. While I struggled with the loss of my father and my mother's drinking, Savannah's mother struggled to support the family. Savannah babysat as much as possible until she turned sixteen, then she started working at the grocery store for money. From that point on, she purchased her own gas, insurance, and clothes. She works hard for her money and strives to provide a better life for herself.

"Oh, you know." Savannah mutters something about an idiot driver before returning to our call. "Work, eat, sleep, work, eat, sleep. It's the story of my life." She lets out a long sigh.

"So, plan another vacation," I suggest. "I heard you snagged a nice rack a few weeks ago during bow season. When are you taking off again for gun season?"

"I have a vacation planned the second week of November. Then, the bakery gears up for the Thanksgiving and Christmas busy season. Don't worry, I still get as many vacation days in during deer season as I can."

I struggle to think of what to say next. I know Savannah has a reason for calling. While she participates in our group calls, she never calls me herself. We text occasionally, but for her to call me, something must be up. I need to wait until she's ready to share.

"I could use some of your iced cookies right now. Just talking to you gives me a sugar craving." We laugh together.

"I need to vent," Savannah blurts.

"Have at it." I anxiously wait to hear the issue.

"People in Athens suck." She pauses.

I hear her car beep as she opens her door, then turns off the ignition. Her breathing increases as she walks.

"Sorry, I just got home. Where was I? Oh yeah, I hate how people are rude to anyone not from around here. You know?"

"Tell me about it. You know it's one of my pet peeves."

"Today, I was helping a customer with his donut order. Ol' Lady Humphreys walked right up to him. She introduced herself to the guy. I'm sure my chin hit the floor when she told him that she'd overheard he was looking to buy a house and that it was a bad idea. She actually informed him it would be smarter to rent as he would only be here a year or two. 'People like you don't last long in Athens,' she told him." Savannah imitates the old woman then groans. "It's like she rules the town, and she came in to inform him he'd need to leave soon."

"I'm not all that surprised."

"I hear all of the gossip at the store. People come in to visit all the time. I waste over an hour a day visiting with shoppers. My boss reminds me it is PR, and I need to stop what I am doing and visit with them. I listen to everyone complain that we don't attract new businesses. Well, duh. New businesses and people will not stay if we don't welcome them." In her voice, I sense her frustration growing with her volume.

"So, who was the guy?" My curious mind needs to know. *Is he an upstanding citizen? Is he a criminal? Why was Ol' Lady Humphreys keen on speeding his exit from Athens?*

"He's a new history teacher at the high school. He comes in a couple of times a week for a donut before school. There's absolutely nothing wrong with him."

"Except he wasn't born in Athens or the surrounding area," I quip.

"Right!"

"So, he's a donut addict?" I clutch on to the nugget of information my friend didn't mean to share.

"Oh, you know, he's always in a hurry, so he grabs breakfast on the way to school several times a week," she quickly back pedals.

Wouldn't it be quicker at the convenience store or McDonald's drive thru? He's not coming in for the donuts. He's interested. This is so awesome! I cheer internally for my friend. I do not let her know my real thoughts—I don't need to scare her.

CHAPTER 8

Madison

We arrive at Alma's room an hour before tonight's game. I unpack a wide variety of activities for Liberty throughout the room. As Alma is already in bed for the night, I don't have to worry about her falling over any of them.

The head of her bed is raised to allow her to easily chat with us and view the TV. With arms up, Liberty signals she wants me to lift her onto the bed.

"Be careful," I prompt.

Liberty sits facing Alma and blabbers. Alma smiles and listens as Liberty shares a story of some sort. After a minute, she wiggles her way off the bed, back to her toys.

"She…happy…" Alma's slurred speech is difficult to understand. The stroke has caused her to lose mobility in the left side of her face. She struggles with word choices and is easily frustrated when she can't communicate.

"She played in the yard again today." This makes Alma smile. "We've been very lucky this October. She didn't need a jacket again today." I pat her arm as I move the chair closer to her bedside. "She was probably telling you I gave her a bath before we came tonight." I swirl my finger in circles near the left side of my head. "This mom went crazy and changed our nightly routine."

A sound resembling a laugh comes from Alma. "Ham… Ham…he…pitch."

"Yes, and I'm too nervous. Memphis sent this picture." I show her my cell phone and the photo of Memphis and Amy with Wrigley in the background. I reach into my backpack. "I smuggled you in some chocolate chip cookies Liberty helped me bake today. You know we have to keep making your lucky cookies so the Cubs will win." I cringe remembering Alma fell while making her last batch of lucky cookies.

Liberty approaches. "Wib-Be."

She's letting us know she needs a cookie. I break one in half, knowing she will want another one later during the game. She smiles toward Alma then returns to her baby doll on the blanket covering the tile floor.

I find the announcers annoy me before the first pitch is thrown. I turn the volume down a bit more. I want to listen occasionally but seeing the game is more important to me. The game begins as all the others have this week with the National Anthem. Tonight Maroon 5 performs.

Next, two little boys throw the ceremonial first pitches

from the mound. The balls barely make it halfway to the catcher. Tears well in my eyes when Adam Levine encourages the two to pick the balls up and throw them the rest of the way home. I absolutely love that he didn't do it for them, rather assisted them in making accommodations to be successful. On the second throw, each ball hit the catcher's mitt. This is why I love this singer.

This week, I've watched as Taylor and Trenton did things for Alma instead of helping her do them. It's important that she learn a new way to do things for herself. I'm going to make it my mission to talk to her kids and assist her in finding success on her own. I'm sure she still wants to be independent as much as she can, and we can help her.

"That's…guy…*Girls Like You*…" Alma slurs, frustrated with her impaired speech.

"Yes." I lock eyes with Alma. It's important that she know, despite her frustration, she can communicate effectively. "*'Girls Like You'*." It's the song and the video we both love by Maroon 5.

I smile, remembering Alma dancing around the house with me one day when we were cleaning to my Maroon 5 playlist. We took a break, and I showed her the video that the band made to go with the song. We discussed the message of empowerment it shares and attempted to name all the famous women in each video. Our short break turned into over an hour of enjoying music and videos together. I hope we continue to make more memories like that.

"When the Cubs win tonight," I only half tease. "We will crank up our song and dance."

Although she shakes her head, believing she can't dance, I know the feisty, fun-loving, try-anything Alma is still inside her.

"What? Are you afraid I will dance better than you now?"

Alma's garbled laughter is music to my ears.

Hamilton pitches a near perfect game, though you wouldn't know it by my nerves. The closer we come to the end of the game, the more anxious I grow. He racks up 12 strikeouts and gives up no walks or runs as we start the eighth inning.

Alma is napping at the moment, and Liberty sleeps on the blanket in the corner of the room with Cubbie Bear tucked under her arm. Alma drifted off a few times, and I attempted to cheer quietly during her naps. I probably should have packed up and left at eight when visiting hours ended. I know Alma needs her rest, but I wanted to watch the entire game with her as if she hadn't had a stroke.

The vibration of my cell phone on the bedside table wakes Alma. I pretend I didn't notice she fell asleep as I pick it up.

Trenton: I'm back in town
Me: I'm with Alma
Me: watching game
Trenton: I'll go to the house
Trenton: past visiting hours

Me: permission to stay late
Me: say you're here to pick us up
Me: watch end of game with me
Trenton: okay
Trenton: I'm 5 min away

The game remains scoreless in the bottom of the eighth. I desperately need the Cubs to score. My nerves will not survive extra innings. Alma's face lights up with Trenton's arrival.

"Bottom of the lineup, not a promising place to score a run," Trenton shares.

"Ham...Hamilton," Alma mumbles to refute his statement.

"She's right," I chime in. "Hamilton is not your average pitcher batting ninth in the lineup." I give Alma a thumbs up.

Trenton smirks. He knew what he was saying. He wanted to get a rise out of us women. We played right into his plan. He winks at me.

Hamilton stands in the batter's box with a full count. I hold my breath as the pitcher winds up, then delivers. His upper body twists, his thighs bulge, his bat cracks, and the ball flies. It soars over the infield and continues over the outfielders.

I rise from my chair. I throw my arms straight up in the air. Internally, I am screaming, "Go! Go! Go!"

The ball's trajectory arcs down past the outfield wall. Stunned, I look to Alma then Trenton. I feel my eyes bulging as my chest tightens and burns. Breath, I need air. I suck in an audible breath. As life returns to my lungs, I begin to react.

"He hit it out of the park!" I hop in place. "Hamilton hit a homerun out of the park in the World Series!"

Trenton hugs me then his mom. I raise my hand toward Alma. Shakily, she lifts her arm to give me a high five. The right side of her face smiles while the left droops. Our celebration continues until Hamilton resumes the mound at the top of the ninth. Trenton adjusts the TV volume.

"Armstrong returns to start the ninth," the announcer's baritone voice states. "It's rare for a starting pitcher to throw an entire game in the Majors."

The second commentator adds, "Armstrong has only thrown 76 pitches. He hasn't shown any signs of arm fatigue. I'm impressed the coaching staff allows Armstrong to go the distance."

Worried about his arm, my mind calculates pitch counts. With three strikes per out and three outs per inning, a pitcher theoretically could throw nine strikes per inning for nine innings. If my mental math is correct three times three times nine is eighty-one. I remind myself Hamilton has thrown seventy pitches in a couple of games this season when he was pulled by the sixth inning. I tamp down my over-protectiveness by telling myself his coaches would not keep him in the game if it might hurt his arm.

The first Yankees batter hits a fly to right-center field where Stan easily catches it. The fans at Wrigley go wild. Goosebumps prickle my skin with the realization that with two more outs, the game and the World Series will be over.

Hamilton walks the second batter. The commentators rationalize that his arm is showing signs of fatigue, and the weight of this game is taking its toll on his concentration. I attempt to block out their words.

Hamilton bounces the rosin bag in his hand while looking toward the runner on first. He positions himself on the rubber and looks to his catcher for the sign. He shakes his head once, twice, then a third time. Catcher's don't like to be shook off like that. *C'mon Hamilton, listen to him, and work together.* Finally, he likes the sign he's given and nods. He glances towards first as he comes set on the rubber.

Hamilton's fastball targets the outside corner of the plate. The batter swings, making contact, and the ball bounces towards the shortstop. The shortstop fields the ball, throwing to second as he falls backward. Hamilton darts to back up the first baseman while the second baseman places his right foot on the bag then throws to first.

The ball arrives at first, simultaneously with the runner who is stretching his stride to cross the bag. Hamilton throws his arm and closed fist over his shoulder, signaling the runner is out at the same time as the official signals.

All air evaporates from the room as Alma, Trenton, and I are frozen. We don't make a peep or look to each other. Our eyes are glued to the screen. A double play means the game is over, and the Cubs win.

The network replays the play at first from three different angles. It's close, however from the outfield camera angle, we see the ball in glove with the infielder's foot clearly touching the bag a moment before the runner's right footsteps onto the bag.

I don't allow my body to celebrate—I don't allow my mind to go there. I wait with bated breath for the official to make his ruling. The head umpire behind homeplate clenches his fist in the air. Out. *Out? Out!*

I don't hear the announcers or the crowd at Wrigley. I only hear Alma and Trenton cheering. *They did it! The Cubs did it! They won the World Series in a four-game sweep. Hamilton pitched an entire game. The Cubs are World Series Champs!*

Two members of the nursing staff remind us to keep it down as most residents are asleep. They congratulate Alma on her team and her friend winning while reminding us to go soon before their shift ends.

I pull out my phone, needing to text Hamilton.

Me: You did it!
Me: World Series Champions!
Me: Fly the W, Cubs Win!
Me: Great game!
Me: I (heart emoji) you

I know he won't see my texts for hours, maybe not until tomorrow. I'm sure Chicago will party all night, as will his team. I hope he joins them—he deserves to celebrate. His homerun and pitching led to the final score of one to nothing.

CHAPTER 9

Hamilton

"He's out!" I signal while jumping up and down and shouting.

The official closes his fist and raises it above his shoulder. "Out!"

Out! That's three! Game over! We win!

We win. We won the World Series. Every muscle in my body flexes as the infielders swarm me. It takes all my strength to remain upright. I can't risk injury on the bottom of a dogpile. Adrenaline courses through my veins as warmth engulfs me.

I struggle to pull in a breath and tears stream down my face. *I'm crying. I'm freakin' crying.* On one of my upward jumps, I notice our large group gathered in the infield. The bench clears and coaches join in our celebration on the field.

Television cameras and the media begin to infiltrate our mob, seeking photos and interviews. Staff from the head office begin corralling us this way and that for the networks. T-shirts and hats declaring the Cubs World Series Champs fly through the air with orders to put them on.

Two sports announcers with camera in tow approach; I close my eyes and attempt to catch my breath. Madison comes to mind. She stands in front of me, excitement oozing from her every pore. Her dazzling smile reaches her bright eyes and beyond. She bounces on her toes, too excited to stand still. It's easy to see her arms twitch, needing to hug me. She's the only person I want to celebrate with in this moment and the one too far away to do so. She had a ticket to tonight's game. She was supposed to be here. I'm glad she's with Alma in her time of need, but it doesn't stop me aching for her to be with me.

"Hamilton," frantic sports personalities greet while their camera persons scramble to find the perfect angle. "Great outing tonight. How does it feel to be World Series Champions?"

What a dumb question. I'll have to answer it just like every other ball player has over the years.

"It's been an amazing season. This is a great group of guys. We worked hard all season long and never lost sight of our goal. I'm proud to be a Cub!" I hope that doesn't sound too cheesy.

"With a World Series win, how will this affect next season?"

"We'll prepare for next season as we do every year." I attempt to keep sarcasm from my voice. They really do ask dumb questions in these post-game interviews. "Perhaps we'll earn another ring to join this season's." I wave five fingers at them.

"I understand that your mother and sister were in attendance tonight. What does it mean to you that they witnessed you pitch in the final game of the World Series?"

"I'm always happy when my family can attend. I wouldn't have made it this far without their support over the years." My thoughts dart again to Madison. "A special person couldn't make it tonight. Although I wish she were here, I know she's celebrating with us in her thoughts."

"Hamilton is this a new romantic interest?" the over-eager announcer asks.

I smirk, raise my palm up, and walk away from the interview. I've said too much. I only wanted Madison to know I am thinking of her in this monumental moment. I don't want the press to hunt her down or follow her around.

With each of my next three interviews, I struggle to keep thoughts of Madison from becoming my answers.

"You have that faraway look in your eye," Stan claims as he and Delta approach through the raucous crowd.

I hug an excited Delta.

"You were on fire tonight," she states, patting my back. "Why isn't your family down here with you?"

"I invited them, but Mom prefers to celebrate privately at the condo later," I explain.

"That's not who you were longing for," Stan prods. "Did you get another update?"

I shake my head–it's much too loud to continue this conversation. When the next media crew approaches, I wink at my friend before composing myself yet again. I don't attempt to move Madison from my mind this time. There's no need to fight it–I can't deny I need her here. She's a big part of my life, she means everything to me, and it's time I told her so.

CHAPTER 10

Madison

Trenton offers to drive Liberty and I home, claiming he will return for his car tomorrow. He even helps me pack the abundance of toys I drug to Alma's room. He carries Liberty to the van and deftly buckles her in the car seat. Once home, he carries her to her crib, tucking her in for the night. He's a great adopted uncle. Liberty needs more male role models in her life like him.

I attempt to wipe the smile from my face as I lie in bed later. My thoughts return to Hamilton's performance in tonight's game. I imagine him celebrating in the locker room with his teammates. *I wonder where they went when they left Wrigley tonight. Did the owner plan an after party at some expensive venue?* Wherever he is, I want Hamilton to enjoy the moment. This is a once-in-a-lifetime moment; well for most it's once in a lifetime. Maybe the Cubs will repeat next year or the year after that. Perhaps Hamilton will collect another World Series ring or two during his career. There's no way I'll miss his next World Series. I won't be in another state–I'll celebrate with him every step of the way.

Baseball season is over, and in two days, it will be November. I only have two months. This time I will do it. Although, the joint Christmas with Alma and Memphis' families is no longer happening, I promised Alma, we set a deadline, and I will keep my vow. Liberty will meet Hamilton by Christmas. I will come clean and deal with the repercussions.

I'm sure Hamilton will be busy for several weeks until the World Series hype dies down. That gives me a couple weeks to plan a time to meet and the perfect words to explain we have a daughter. You'd think I would have figured it all out in the two years following my positive pregnancy test, but I've found it difficult. It seems finding the right words to say I'm sorry, share the reasons for my actions, and not lose the love of my life vexes me.

Add to that the fact that I need to find a new place for Liberty and I to live, and my life is very complicated right now. Memphis mentioned staying with her while I figure out my next move. In order to do that, I need to speak to Hamilton about Liberty first. I know I don't want to be here when the realtor starts showing the house to potential buyers, so I need to figure something out fast.

Last week, I felt safe as Alma and I shared this happy home. With one fall, one accident, my entire world shifted. I can't stay in this house. Liberty and I need to come up with a new plan and life that no longer depends upon Alma.

Alma is my pillar, my foundation, my friend. Now everything seems to crumble around me. I feel her loss more with each day she's away from home. Once again, I'm alone trying to find my place in the world. The 18-year-old me thought my college degree would secure my place and path. I even thought leaving Athens for college would ensure I left loneliness behind. How silly of me to think that something like that could change.

Fate is cruel. Our loving family ended with my dad's death. My once loving mother transformed into a tortured soul. It brought Hamilton into my life in middle school then tore him away with the draft. It brought Alma into my life, and now she falls away. *Where will it lead me now? Who will be the next to make me love them only to be ripped from my life? Will the cycle ever end?*

Realizing it will be hours before my mind allows me to sleep, I turn on my lamp to write. *Without Alma's help, when will I find the time to write?* While Liberty plays by herself, she still does require my attention–when I write, my mind is on one track. I can't watch her and write at the same time.

Try as I might, I can't think of anything but Hamilton. Instead of my story, I decide to send Hamilton an email.

From: alwayswrite@gmail.com
To: armnhammer@gmail.com
Subject: Freakin' World Series Champs

The word congratulations isn't big enough. You and the Cubs are World Series Champions!
You dominated the mound with every pitch. I'm so proud of you. (That sounds stupid & maternal.) You've worked hard for many years, and tonight, it showed.
I'm so sorry I wasn't there. I hope you know that. I wanted to be there so bad. It's not the same watching it on TV.
Alma stayed awake for most of it. Trenton came back for the last inning. The three of us struggled to celebrate quietly for your home run and again at the end of the game.
I'm home now and can't quiet my mind. I'm lying in bed, celebrating. I'm imagining you celebrating in the locker room and at the after party. I hope Stan kept you from leaving early. You've earned the right to party with your team all night (scratch that), all week long.
I must admit, I laughed at your post-game interviews and the silly questions they always asked. You smiled like a kid on Christmas morning. You're a celebrity, and I often forget that. I'm not sure how you handle it. It's gonna change now. You'll have trouble walking down the street or going to your favorite restaurants from now on. Your hand is gonna get tired from all the autographs you'll be signing.
Don't let it go to your head, or I'll drive to Chicago and knock you down a notch or two. Remember what you

were like in Athens and how much your favorite players influenced you. Oh, and I need an autograph, too.

Alma still stutters and slurs her words. She becomes frustrated when she can't get the words out. The staff mentioned she'll be transferred to a rehab facility or nursing home soon. While they state she'll improve, she'll never be able to return home. Trenton is meeting with a realtor about the house. Taylor and Cameron are letting him handle everything.

I'm so glad Memphis and Amy were at Wrigley for the game. I wish they could have stayed more than one night. I'm sure they wanted to celebrate with you. Amy's "friend" saw a great game with my ticket. Does she admit he's her boyfriend yet? Memphis and I laugh about her denial.

I really should do some writing and let you sleep or celebrate. I'm sure from this email you can see my thoughts are all over the place.

Love Ya,
Madison
P.S. I'm still your #1 fan.

CHAPTER 11

Madison

Liberty calls to me through the monitor. "Ma-Ma."

I want nothing more than to sleep late today. The adrenaline high of the World Series game took hours to fade. I wrote until two a.m. knowing Liberty rarely sleeps past seven.

I'm surprised to find Trenton already up and working in the kitchen as Liberty and I enter.

"Good morning," he greets without looking up from the laptop and legal pad in front of him on the table.

"It won't be good until after 10 or several cups of coffee," I mumble. Although I'm up with Liberty daily at 7, I am definitely not the morning person she is.

"There's a huge article about your man on the cover of

today's paper." He motions toward the paper opposite him on the table.

I secure Liberty in her chair and hand her a bowl of lukewarm oatmeal and a spoon, knowing full well she will opt to use her fingers instead. With coffee in hand, I focus on Hamilton's cover story.

As the journalist describes the plays in last night's game, I relive them in my mind. I'm lost in the excitement and staring at the photo of Hamilton's teammates surrounding him on the mound at the end of the game.

In a perfect world, I would've been at his game. I'm bummed I gave my ticket away, but I know my place was with Alma yesterday.

"Madison," Trenton calls to me, breaking my trance. I look to him, confused. "Your daughter's done eating."

I look up from the paper and can't help but giggle at the sight of my daughter covered in oats.

"On a positive note," I tell Trenton while moving to the sink, "her bowl is empty." I wet two paper towels. They won't be enough, but it's a start.

Liberty sucks on her fingers while I begin at the top and work my way down. I free her springy curls then wipe down her face. The doorbell rings as I start at her elbow and wash to her fingertips.

"Can you get that, please?" I ask Trenton as my hands are now covered in oatmeal paste. I continue removing cereal from my daughter until a throat clears behind me.

"Madison, it's for you." Trenton steps by me to take Liberty from her chair.

A gruff male voice greets me as I turn. "Madison Crocker?"

All air flees my lungs and my hands fly to my mouth. Bile rises in my throat and I fear my worst fear has come to fruition.

"Yes," I assure both officers now standing in Alma's kitchen.

One shifts nervously. "Ms. Crocker, I'm Officer Blackburn. We're here in regard to your mother…"

"What's she done now?" I blurt. "And how much is the bail?" Heat floods my veins. I fume, and I don't even know what I'm fuming about.

"Ms. Crocker, there was an accident."

I knew this day would come. Her repeated attempts at drunk driving after late nights at the bar could only lead to this. *Please let there be no one injured. Please let there be no one else involved.*

"Ms. Crocker, a neighbor drove by her house twice this morning. He called the Sheriff's office in Athens because the front door stood open both times." He adjusts his hat before returning his hand to his belt loop.

I hear the officer's words but cannot process their meaning.

"Ms. Crocker, your mother passed away last night." He clears his throat with a horrifying half growl, half croak. "Now, they aren't sure of the specifics and are currently investigating."

I hear my heartbeat in my ears. Suddenly, I'm sweating.

Dead. My mother is dead. I can't believe it. She's dead. I never get to say goodbye. What happened? How did she die? Was she in pain? Did she think about me? She was alone. I never wanted that. I never expected this.

"Madison." Trenton grips my shoulders, bending down to look directly into my eyes.

I shake myself out of my thoughts. "I'm sorry," I look toward the entry to the kitchen. The officers are no longer there. "Where'd they go?"

"Sit." Trenton pushes me down into his chair. "Drink." A bottle of water is forced into my hand. "You need Taylor or Mom right now. Anyone is better than me." He laces his fingers together, hands resting on top of his head.

"I'm fine," I inform him. "It just caught me off guard for a minute."

"Try five minutes," he states. "They didn't have any other details but wanted you to know that the house is roped off as a crime scene. The sheriff's department is retracing her steps of the previous 24 hours and anxiously waiting on the toxicology screen results."

I thank him for stepping up for me and brush my fingers lightly over Liberty's cheek before she darts from the room.

"Can you keep an eye on Liberty while I pack?"

"Madison, you don't need to pack right now. Take a minute. Take an hour. Hell, take all day. There's no rush. You can drive to Athens tomorrow." Trenton's frustration over not knowing exactly how to assist in this situation exudes from him.

"I need to keep busy," I explain. "I think better while I work. It will only take 30 minutes."

When he agrees, I excuse myself to pack upstairs. Unsure if I will be away a couple of days or a week, I pack several outfits for both Liberty and me. I fight the tears that threaten as I grab my writing materials for the sleepless nights that lie ahead and pack a separate suitcase of toys for Liberty.

It doesn't escape me that as I pack now for a trip to Athens, soon I will be packing for a permanent move from this house. I've become very comfortable in Alma's home for the past two years–it will not be an easy move.

Looking to heaven, I ask for mercy. "Please. I've had enough," I whisper. Alma's fall, her stroke, my need to move, and now my mother's death press down on me. I feel so helpless…It's too much. I want to roll up into a little ball and hide for a day or two. That's an option I don't have. I must be strong for Liberty, I need to help Taylor, Trenton, and Cameron, and as her only relative, I need to make funeral arrangements for my mother.

I pat my cheeks and mentally tell myself, "Suck it up, Buttercup."

I make two trips, carrying our bags down the long staircase. I find Trenton entertaining McGee and Liberty in the sunroom. I take advantage of their distraction to load the mini-van with four suitcases, a portable crib, a cooler for drinks and snacks, and my purse; it takes several trips.

The two-hour drive to Athens gives me much too long to think. With Alma in the hospital, I have Liberty with me. The big secret can no longer hide. All of Athens will soon meet my daughter.

Looking back, I wouldn't change a thing. I requested a

favor—Hamilton granted my favor, and we followed through on our plans. If I changed anything, I wouldn't know Alma and her family, I wouldn't have my degree, I wouldn't be a published author, I wouldn't have watched Hamilton pitch in the World Series on TV, and I wouldn't have Liberty. I leave pieces of me everywhere. Some break off–some I willingly give. Part of my heart remains in Athens and part now resides in Columbia. A large chunk of my heart lives in Chicago.

I allow tears to fall as I drive.

For two years now, Hamilton and I chased our dreams, were apart, but kept in touch. Hamilton is my oldest friend, my best friend, my go-to-person, my emergency contact, my voice of reason—I cannot lose him.

My thoughts swirl to my mother. I assumed I'd have another 20-plus years to work things out with her. Of course, I imagined she'd eventually seek help for her addiction. She'll never meet her granddaughter. She'll never give me advice on being a mother.

I swipe away the river of tears, covering my cheeks. I need to mentally prepare myself to bury my mother while introducing Liberty to her dad and grandma. I shake my head; this will be a week from hell.

As Alma's minivan carries me through the main streets of Athens, I feel the eyes of the locals assessing me. A vehicle with an unrecognizable driver will cause the rumor mill to kick into overdrive. Several residents glue themselves to their police scanners. They will have shared that the sheriff was at Mother's farm and that the coroner was summoned. Law enforcement agents on the scene often share a few details with their families, neighbors, or friends. Privacy is not practiced in this town. The town of Athens, Missouri runs on the spreading of gossip.

Placing the van in park at the small grocery store, I cringe knowing inside I will be recognized. Within an hour, more than half of Athens will know I have returned for the funeral with a little girl in tow. It will spread like wildfire, everyone in this little burg knows the reason I am here—most know of my strained relationship with my mother and assumed I would not show.

I assist Liberty from her car seat, and we walk hand-in-hand into the small market. I lift her into the child seat of the shopping cart while reminding her we only need a few items today and plan to return again tomorrow. The sweet smile on her cherub face warms my heart.

As we make our way up and down all eight aisles of the store, I place the items we might need this afternoon or tonight in the metal cart. Liberty requests macaroni and cheese for supper, so I purchase a box along with margarine and two-percent milk. I buy a case of diet cola—caffeine is a necessity for me. I procure cereal for breakfast and tissues, just in case there is none when we arrive. At the pharmacy section, I place a bottle of Benadryl in the cart to assist my sleeping before making my way to the check out.

Liberty enjoys looking at the varieties of candy placed conveniently as we wait our turn. She understands these are not items we consume except on special occasions. One might claim this is indeed a special occasion–I see it as much needed closure to a traumatic portion of my past. It's come much too soon. Every time I try to process her death, I long to run to Alma, but I can't.

"Madison Crocker," a much-too-high voice greets. "How long has it been?"

I close my eyes, bite my lips, and attempt to gather myself to politely greet her. I slowly turn around with a fake smile upon my lips to find, a former classmate, Waverly Fleming behind me. Her grocery cart overflows with processed foods. Two toddlers sit in the child seat of the full cart, their fingers gripping the push handle. A boy about seven stands behind the cart next to his mother. In his hands, he holds four chocolate candy bars.

"Waverly, how have you been? Are these your children?" I attempt to be polite and interested in her life.

"The twins are my oldest; Mom is in the car with my youngest," she answers then points to the boy, "This is my husband's son. I'm so sorry to hear about your momma, my Aunt is the night dispatcher at the sheriff's office. She shared the tragic news with us over breakfast at Mom's. I am glad you came back to town. Will you be here long?"

"I'm here to make her arrangements; that's all," I claim not wanting to share too much for the gossip mill.

"Is this your daughter?" Waverly points as she asks the question I've been dreading.

"Yes, this is Liberty," I twirl her dark curl around my finger.

"She's adorable," Wendy draws out, her voice rising an octave.

Fortunately, it's now my turn at the register. As I place our few items on the black conveyor belt, Liberty waves at the little ones behind her, and Waverly continues talking. She fills me in on all the latest gossip on my former classmates. I pretend to listen as I block her out.

Waverly and I graduated together from Athens High School. It seems she married right after high school, choosing to remain local. In the two years I've been away, she has given birth to three children. In this small rural town, it's common for women to choose to forego college to start families immediately.

Once I pay, I wave goodbye to Waverly, quickly escaping with Liberty to my car. I'm sure she is not the only one that recognized me. Others will also be spreading the news of my arrival. I will be a hot topic as I have Liberty with me for the first time.

Liberty runs playfully through the grass ahead of me. Out of the city, on this seldom traveled gravel road, my constant, watchful eye is unwarranted. I know this, but I can't turn off my mother-hover gene. I attempt to corral her closer to the front door.

I freeze fifteen feet away, taking in the scene in front of

me. As promised by the officers this morning, bright yellow tape hangs as a makeshift fence to keep non-law enforcement out. The front door is closed. I imagine it open, picturing the scene as it looked when they found her... Somewhere inside, my mother lay for hours, alone. *Was she in pain? Was it quick? Did she long for me?*

While Liberty sits nearby playing with sticks, I peek in a window. It's dark inside, and I can't make out anything. I should have known stopping here was a bad idea. I want answers to so many questions I fear I will never find answers to.

I long to visit my favorite spots, the cemetery across the road and the treehouse Dad built for me. I need time to think. I fight the urge to help Liberty climb up into the treehouse in the backyard with me; instead we climb back into the van. I pull from the gravel driveway with a pit in my stomach. I don't want to spend tonight in the motel room with Liberty. Athens only has one motel and to say it is lacking is an understatement. It seemed like a good idea when I made the reservation this morning, but now, I don't believe it is.

Instead of turning towards Athens, I head in the opposite direction. I've taken this road a million times. The farther I drive from my mother's home toward my new destination, the lighter I feel. I can do this—we can do this. It's time. I can take this sad situation and make it somewhat better.

When I place the van in park, my stomach drops, and my heartbeat quickens. *I'm really doing this. Take a breath. Just like pulling off a bandage, quick is best.* As I ease my driver's door open, Memphis steps out her back door.

"I'm so glad you're here," Memphis greets, opening her arms for me.

When I pull from her embrace, I ask, "Can I stay with you?"

"Psst," Memphis swats at me. "You know you are always welcome here."

"Well, I need to tell you something first." I signal for her to stay put as I back toward the vehicle. I open the back, driver's-side door, unbuckle then lift Liberty from the van. "Liberty, this is…"

"Grandma!" Memphis stands beside us; tears fill her wide eyes as her left hand presses against her chest and her right fans her face. "Oh, my!"

I'm not surprised; it's easy to see the resemblance between Liberty and Hamilton. She looks like his sister, Amy, as a little girl.

"Libby, this is Na-Na." I point as I speak. "And this is Liberty."

"Wib-Be," Liberty tells Memphis while pointing to herself.

"Yes, Libby," I point to my daughter. I love that she's attempting to introduce herself.

"Hi, Libby."

I absolutely love the smile on Memphis' face. It gives me hope.

"Mommy," Liberty places her hand on my cheek to get my attention. She then extends an arm towards Memphis.

"Um, this might be a little weird," I nervously tell Memphis. "Can you let Libby touch your face for a minute?

She does this thing where she likes to look in your eyes." I love when Liberty does this to Alma and me. I hope Memphis will allow her to do her thing.

I step closer to Memphis. Liberty raises her two hands, placing them on each of Memphis' cheeks. Although I can't see it, I know her eyes are peering straight into her grandmother's. I witness tears form in Memphis' eyes while she smiles at Liberty. I'm not exactly sure what Liberty looks for when she does this, but happy with what she sees, she lets go of Memphis and looks around the farm.

"Mow-Mow!" Liberty claps. "Mommy, Mow-Mow!" She points at two kittens near the house. She wiggles trying to climb down.

"She's saying meow." I ask Memphis, "Are they somewhat tame?"

Memphis nods. "Let me get one for you."

I lower my daughter to the ground, and I hold her near me. Liberty claps as Memphis approaches with the kittens. She wiggles harder to escape my hold. I release her as Memphis walks back with a kitten in her hands. She sits in a nearby chair, and Liberty quickly approaches.

"Mow-Mow," Liberty calls then giggles, placing her hands over her mouth.

"You want to touch it?" Memphis gently asks.

I slowly ease Liberty's hand out to touch the fluffy kitten. She tugs her hand back immediately after contact. With her hands over her mouth, she giggles.

"Our neighbor has an older, male house cat," I explain to Memphis. "He hides from her. This is the first cat she's ever seen up close and touched." I shrug. Growing up on the farm, touching animals was the norm. I suddenly feel embarrassed that my daughter has never touched a cat and need to explain it to Memphis.

"Libby," Memphis calls to her. "Want to touch it again?" When Liberty nods, she slowly extends the kitten toward her.

Liberty slowly holds out her hand. She hesitates within an inch of it. Memphis gently pets the kitten with her free hand and encourages Liberty to pet it just like she does. Liberty places her hand near the kitten's ears and rubs down its back. She imitates Memphis' petting over and over.

I love watching the world through my daughter's eyes. Her sense of wonder and desire to try new things amaze me. I hope to foster this in her and encourage her to be a life-long learner.

"Mind if I unload while the two of you..." I motion from Memphis to the kitten.

She nods, and I carry in the portable crib, our luggage, the cooler, the groceries, and the backpack. After my last trip, Liberty now sits in the chair with a proud smile upon her face while Memphis helps her hold the kitten in her little lap.

"Look at you!" I praise.

On Liberty's next pet down the kitten's back, a little meow emits. Liberty's eyes bug out as her mouth forms an "O". She quickly looks from Memphis to me.

"Mow-Mow!" Liberty announces.

"Yes, I heard the meow," Memphis states. "The kitty likes you. Cats meow when they are happy."

Liberty proudly nods at her grandmother's words.

"Libby," I bend in front of my daughter. "It's time to let the kitty go back to its mommy. We need to eat dinner. Aren't you hungry?" I nod trying to encourage her agreement.

Memphis rises, takes the kitten from Liberty's lap, and lets it down near the house. We watch as the kitten jogs towards the other cats near a tree in the backyard.

"Let's go see what Grandma has for dinner." She extends her free hand to Liberty.

"I bought some food on my way through town," I say as I follow the pair into the house.

Memphis shakes her head. "Nonsense. I'm sure I have something. We can save your food for tomorrow." She lifts Liberty to stand on the counter in front of her as she opens a cabinet door. "Hmm…"

Liberty points, and Memphis pulls a box of macaroni and cheese from the shelf. I nod, telling Memphis it works for dinner.

"Before we cook, let's go wash our hands." I say and Liberty hurries to follow me.

"Pod-de! Pod-de, Mommy!"

"Okay," I acknowledge. "Potty first."

I assist with removing her leggings then her Pull-up. It's still dry. She's really taken to this potty training. I lift her up to sit on the toilet seat then step back to wait and listen.

"Big girl potty already?" Memphis asks, approaching the restroom door.

"I tried it once a week ago, and she enjoys it. Sometimes she's wet overnight or after a nap; otherwise she potties in the big girl potty. I know at one-and-a-half, it's early. I anticipated her fighting me. I thought we'd attempt it once or twice a week for several months before I focused intently on it," I chuckle. "I should have realized she'd be tenacious in potty training, just like she is in everything she does. When she attempted to feed herself and walk, she demanded to do it on her own and didn't give up."

"Shh!" Liberty places her finger over her mouth. Her eyes grow wide as the sound of urine hitting the water fills the quiet room. When finished, she claps and cheers, nearly plunging into the toilet.

"Wow!" Memphis looks to Liberty. "You are a big girl."

Liberty nods. I help her finish the task and redress before we wash our hands. I squirt a small dab of hand soap on Liberty's hand then mine.

"Ready?" Liberty nods and I begin. "A-B-C-D…"

Memphis joins in, singing the alphabet song with me as Liberty and I rub soap over our hands. When we finish the song, I turn on the warm water, and we begin removing the bubbles from our hands. I dry Liberty's hands, and she helps dry mine. I scoop her up, and we return to the kitchen.

Liberty sniffs her hands then gestures for me to smell them. At Alma's, we use unscented soap. Memphis has a sweet pea hand soap, and Liberty won't stop sniffing the sweet scent. In the kitchen, she urges Memphis to smell her hands.

"Smells good," she tells Liberty, much to the joy of my little one. "I have a bottle under the sink. Would you like your own bottle of the soap?"

Liberty nods excitedly and claps.

Memphis pulls an old highchair from the utility closet. "I pulled it down from the attic to use when Amy brings the twins over."

"How often do they visit?"

"A couple of times a month, she brings the boys over for a change of scenery." Memphis places two plates and a bowl on the table. "They are a handful now that they can walk. Sometimes, they are too much for even the two of us to keep an eye on."

While I prep a salad, Memphis keeps an eye on the macaroni on the stove top, and Liberty entertains herself, eating dry cereal in the highchair.

"I'm sorry," I blurt. I can't wait, and Memphis hasn't asked. She hasn't pried for details. I need to know how she really feels about my actions.

"Uh-huh. You don't owe me an apology." Memphis leans back against the counter beside the stove with a wooden spoon in her hand and arms crossed. "You've given me a happy, healthy grandbaby. You made decisions you thought you had to. You sacrificed, and I'm sure you struggled. I now understand why you separated yourself from everyone you knew; it was to give my son his dream." She stirs the pasta, lays the spoon on the counter, and approaches me at the table. She places her hands on each of my shoulders. "Thank you for giving me a granddaughter. I might be biased, but I believe she is absolutely perfect."

I love her words but find it hard to believe she isn't mad at me for keeping my secret for so long.

"I kept a video journal during my pregnancy and after." I

hope my videos prove I always planned to reveal Liberty to Hamilton and his family. "I'll give you the login information after dinner so you can view them. I know it can never make up for the time I robbed from Hamilton."

The timer interrupts my explanation. Memphis preps the macaroni, I fix each of us a drink, and Liberty talks to herself. We fix our plates and eat in silence for a bit.

CHAPTER 12

Hamilton

I pour myself into bed at 10:30. The past few days begin to wear on me. The appearances and the interviews take their toll. Tomorrow, my day begins promptly at 5:00 a.m. at the local network via satellite with ESPN on the East Coast.

My cell phone vibrates on the nightstand.

Mom: Madison is staying with me
Mom: her mother died
Mom: & she needs you
Me: I'm slammed with interviews
Mom: I know
Me: services scheduled?

Mom: sheriff still investigating
Mom: rumors of foul play
Me: Let me see what I can arrange
Mom: it's a family emergency
Mom: Cubs will understand
Me: I'll let you know

My heart aches, and my chest feels heavy. It's not like my upcoming interviews will ask any questions I haven't already answered five times in the past twenty-four hours. I want to be with Madison. I decide to shoot a text; if I don't hear back, then I'll email my publicist, Berkeley, to see if I can get out of the appearances.

Me: Are you up?
Berkeley: Yes, want me to call?

I dial her number instead of replying.

"Hello," Berkeley answers, always perky. "What's up?"

I'm sure the late hour leads her to believe I have a problem. "There's been a death in the family, and I need to get to Athens." It's not a total lie. Madison has been a part of my family since eighth grade.

"I'm sorry, Hamilton. Who passed away?" Berkeley quickly inquires. "How's Memphis?"

"Madison's mother passed away yesterday." I prepare for her stating the obvious--that she's not family.

"Just a second," Berkeley pauses, and I hear her murmuring to herself as she opens the calendar on her iPad. "Okay. Hmm. Okay. Maybe. No, that can't work. Okay…"

Realizing I could be on the phone for hours trying to help her rearrange each appearance, find a replacement for me, or cancel a function, I decide I'm going, no matter what. I've been the perfect client, public figure, and player. I've done everything asked of me and never been a no-show. I need to do this for Madison–I need to do this for me. I'm going to do this.

"Berkeley." I interrupt her thought process. "I'm packing as we speak. I'll be in Athens by morning. I need you to take care of everything for me."

"Sure." I hear the frustration in her voice. "How long do you need?"

I'm relieved she didn't fight me on this. "A week?" I run my hand over my face. "I'm not sure. Mom says she's not handling it well. Law enforcement suspect foul play. She can't schedule a funeral until the investigation is complete and they release the body. Let's say a week. I'll keep you updated."

"Um," Berkeley hedges. "Okay. You've got to be tired, and it's over a six-hour drive. Can I talk you into waiting until morning to drive?"

I groan. She's right. The smart thing to do is wait until morning.

"Can I ask a favor?" Berkeley clears her throat and

quickly continues. "Can you do the ESPN gig at the station in the morning? I won't be able to get anyone to replace you in the next six hours. You could leave Chicago by nine and be in Athens around dinner time."

I release a deep, audible breath. "Yeah, if you can get me out of everything else, I can be there in the morning."

"Good. Pack quick and get to sleep. We don't want dark circles under your eyes on ESPN."

I agree with Berkeley and say goodbye. I pack a bag and hang my suit over it in the closet before climbing back into bed.

Me: I'll head out in the morning
Me: text when I'm on my way
Mom: Thank you
Me: be there by dinner time
Mom: She'll be glad to have you here
Me: gotta be up @4 am
Me: need sleep
Me: talk to you tomorrow
Mom: I love you
Me: (2 heart emojis)

CHAPTER 13

Madison

I barely keep my eyes open as Memphis clicks another video entry in the journal I created for Hamilton.

"I'm gonna go lay Liberty down for the night," I state after my next yawn.

"Why don't you turn in for the night, too?" Memphis' words catch me off guard. I thought I was hiding my exhaustion. "I'll just be here, watching Liberty grow before my eyes. You've created a terrific chronicle of her life. Get some sleep. I'll see you in the morning."

I nod and carry Liberty upstairs. I hesitate at the door to Amy's room. I set up the portable crib in the corner earlier. I look to my pajamas on Amy's twin bed. This is not where I need to be. I turn, walking back down the hallway.

I step into Hamilton's room. "This is Daddy's room," I inform Liberty.

"Daddy," my sleepy toddler murmurs around the two fingers in her mouth.

I sit her on the bed Hamilton used for 18 years of his life. "I'll go get a book; you stay right here." When Liberty nods, I grab the bag I packed for her from Amy's room and return with it in hand.

I choose one book then slide onto the bed, urging Liberty to lay beside me. I open the book, and she begins playing with one of the curls that frame her face. As I read, her eyes grow heavy and eventually close. I shut the book midway, rolling to face my baby girl.

My head lays on Hamilton's pillow just as his has so many times before. The heady scent of him surrounds me. It wraps me like a warm blanket, letting me know everything is going to be okay. In my heart, I know Hamilton will love and accept Liberty on sight. It's his feelings towards me that I fear. I know he loves me, but I'm unsure if he will continue to love me when I share Liberty with him. Now that Memphis has met her, Hamilton will learn about our child very soon. I can no longer hide her. As more people in Athens meet Liberty, I risk Hamilton finding out from someone other than me, and I can't let that happen. I need a plan, and I need it now. I grab my phone.

Me: I'm @ your mom's
Me: I know you're busy

Me: will you be @ funeral?

I plug the phone into the charger and quickly fall asleep.

The first day of November arrives with heavy dread as I slip from Hamilton's bed. I quietly take care of my morning business in the attached bathroom then sit on the floor, leaning on the bed, and open my cell phone.

I don't see a text from Hamilton. The timestamp shows I texted him at 11:15 last night. It's now 7:00 a.m. I guess he could have been asleep and not have seen my text yet. I turn as Liberty stirs on her side of the bed.

"Good morning," I call to her, a smile upon my face.

"Na-Na?" She sleepily rubs her eyes and stretches.

"Let's go potty, then we can go down to see Grandma."

I follow along as Memphis tours the farm with Liberty in her arms. We pet the horses and prepare to bottle-feed a calf. Liberty enjoys making each animal sound with Memphis. I marvel at the ease at which the two have bonded.

I know it will be the same with Hamilton. I dread his reaction to my betrayal. I fear he won't forgive as easily as his mother.

I force my mind to focus on my daughter feeding the calf in front of me. I snap a couple photos with my phone. Lifted by her grandmother, Liberty tips a large bottle into the mouth of the week-old calf. As the calf nurses and nudges, it reminds me of helping my dad with chores on the farm. I shadowed him as often as I could. My favorite memories are riding the tractor with him. Maybe tomorrow I'll take my daughter on her first tractor ride.

"We should clean up," Memphis suggests. "We'll need to leave soon for the funeral home."

I'd forgotten all about the appointment Memphis made for us to discuss arrangements for a funeral. She's promised to help me every step of the way, and I'll surely need her help.

CHAPTER 14

Hamilton

My mother's house comes into view. I find it odd that no vehicles are in the driveway. Mom knew I'd be here for dinner, and it's 5:30 p.m. That's weird. I shoot Mom a text before I exit my parked truck.

Me: I'm here
Me: where are you?

I decide to carry my bags inside while waiting for Mom's reply. The house is dark. I turn on a light as I walk through the kitchen and upstairs to my room. I hang my suit in the closet and place my duffle on the bed. A stuffed toy lays on a pillow. Amy must have left it last time she had the twins over to visit Mom. I check my phone as I descend the stairs. Still nothing.

Me: Hello?
Mom: Sorry, I'm at store
Mom: be home soon

I peek out the kitchen window at the sound of a vehicle coming up the lane. I don't recognize the light blue minivan. I walk outside to greet the stranger. Perhaps they're lost and need directions.

As the van parks, I recognize Madison in the driver's seat. I approach, a smile on my face.

"Hey," she greets, exiting from the driver's seat. "This is…a surprise." She doesn't sound like herself. Her hands shake as she plays with the zipper on her jacket.

Why isn't she coming to me? A surprise? Why didn't my mom tell her my plans? Mom said she wasn't handling her mom's death very well, maybe Madison forgot I was on my way. She stands frozen in place, pale as a ghost.

"I told Mom I would be here for dinner." Unable to resist any longer, I wrap her in a tight hug. In her ear, I whisper, "How are you doing?"

She shakes her head, unable to answer me. She pulls

away as tears stream down her cheeks. "Let's go inside." Her voice is shaky and barely above a whisper.

As we enter Mom's kitchen, I turn her to face me.

"Madison, you're scaring me," I confess. "Please talk to me."

Her cell phone beeps from her pocket at the same time mine vibrates in mine.

Mom: I'm leaving store now
Mom: Please talk to Madison
Mom: Tell her how you feel
Mom: give her some good news

I quirk my head to the side, trying to interpret Mom's texts. *Does she mean our conversation last Christmas? Does she want me to share everything we talked about then and in the year since?*

"That's weird."

I lift my head at Madison's statement. "What's weird?"

"Your mom just texted me, and I quote, 'Make Hamilton tell you the secret.' What does she mean?"

Damn it, Mom. She leaves me no choice. My pulse speeds up and my palms sweat.

Dark shadows lie beneath Madison's sad eyes. Exhaustion and stress darken her beautiful face. "Um..." I rise, walking to the refrigerator. "I'm going to have a beer. You want one?"

"No, thank you."

"So..." I pause, trying to decide how to start. "Last year, last winter, I had a long talk with Mom about my life in Chicago." I sit and take a long pull from my beer. "Okay. I'm going to share some things with you, but you have to promise you won't be mad at me."

"Mad at you? Why would I be mad at you?" She tilts her head, her eyes imploring me for answers.

"I didn't share some things with you. I didn't share them with anyone until I told Mom last Christmas." I shrug apologetically. "I live in a town with millions of people, and I am alone. When I leave the ballpark, I'm alone. I eat alone, I watch TV alone, and I live in a large condo all by myself." I groan on my exhale. *Thanks Mom. Is this really why she texted me to come here?* I attempt to take in a calming breath.

"It's hard to trust anyone I meet. I learned in my first short season in the Majors that people want to use me. Other players, women I meet, and even businesses want to exploit my celebrity for their gain." I run my fingers through my hair. Madison nervously picks at her cuticles while her eyes are on me. She doesn't look away. I continue before I chicken out.

"I quickly learned it's just easier to avoid these situations. It's so different from life here in Missouri. So, if I'm not working, I'm home alone. Mom, Amy and you are the only people I trust aside from my agent and publicist. It's the way it has to be."

Madison places her palms on the table in front of her, leaning in my direction. "What about Stan? You talk about him and his family sometimes." The corners of her mouth curve slightly. She perks up a bit at the chance to help me through this.

"Yeah, I hang with him and the family from time to time. But as you can imagine, they are busy, and I don't want to be a nuisance." *Wow! I sound pathetic.* "I spend most of my free time imagining you with me."

Her cheeks pink infinitesimally as her eyes grow wide. I smirk, knowing what she thinks I meant.

"When I walk down the street, I imagine you walking beside me. I daydream about you being at the condo when I return from a road trip." I draw in a deep breath, preparing for the big reveal. "So, last winter I asked for Mom's help."

I shift in my seat to pull the tiny black velvet box from my front pocket. "I've carried this with me since January." I fall to one knee in front of her.

Madison's hands fly to her mouth. Her eyes grow wide, and her breath hitches.

Smiling, I continue. "My life changed on my last night in Athens. I've missed you more every day since. I can't tolerate my life, any life, without you by my side. Madison Crocker, will you save my lonely existence and marry me?" I extend the open ring box toward her.

I attempt to regulate my racing heart. *I did it. I finally admitted everything. I've placed my heart in her hands.*

"Ham," she whispers as large tears flow down her face. "I have to tell you something first."

"No, you need to answer me. Then you can tell me anything you like."

"Hamilton, I'm afraid you may not want to marry me after I tell you…"

I realize the exhaustion I recognized earlier on her face was also fear.

"There's nothing you can tell me that will make me change my mind." I need her to trust my love.

She shakes her head vigorously. "You say that now, but I need you to know…"

The door swings open; I witness true fear in Madison's eyes before she turns. A tiny girl toddles into my mom's kitchen like she owns the place. I'm still kneeling as she rounds the table on her way to Madison, her chocolate curls bouncing with each step.

"Mommy, ice-me. Ice-me." She extends her tiny jacket covered arm, allowing Madison to remove the plastic grocery bag.

Madison's attention is glued to the child. Warmth speeds throughout my body and my heart drums in my chest. My brain rapidly processes the fact Madison is a mother. Instantly, I know the child; I've seen her before. She's a mirror image of my sister, Amy. I peel my eyes from the darling girl to my mother, standing behind Madison. Mom beams and nods. I open my mouth in an attempt to draw more air into my burning lungs.

"Grandma bought you ice cream?" Madison asks the child.

The girl nods once before clapping.

"Ice cream after dinner," Mom reminds the toddler and places several small tubs of ice cream into the freezer.

The little girl proudly carries her own tub to Mom, and she tucks it away with the others. I glance back to Madison. She stares anxiously at me.

This is it. This is the secret she mentioned so many months ago. She wasn't raped as I worried when she fell deep in her depression. This is the secret she worries will cause me not to love her. This is the reason she didn't reply to my proposal moments ago.

I move the ring box from the table into my open palm and extend it in her direction. She shakes her head, tears falling faster now. "I love you more now than I did minutes ago. I love everything about you. Please?" I choke on the words I need to say. I attempt to clear my throat. I hate the hoarse sound of my voice when I continue. "Marry me. Let me love you. Let me love both of you. I'm lost without you."

I pull my grandmother's ring from the box. Slowly, I slide it upon her left ring finger and lock my eyes with hers. She doesn't refuse my action. She doesn't argue.

My mother claps excitedly as I rise. I pull Madison from her chair into my arms. "I'm sorry I hurt you," I whisper. "I can't imagine how scared you were. I didn't know…"

She pulls from my embrace. "I didn't want you to know." She shakes her head. "I mean I didn't want to tell you right away. I wanted you to chase your dream, and you did. It was even better than my wildest dreams. I needed you to settle in before I told you."

Wait. What? She's protecting me. I failed to protect her on our first night together. And she thought she needed to protect me?

"I…" I begin, but Mom interrupts me.

"Let's wait 'til later tonight to share all the details," she points to the little one she's holding. "I've got a hungry granddaughter to feed."

Granddaughter. She has a granddaughter. I have a daughter.

As a tsunami of emotion floods over me, the little girl squirms free and walks toward me. I squat in front of her, never taking my eyes off of her. She extends her tiny hands to my face. Her dark eyes scan mine. I marvel at her actions. She's never met me, yet she peers into my soul like she knows me. This precious miniature version of my older sister standing before me, eyes scanning mine. But what is she waiting for? What should I do? What would a dad do at this exact moment, meeting his daughter for the very first time? How old is she? I scan this confident little person still clutching my face from head to toe. She could be one or maybe… My thoughts stop in their tracks when her perfect lips grace my cheek with a kiss.

She steps back, pointing to her chest. "Wib-Be," she says.

Wib-Be? Fear engulfs me. She's trying to tell me something, and I don't understand. I look to Madison for a lifeline.

"This is Liberty, or Libby." Madison smiles for the first time tonight.

Liberty points to me. "Daddy."

It's not a question. Her voice doesn't rise at the end of the name. *She knows I'm Daddy. How can that be?*

She turns to her mom when I don't respond. Madison

picks her up, quickly placing a kiss on her chubby cheek. I remain frozen in my squat, and my hands tremble.

"I think Daddy needs another drink." Madison looks from me to Liberty. "Should we get him a drink?"

My daughter smiles my way, nodding. Her smile melts me to a puddle. I've never seen anything so beautiful, so perfect. Instantly, she's my whole world, the center of my universe. I try to remain calm and look casual as my world has just doubled in size. Instead of one woman, I now have two.

"She's a miniature Amy," I blurt.

They turn back from the fridge with a beer for me while my mom pulls me into a hug.

"Isn't she perfect?" Mom whispers into my ear before pulling away.

"Daddy," Libby calls to me as Madison extends the cold beer bottle. "Pod-de!" her little voice yells without warning.

I marvel at the speed in which Madison sweeps her into the bathroom and closes the door. I look to Mom, my brow furrowed.

"Potty training," Mom beams proudly. "She's smart."

"She got that from her mom," I state.

Mom waves a paper plate at me. "She gets her looks from you."

"Um," Madison calls from a slightly open bathroom door. "Libby wants Daddy to watch her."

Watch her potty? Is that allowed? I'm a guy. Stone-still, my wide eyes beg Mom for guidance.

My mother turns me in the direction of the bathroom and gives me a shove.

"Should I...?"

"You're her Daddy. It's okay if you're her dad." Mom states, understanding my hesitation. "You'll be by yourself with her, so you better get used to it."

"Daddy!" My daughter waves at me.

I stand frozen awkwardly in the door frame. It feels pervy to watch a child sit on the toilet.

Liberty's movements cease as the sound of pee fills the tiny room. The widest smile I've ever seen glows as bright as the twinkles in her dark eyes. She claps at her success. When her tiny bottom sinks, Madison quickly saves her from falling into the water. *That was close.*

I'm lost in the routine as they redress, squirt soap on hands, sniff the soap, and sing the alphabet song. *How will I ever learn all of this? There's got to be a book. I'll ask Mom about it later.*

Libby raises her freshly washed hands in the air, signaling for me to lift her up. When I do, she places her tiny hand near my nose. I inhale the scent as she giggles.

"She's enamored with your mother's sweet pea hand soap," Madison explains. "We don't have it at Alma's."

Libby again places her hands on my cheeks. This time her eyes don't examine me. She places a kiss on my lips.

Again, this tiny girl knocks me to my knees. Her kiss, her acceptance of me, her calling me Daddy within minutes of meeting me is humbling. Suddenly, everything I've accomplished pales in comparison to creating this perfect, tiny person.

Madison and Mom fly around the kitchen, distributing paper plates, napkins, pizza and drinks for everyone while I hold my daughter in my arms, never wanting to let her go.

CHAPTER 15

Madison

I snap Liberty into her highchair, placing a paper plate in front of her. From mine, I cut tiny pieces of cheese pizza then slide them onto hers. I tear a piece of thinly sliced ham for her and move her toddler cup of milk within her reach.

As I turn toward our table and my plate, I find Hamilton staring at me. "What?"

He shakes his head. "I've got a lot to learn," he murmurs, brow furrowed.

"You'll be fine," Memphis assures him. "Most is common sense, so you will be fine."

I guess I didn't think that Hamilton might feel overwhelmed by all of the day-to-day parenting activities. I worried about all the important moments he missed and created videos to help with that.

"Believe it or not," Memphis continues, "you've watched parents your entire life. All that info is stored deep in your brain and will slide to the front as you need it."

I know it may not help with his current fears of knowing what to do and when, but I feel I need to share now. "Ham, I've created a video journal for you. It has videos from my growing belly, the birth, first words, first steps, and attending Cubs games."

His eyes sparkle.

"I know it can never make up for the moments you missed, but I wanted you to be able to see her life up 'til now." I shrug apologetically, knowing my videos will never be enough.

He reaches across the table to hold my hand, tilting his head. He opens his mouth to speak but is interrupted.

"Daddy!" Liberty raises her little voice and extends her hand to him.

Hamilton takes her hand just like he holds mine. She smiles at him and continues to eat with her free hand. I chuckle. Seems Liberty will be jealous of the attention her daddy gives me. His hands will be full, and I love it.

"I watched four hours of videos last night," Memphis brags. "I couldn't take my eyes off the laptop screen. I even had to rewind and watch several of them a second time."

Hamilton looks from his mom to me, a crooked smile upon his face. His brown eyes dance with excitement.

"I'll give you the site and log in tonight." I smile,

knowing he's excited to view them. "You can watch on your phone or computer anytime."

"Don't start if you don't have an hour to two," Memphis warns. "It was hard for me to shut them off to sleep last night."

I love that she enjoyed them so much. I hope Hamilton will, too.

"Cubbie," Liberty wines while Memphis and I clear the table.

I place the leftover pizza in the refrigerator then turn to face Hamilton, who's holding Liberty. One of her hands twirls a curl while Hamilton spoon feeds her the ice cream, her head on his shoulder.

"Liberty," I attempt to draw her attention from her father's large bowl of ice cream to me. "First bath time, then Cubbie bear."

Memphis announces, "It's bath time! I love bath time!"

Liberty lifts her head from Daddy's shoulder, and she slides from his lap, abandoning the shared ice cream. She looks over the edge of the bathtub as I run warm water and place a few of her favorite bath toys inside. Happy with what she finds, she hurries back to Hamilton. "Daddy," she clutches his right hand in both of hers. "Baff!"

Hamilton promises, "You go. I'll eat my ice cream quick then come watch you in the bathtub."

My daughter, happy with his promise, runs toward the bathroom yelling at Na-Na the entire way. It may be very crowded for three adults to watch her in the tiny bathroom tonight.

I shut off the water, strip Liberty, and prompt her to potty before I place her into the tub. As she always does, she begins swimming, splashing, and blowing bubbles immediately. I step back to allow Daddy and Grandma to witness the bath time fun.

As they enjoy Libby and her bath time play, the pit in my stomach grows. Soon, Liberty will be asleep, and Hamilton and I will be alone. It'll be our time to talk.

I want him to tell me honestly how he really feels. He needs to yell at me or throw something. He should say he'll never forgive me. I deserve his ire. I deserve it all–I cheated him out of a year and a half of Liberty's life. I stole moments; although I tried to record many, it's not the same. I didn't give him a choice–I chose for him to go after his dream rather than be with his daughter. I'm selfish. *How can I hope for him to keep loving me?*

CHAPTER 16

Hamilton

Wrapped in a towel, Liberty stands on a mat outside the tub while Madison attempts to dry her springy ringlets. I shake my head. It's like I'm looking at Amy in our childhood. It's uncanny.

My cheeks ache from smiling so much. My heart swells tight in my chest. I never dreamt I'd know such love. The shear amount of love I hold for the two girls in front of me overwhelms me.

"Daddy," a sweet little voice calls as her arms reach upwards. Now in a Cubs nightgown, I lift her into my arms. "Cubs," she points to the front of her chest.

"I love your pajamas," I respond.

"Daddy gave you those for Valentine's Day, didn't he?" Madison prompts, and Liberty nods in agreement.

I go along with it and add the gift to all the questions building in my head.

At Madison's prompting, we say good night to Grandma before I carry my daughter up to bed. Liberty's head rests upon my shoulder as we climb the stairs, Madison following behind.

"I set her crib up in Amy's room," Madison states, placing a hand at my side.

"Daddy's," Liberty demands.

For the life of me, I don't understand.

"Her books are in your room," Madison explains.

I hold Liberty in the center of my chest, unsure what to do next.

"Cubbie!" Liberty points to the stuffed toy on my bed.

Unsteady in my actions, I lower her onto my bed where she hugs the bear tight to her chest and rests her curls on my pillow. I sit carefully on the edge.

Madison approaches, a couple of books in hand. Without a word, she slides between Liberty and the wall.

"Pick a book," she prompts, holding three books above them.

Liberty points to the weirdest book I've ever seen. Madison lays the other books down and settles into the mattress, opening the cover.

"Daddy sweep," my daughter demands, patting a pillow.

Madison turns her head and smiles encouragingly. It's clear they have a routine. I feel like I am interfering.

"Wib-be wead,"

Will I ever learn this new language? I feel lost with no translation manual.

"Okay, Libby can read to Daddy." Madison throws me a life raft by interpreting.

"Wib-be wead" equals Libby read. That makes sense. Maybe I'll get the hang of it after all.

Liberty begins to point at each photograph in this four-by-six book and declares who is in each photo. The first photo is Madison then Alma. I look at the picture of Alma holding Liberty. It's the same woman I've seen a few times while Face-Timing Madison. Next is McGee then my mom and me. So, this is how she recognized me tonight. Madison shared photos of me to help my daughter connect. It's all coming together now.

A giant yawn engulfs Liberty's entire face.

"Can I read?" I offer to allow her to fall asleep.

Her approving nod clutches my heart. Surely not all kids are this agreeable.

I steal peeks frequently at Liberty's tired eyes as I read the label secured at the bottom of each picture. The book contains photos of my family, Alma's family, and all of our mutual friends from Athens. I continue to read a few more once she loses the battle to keep her eyes open.

I move my glance to Madison to find her eyes glistening with tears. I lay the book down, my hand moving to her face on its own. Gently, I caress her cheek.

"She's perfect," I whisper in an attempt to keep from waking Liberty.

"Far from perfect, but I know what you mean," Madison corrects.

"I'm sorry I didn't protect you." A lump forms in my throat.

Madison's hand covers mine on her cheek. "You never hurt me."

"You were alone, pregnant, in a new city, a new school, with no money, I…"

She places a finger on my lips to silence me. Slowly, gently, I kiss her fingertip before pulling her finger away.

"I should have been there. If I had visited during my off-season as I promised, I would have known you were pregnant," I clear my throat. "I would have helped Mom with the farm and cared for the two of you. You didn't have to do it all alone." Tears wet my cheeks as I spill my heart to the woman I've loved for so long. "Please forgive me," I beg. "I've known for a long time that I should have taken over the farm after Dad's death. A good son would have."

"Ham," her voice cracks. "I'm the one that needs your forgiveness. I didn't tell you. I wanted you to have a career in the Majors and didn't want to be the reason you gave that up."

I long to pull her into my arms as her sobs strengthen. "Shh," I urge. "I know why you kept the secret. I'm just sorry I didn't protect you better on our night together. I never meant for this." I swipe tears from her cheeks. "You allowed me to earn a World Series ring." I smile at her. "Tonight, we admitted we'd rather be together than apart. We've both apologized. We're good, right?"

Madison nods, a slight smile upon her lips.

"Now, what's the update on your mother's investigation?" I ask.

"I can't," she whimpers. "Distract me. Tell me all about the World Series."

Her tears dry and eyes grow heavy as I play with her hair and share everything I remember about our celebrations. I stare at my fingers in her hair as I talk. When she no longer asks questions, I find her eyes closed.

She snores softly. I study her relaxed face. I don't like the dark shadows under her eyes. She hasn't been sleeping. Taking care of Liberty and Alma while watching ball games each night has taken their toll.

She needs sleep. I tug my phone from my pocket and snap a picture of my sleeping girls. I stare at them for several long moments. My world will never be the same.

Realizing I neglected to get the login information from her before she fell asleep, I tiptoe downstairs to see if Mom's up. I can't wait to see the videos she rants about.

CHAPTER 17

Madison

My head swims with all I learned at my family's lawyer's office today. Hurt slices through me with the secrets my mother kept. *Why wouldn't she tell me?* With my dad's death, the farm was paid in full. I never knew this. My mother had a thousand more dollars per month that she apparently squandered on her drinking. A tiny part of me hopes she didn't spend it on alcohol but on something responsible. Maybe I will uncover it in the days to come, but I'm not holding my breath.

Also, with my dad's passing, a trust fund was created for my secondary education expenses. *Why did she not tell me this?* I get why she didn't tell me at age 13 it existed. Perhaps she wanted me to strive for good grades and thought if I knew my education was paid for, I wouldn't care about the grades. But she didn't tell me my senior year, at graduation, or when I moved in with Alma in Columbia. I worked my butt off to get straight A's. I took all of the dual credit classes I could while they were free in high school to save me money. I saved my money from babysitting and my part-time job. All the while, she knew more than 50,000 dollars gathered interest in the Athens Bank while I scraped for every penny I could save. I nursed my twenty-year-old, beat up car along for years to save money. I didn't have an air conditioner in the ninety and one-hundred-degree July and August days. *Why? Why would a mother do that to her child?*

Top that off with the fact that I didn't know my dad's parents' farm remained in our family. As of now, it's in my name. I'm 20 years old, and I own two farms, free and clear. Fortunately, when my dad passed, their farm waited in a trust until I turned 18 instead of transferring to my mother's name. This farm is valued at over 1.5 million dollars and constantly growing. I became a millionaire at age 18 and didn't even know it. The land and the old farmhouse are rented on a year-to-year basis. All of the income from the property rolls back into Crocker Farms, so it's constantly growing for me.

Their lawyer, now my lawyer, states I need to decide what to do with my parents' farm as soon as possible. He offered to help me rent the land and the house or sell it. My grandparents' farm has already signed contracts for the next 12 months, so I have a year to decide whether to continue with it kept in the trust or to sell. Hours later, my head still swims with all I inherited years ago and this week along with all of the responsibility and decisions that lie ahead.

I sat quietly during the meeting, taking it all in, while Hamilton asked several questions. He shared the contact information for his financial guy with the lawyer and seemed to understand the ins and outs of the financial mumbo-jumbo.

I'm grateful he's with me. When the funeral is over, I plan for him to walk me through it all and give me some lessons. It's important that I understand it all to ensure a better future for our daughter.

"Mady," Hamilton's voice calls to me. He stands outside my open passenger door. We've arrived at the sheriff's office.

"Sorry." I shake my thoughts from my head, preparing to face news of my mother's death inside these walls. "I'm not sure I can handle much more."

He pulls me into a tight hug. "I'm here." He places a long kiss to my temple. "After this, I'll take you to Liberty." He tucks my hair behind my ear. "We can hold 'Mow-Mows' and eat ice cream."

I love the speed with which he's learning everything about Liberty. Looking into his eyes, I see he believes once we're at Memphis' farm in the presence of our daughter that all will seem better. He's right—when Liberty is in my arms, the present and future seem less daunting.

I take his hand, shut my door, and allow him to lead me into the county sheriff's office. We don't need to introduce ourselves. Several office staff members, Athens Police Officers, Highway Patrol Officers, and deputies swarm Hamilton. Rumors of his return to Athens tipped them off that he might arrive with me today. They congratulate him on the Cubs winning the World Series, ask for autographs, and pose for photos with him.

It's easy for me to forget he's a famous athlete. When I'm with him, he's still just Hamilton. It isn't until we go out in public and he's surrounded by adoring fans that I remember he's more than just my hometown boy now. He glances my direction with an apologetic look. I smile, letting him know it's okay. Watching him with his hometown fans eases my mood.

"Ms. Crocker," the sheriff greets, extending his hand. "I'm sorry about all of that." He nods towards Hamilton.

"It's fine; he needs to come home more often. Most of them were his fans before he left for the Major Leagues."

"Guys!" He yells through the office. "Mr. Armstrong, please join us as we head to my office." He shoots a stern look to the crowd.

Hamilton assumes the seat beside me while the sheriff closes his door and seats himself on the other side of his desk. Moving a file folder from a tray to the empty area in front of him, he begins.

"In our investigation, we have interviewed several people that saw your mother on October 30th." He's careful to keep the crime scene photos covered. "The coroner suspects she was poisoned, and we are still waiting on the tox reports. They should be in later today or tomorrow." He sighs, clearly not wanting to share the next part. "Arnold Ballwin confessed to having a sexual relationship with your mother for the two months prior to her death."

Well, I wasn't expecting that bit of information. I thought he'd share a suspect list, the events of her last day, time of death, but not that my mother was having sex with the married owner of the bar she practically lived at.

"He confessed to entertaining your mother around four p.m. on the 30th. Then, she went to the Black Jack, and he waited an hour before he arrived at the bar. Apparently, this was common on the days his wife would open and close the bar." He closes the folder. "Several people verified your mother arrived at the bar around 4:30 and remained until closing. Arnold was said to leave the bar at 10:30 p.m. We confirmed with neighbors that when he arrived home, he stayed until his wife arrived home after the bar closed for the night."

"We have two more interviews this afternoon. Arnold's wife, Henrietta, was the last to see your mom when she closed the bar at midnight. She is one we will be talking to this afternoon." The sheriff takes turns looking at Hamilton and me as he talks. "Your mother's car wasn't found at her home. We found it still parked around the corner from Black Jack Bar on the thirty-first. We are trying to piece together the events that occurred when she left the bar, how she got home, and what happened when she arrived home."

Hamilton squeezes my hand in support.

"I hope to have more information to share after today's

interviews and the tox results. I'll call you around dinner tonight to give you an update." With that, the sheriff escorts us back to our car and sends us on our way.

"Thoughts?" Hamilton prompts as we drive home from Athens.

What a loaded question. My thoughts. Well, right now, they are all over the place. "Part of me doesn't believe she was poisoned. Or at least not by anyone but herself. I mean, why would anyone do it? They didn't steal anything; her purse and phone were found still in her possession." Hamilton nods in agreement as I continue. "I could do without knowing she was sleeping with Arnold."

"I know," Hamilton cringes while keeping his attention on the road.

"Honestly, I'm more upset with all she kept from me." I lean my head against the window, not seeing the farmland passing by. "I struggled through high school then even more the past two years, and I didn't need to. It blows my mind that she never told me. Why do you think she did that?"

"Honey, you will never know why. Just like so many other things she's done. All you can do is focus on what you plan to do now that you know about the two farms and the trust fund." He quickly smiles at me before facing the road again. "It's important that you take care of yourself and then do a little good with it. You know?"

I love that he gets me. Several people in Columbia took care of me when I thought had nothing. I need to find a way to pay it forward while thanking them for all they did for me.

"It's overwhelming," I confess. Lifting my head, I take his free hand. "Will you please help me with the farms and financial stuff?"

"If you want. I meant it when I said we'd discuss it with my financial guy. He really helped me organize and plan; I'm sure he will have lots of options for you." He squeezes my hand reassuringly. "First thing is you need to decide if you want to keep each farm and if you plan to live at either one."

I pull my hand from his and turn in the seat, pulling my knees up, facing him. "I plan to live with my husband."

Hamilton squeezes my knee. He tears his eyes briefly from the highway. His face says all I need to know. He likes my statement a lot.

"I don't know if I will ever live on either farm, but I think I'd like to keep them, at least for a while." I shrug and purse my lips. "I thought I would have to sell the farm since I couldn't keep up with the payments. Now that I know it's paid off; I want to keep it. I have many great memories of my dad on the farm. Even the last seven years didn't erase the fun I had with Mom and Dad before that."

"So," Hamilton summarizes, "I'll contact Foster; he can get in touch with your lawyer and share some options with you."

"Um, with us," I correct. "As a couple, what's mine is yours."

"I get that, but…"

"No buts!" My voice raises sternly.

Hamilton's sigh lets me know he doesn't plan to argue me on this topic right now.

"I'd like to plan a get together with the entire gang," I state, staring out the window once again.

"To tell them we're getting married?" he assumes.

"Well, yes," I agree. "I need to tell them about Liberty."

He swiftly pulls to the side of the gravel road and puts the truck into park. He turns to face me. "I assumed they already knew."

I shake my head, internally cussing my burning sinuses.

"Adrian and Bethany only know because they surprised me in Columbia," I confess. "I swore them to secrecy until I could tell you."

He pulls me onto his lap and holds me tight. As I cry into his shoulder, I feel him pull his cellphone from his back pocket. I'm still trying to stop my tears when my own phone vibrates.

He chuckles. "Group text. It's from me."

I wipe my eyes, struggling to read my cell phone through them.

Hamilton: bonfire tomorrow
Hamilton: 7 @ farm
Me: hope to see you
Salem: we're in
Adrian: count us in
Bethany: what can I bring
Me: nothing
Savannah: (thumbs up emoji)

When we pull up to the house, Memphis and Liberty hold two kittens in their laps on the porch swing. Liberty's big wave greets us as we exit Hamilton's truck.

"Daddy, wook!" She hollers. "Mow-mow. One. Two." She points from her lap to Memphis'.

As we near, she lifts her kitten, presenting it to him. "Daddy do."

Without missing a beat, he cuddles the kitten in one arm and lifts Liberty into his lap on the swing with the other. I take some pictures of the three of them and a few more including Memphis and her kitten.

"Hop over here and let me get a family picture," Memphis orders, passing the kitten to me.

I want to argue. I'm sure I look horrible. I haven't worried much about my hair or makeup since Alma's fall days ago. I'd imagined our first photo of the three of us to be during happier times.

"Someone hasn't napped yet," Memphis pretends to whisper.

Liberty's eyes dart to mine. She knows she must nap every day. "Mow-mow, nap," she nods as she speaks.

Memphis explains, "We decided to pet the kittens then take a nap." Liberty still nods. "We just played with the cats too long."

Liberty's face awaits my verdict, eyes locked on mine.

"Daddy." I lean forward, looking toward Hamilton, hoping he'll play along. "Does your kitty look sleepy?"

He lifts the kitten to eye level. "What do you think, Libby? Is this kitten sleepy?"

Liberty nods.

"Here Grandma," I suggest. "You help the kitties go take a nap, and I'll help Libby."

"Bye, Mow-mow," she waves over my shoulder as we enter the house.

After she potties, we sing the ABC song and rinse our hands.

"I'm going to make a few calls while you lay her down if that's okay?" Hamilton asks, peeking into the bathroom.

I nod and carry my sleepy girl upstairs.

"Hey, sleepy head," Hamilton greets as I slink into the kitchen.

"I can't believe I fell asleep," I croak.

"Apparently, you needed it," he teases.

"What's all that?" I point to a legal pad and papers strewn in front of him on the table.

Hamilton explains he called his money guy and the firm jumped into action. He points to an email. "Seems your grandparents' farm has been in the family over 100 years." His eyes continue to read the email. "He has forwarded the information necessary to have it listed as a Century Farm. Once confirmed, you may display a Century Farm sign on the property."

Pride grows within me. For so long, I believed my family

history and my connection to them passed with my father. I'm finding my connection to my family through the land quite appealing.

"Foster will be at the lawyer's office at 10 tomorrow morning. He'd like to meet with you after lunch, if that's okay."

I nod. He's been a busy man during my nap. The sooner I begin understanding my new financial situation, the better. For now, my head continues to swim with too much information and too many possibilities. I crave for the order and normalcy I knew as my life a week ago.

Hamilton moves toward me; I sense he's something else to share with me.

"I asked him to do something else," Hamilton hedges, takes a deep breath, then continues. "I want my name on Liberty's birth certificate. Foster says it's easy, as long as you're okay with it."

In his eyes, I see worry. *Does he seriously think I would fight him on this? Why wouldn't I want it?* I tried to put it on the certificate when she was born, but I couldn't.

"I tried to do it when she was born," I explain. It's important he knows this. "Since we weren't married and you weren't with me, the law wouldn't allow me to list you as her father. I was able to give her your last name, but it was all I could do at that time."

He chews on his thumb nail while I explain. "So, I can?"

"I'd always planned for you to be on her birth certificate," I murmur, my throat tightening. "You've always been her father. I made sure she knew that. I'm glad you're wasting no time. I'm just sorry I took so long…"

He silences my apology, his lips smashing to mine. He wastes no time pressing his tongue between my lips, seeking entrance. He consumes my mouth, just as he consumes all of me.

CHAPTER 18

Hamilton

Looking at my watch, I sigh. She's just awakened, and I need to leave. With all that she's got going on in her life, I should really stay here with her.

"What's wrong?" Madison's brow furrows.

"I need to run to town for a bit," I admit reluctantly. "I bought something a month ago with the promise to pick it up my next time in town." I run my hands down my face. "It should only take an hour."

A small smile slides upon her face. "You should go. We'll be okay." She tightens the messy bun on top of her head.

"You can come with me." The words fly out of my mouth. I should have considered it earlier. "Liberty should come, too. I can't wait to see her reaction."

Although I purchased the puppy to keep me company in Chicago, I love that all three of us can share it now. *What little girl wouldn't love a puppy?*

Madison mulls over my offer for a few moments. I watch as she processes the rest of the day and an impromptu trip to town with Liberty.

"Okay," she sing-songs. A flicker of excitement appears on her worn out face. She grabs a backpack then informs our daughter we're going for a car ride.

I park beside the two trucks in the gravel lot. I spot Marshall and his mother across the park. It seems like yesterday we were playing ball and she attended every game.

"Pway!" Liberty squeals when the playground comes into view. "Mommy, pway!"

Madison widens her eyes in my direction. I promised a surprise and gave no details.

"I'm going to talk to Marshall for a minute." I point in his direction as I talk. "You can play for a bit." I jerk my chin towards the playground equipment.

Madison squints, trying to read me. I love her reaction to my mention of a surprise. It places a smile upon her face and a pep in her step, if only for a little while.

Approaching Marshall and his mother, I can't pull my eyes from the fluffy ball of black and white fur at the end of the leash. I kneel, and the Siberian Husky puppy pads my way. While I pet my new friend, Mrs. Harris informs me of the shot records and paperwork in the envelope she holds. I'm picking the dog up two weeks earlier than planned, but she assures me I won't have any issues.

Marshall and I chat a bit about the final World Series game he attended with my sister and Mom. It's clear he would have liked attending the after parties with me instead of heading back to the condo with them.

"I promised my girls a surprise, so I better head over there." I motion toward the playground. We say our good-byes, and I walk toward the playground with my puppy in one arm and an envelope in the other.

Madison notices the puppy immediately and shakes her head at me, a huge smile on her face. I bend down, placing the puppy in the grass as I walk the final yards toward them.

"Daddy!" Liberty waves from the bottom of the small slide. "Puppy!"

Cute little girl squeals emit as she toddles toward me, her little hands waving at the puppy.

"Who's this?" Madison inquires as she squats and extends an open hand for the puppy to sniff.

Liberty stands just out of reach of the fluffy creature. Clearly, she longs to play, but waits for confirmation it's okay to do so.

"This is our new puppy," I explain. "She's gonna need a name."

As if sensing Liberty's apprehension, the puppy sits between us, its little tail wagging with anticipation.

"Libby, come pet our puppy," I urge calmly.

She looks to her mom. With Madison's nod, she slowly

walks over and plops down near the eager puppy. She's immediately awarded kisses on her cheeks. Giggles fill the air–they're music to my ears.

"So, we have a husky puppy," Madison murmurs, nudging my shoulder.

"I reached out to Marshall a month ago to see when his mother would have her next litter. I made arrangements to pick her up when I came to Mom's for Thanksgiving." I pull my eyes from our happy daughter and her new friend. "I figured if I picked her up a little early, it might help entertain Liberty for you this week."

The light in her eyes and her megawatt smile assure me; Madison is glad I did.

"Liberty," I call to the little girl on the ground with a puppy on her chest. "Let's go show Grandma our new puppy."

"What should we name her?" Madison asks as she buckles Liberty into her car seat and I secure the leash to the seat belt beside her.

"I have one name I like," I admit, opening the driver's door. "But we can…"

"What is it?" she interrupts.

"Indie," I respond. "Indiana from the Indiana Jones movies." I smile sheepishly.

"We named the dog Indiana." Madison recites the line from the movie. "Indie it is," she states.

I love that we share similar tastes in movies.

———

Amy's truck is at the farm when we arrive. When Mom mentioned she'd be over today, I immediately started dreading her arrival. I love my sister, but when she's upset, she doesn't handle it well. I realize Madison is not new to our family. I worry that Amy will let her have it for keeping my daughter, her niece, a secret for nearly two years.

I notice Madison's spine straighten and shoulders move backward before she exits the truck to pull Liberty from the car seat. She's preparing for battle—I ready myself to allow her to fight her own battles while I also protect her.

I lead Indie to the nearby patch of grass. "Go potty," I prompt and wonder how much harder it will be to potty-train at four weeks instead of the normal six weeks.

My eyes track Madison as she carries Liberty into the house. Distracted, I'm unsure if the puppy went potty or not. I decide to risk an accident rather than let Madison face Amy alone.

Liberty anxiously waits at the door. "Puppy!" she squeals and points. "Na-na, puppy!"

I hand her the red leash, and she proudly parades her puppy to Mom. I hear Amy's raised voice in the front room. My mom gives me a knowing look as I pass her in the kitchen.

Madison stands, arms folded across her chest. Amy's a couple of feet in front of her, hands on her hips, in a wide stance.

"You'll get no money," Amy spits. "If that's what you're after, you're barking up the wrong tree. You'll have to share custody."

"Amy, I didn't plan to get pregnant, nor do I want any money." Madison's voice is low. "I love..."

Amy throws her palm out towards Madison's face, halting her words. "Don't play dumb. You hitched yourself to my brother years ago. You wanted him to be your way out of your miserable life in Athens. I've been on to you for years." She waves her finger in Madison's face. "I won't allow you to hurt him, and we'll be demanding a paternity test."

I can't allow her tirade to continue. "Enough!" I step beside Madison, tugging her tight to my side. "A paternity test? Really?" I swing my arm wide toward the kitchen. "Why don't you take a quick peek at your niece before you spew more crap."

As Amy stomps over to the doorway, I whisper in Madison's ear, "I'm sorry. Are we okay?"

She only nods. She's trying to keep a tight hold on her emotions. She doesn't want Amy to see she's rattling her.

"She's trying to protect you," Madison murmurs. "I've hurt her with my secret, and she needs to let me know it. I'm ready for it." She fakes a smile up at me.

Realizing several minutes have passed, I look to the doorway but don't find Amy. I guide Madison with me into the kitchen.

"Mommy," Liberty greets and points. "May-me!"

My sister sits crossed-legged on the linoleum floor, building blocks in her hand and a big, dopey grin on her face. It's clear she loves that Liberty knows her name.

When Amy's eyes meet mine, I inform her, "Madison created a book with all of our photos. They read it before naps and at bedtime." With my stare, I hope she understands Madison never tried to keep us from knowing Liberty.

Amy's slight nod acknowledges my statement. I won't delude myself by thinking she'll apologize and move on. She'll be rude a couple more times before she moves on, but the worst is over now.

CHAPTER 19

Madison

My phone rings after dinner. Seeing the sheriff's number on the caller ID, I choose to answer on speaker phone. "This is Madison," I greet. "Hamilton is with me, and I've put you on the speaker."

"I have an update," the sheriff informs. "Although the toxicology report hasn't arrived, we have a suspect in custody and a signed full confession."

I feel as though I've been punched. I attempt to pull in a breath without success. I pull my knees to my chest and wrap my arms around them. This allows me to gulp shallow breaths.

Standing behind my chair, Hamilton rubs my shoulders and asks, "Who confessed?"

Memphis enters the room, fetches me water, and encourages me to sip. When Indie and Liberty run into the room, she herds them back into the front room. Amy assists her in blocking the doorway.

"Henrietta confessed she knew of her husband's affair. She admitted to driving your mother home from the bar that night." He clears his throat. "She also admitted to slowly poisoning your mother's drinks each night at the bar with a variety of toxic houseplants. Seems the Athens Garden Club recently had a presentation on dangerous houseplants for pets and humans. She listed five plants in her home she added over and over to your mother's drinks at the bar. She even confessed to ordering two Oleander plants on Amazon that will arrive later this week. She planned to use them to finish the job if the other houseplants didn't work."

"Does this mean you will release the body to the funeral home?" Memphis asks for me from the doorway.

Hamilton moves to squat in front of me, holding my hands.

"Yes, I've already contacted them to officially release the body. With her confession, we do not need to wait on the tox report as it may not screen for the poisons she confessed to using. The house has also been cleared for you to enter."

"Thank you." My timid voice breaks. I take another sip of water before speaking again. "I appreciate all your department has done to quickly solve this."

My mind boggles with the words "poisonous houseplants." I didn't even know houseplants could harm a human. Seems weird to have such items out in a living space. He said

Athens Garden Club. My mom was a member of the garden club. I wonder if she and Henrietta attended the same meetings. Repeated poisoning. I guess my mother's copious amounts of alcohol made it easier to poison her repeatedly night after night.

"Hey," Hamilton's soft voice calls to me. "Let's take a minute and go upstairs. Amy and Mom will play with Liberty."

I don't resist as I allow him to lead me up the stairs. He pulls me through his room into his bathroom. He places a stopper in the drain and proceeds to fill the tub with hot water. Walking to his shower, he removes his shower gel, and squirts it into the stream of water. White bubbles quickly multiply beneath the spout while he adjusts the water to a tolerable temperature then turns back to me.

"A nice, long soak in a warm bath is just what the doctor orders for you after the day you've had." He flashes his boyish smile at me. "You climb in. I'm going to fetch you a large glass of wine." He places a warm, heavy kiss to the corner of my lips before exiting his bathroom.

Turning toward the vanity, I cringe at my reflection. The weight of the day shows on me. My eyes are tired, and dark circles shadow below them. I place my hair in a messy bun on top of my head, strip, and slide beneath the blanket of bubbles into the decadently warm water. I rest my head on the back of the tub and place my toes against the opposite end. I submerge myself from the neck down, relaxing in the warmth.

As promised, Hamilton returns with a large glass of rosé.

Without a word, he places it on the edge of the tub, lights two candles, turns on a playlist, and turns off the bathroom light before he leaves.

"Ham," I whisper while he spoons me in his bed.

"Yes," he murmurs back.

"I'm sorry." Even at a whisper, my voice quakes. "I'm sorry I kept Liberty from you and your family. I can never make it up to you."

He spins me in his arms and silences my apology with his lips upon mine. While I want to fight him to finish my apology, my traitorous body succumbs to my desire for him. He kisses me senseless, only pulling away when I gasp for breath.

"Now that you can't speak," he begins, "listen to me. I love you. I've always loved you, and I will always love you. You don't need to apologize to me. I know why you chose to move away from Athens and care for Liberty on your own. I believe it when you say you always planned to tell me; your videos are proof of that. It hurts me when you think you need to apologize, because if I had protected you that night, you wouldn't have had to make such a big decision on your own."

I begin to protest, but he places his fingers upon my lips, silencing me. "If I had protected us better, we wouldn't have that precious little girl in our lives." He points his thumb over his shoulder at Liberty, sleeping in the portable crib on the other side of his room. "If we changed one thing, it would change all of them. I've only known her a day, yet I know I don't want to live in a world without her in it." He lifts my hand to kiss my fingers. "You've apologized too many times. I accept your apology, just as you've accepted mine."

He rolls me to my stomach, placing his hand under my shirt upon my back. As he rubs his fingertips up and down, he whispers, "I love you, can't wait to marry you, and to live as a family."

He rubs my back until my mind drifts off into dreams of the three of us happily living in Chicago.

My worry grows the closer we get to seven. Of course, Hamilton doesn't stress at all. I remind him that I'm the one that kept the secret and told lies to cover it. He was innocent in it all.

As the caravan of four trucks stir up dust on the gravel lane, I nearly experience a panic attack. Memphis distracts Liberty in the house until we are ready for her to make her big appearance outside. On the porch, watching them park, Hamilton kisses me. It starts sweetly and quickly heats. His lips surround mine, his hot tongue tangles with mine, so deep and so long I forget where we are.

As my thoughts come back into focus, our friends stand in front of us, clapping.

"We're engaged," Hamilton declares, squeezing me tight to his side.

Adrian lifts my left hand, and they admire his grandmother's ring.

"It's about damn time." Troy pats Hamilton on the back with a loud thump.

Hamilton turns to me. His furrowed brow and tight mouth signal his confusion by Troy's statement.

"They've been looking for this since Salem's wedding," I whisper, raising an eyebrow.

His face lights up, recalling our interactions and dancing that night.

"When's the big day?" Bethany inquires, beaming.

"It's new, and we have other stuff to focus on this week." Hamilton answers to fend off further questions.

We usher our friends to the chairs circling the fire pit in the backyard. Excited conversation flows from our engagement to jobs to Bethany and Adrian's little ones.

"We have another surprise," Hamilton announces, rising to his feet.

Bile rises in my throat; I actually feel my airway tighten. Not now. I need to visit with our friends for a while and then ease into it. But with his declaration, it has to be now.

He prompts me to stand from my chair, looks into my eyes, then whispers, "You can do this."

I watch as he leaves our circle and enters the house. I turn back to the group, finding all eyes anxiously waiting on me.

"I've needed to tell you something..." I pause as their attention shifts from me. Turning, I see our daughter waving to the group from her daddy's shoulder. When I spin back around, seven pairs of eyes await my explanation. "This is Liberty. Libby, these are Mommy and Daddy's friends."

"Befan-ney," she squeals before wiggling down from Hamilton. "Baby?"

I grab her around the waist and lift her away from the fire. As we walk to Bethany and Adrian, I explain the babies stayed home. Liberty's lower lip protrudes in disappointment.

"Maybe you can come play at our house later this week," Adrian offers.

Of course, this raises red flags amongst our other friends. "I didn't share this with Hamilton or with any of you. I wanted Hamilton to be settled with baseball before I introduced him to our daughter." I take a few calming breaths. "Bethany and Adrian made surprise trips to see me last year, so they were sworn to secrecy until I could tell Hamilton." I look at Winston and Troy. "Please don't be mad that they kept my secret."

The guys nod at me.

"So, an engagement and telling your secret to him, when did this all happen?" Savannah asks, standing with hands on her hips.

"Memphis arranged alone time for us last night," I begin. Savannah's hurt, I can sense it.

"She tricked the two of us into being the only ones here at the farm for an hour last night. Madison didn't know I was coming. Mom urged me to talk to her, knowing I've been trying to find the time to ask her to marry me since last Christmas," he shrugs with a crooked smile. "Once I proposed, Madison told me everything." He wraps his arm around my shoulders and tugs on Liberty's curls.

"Just last night?" Savannah seeks affirmation. "So, Hamilton you've only known…"

Nodding, he confirms, "24 hours."

This appeases some of Savannah's anger at being left out of the loop. We're close and keeping this from her causes some damage. I'll need to find time for just the two of us after Mother's funeral.

"Well look-y here," Memphis greets the group in her backyard. "Libby, your bath is ready."

Excited, Liberty wiggles this way and that until I pass her to Grandma. I instantly miss her calming effect on my emotions. Hamilton's arm squeezes me tight, as if he senses my hesitation in letting her go. Memphis and Liberty say good night to our guests on their way back inside.

We truly have the best friends. The rest of the night flows easily. They have a million questions about my life in Columbia and Hamilton's World Series week. Slowly, as time passes, my nerves calm, and my heartbeat regulates. When I can't stop yawning at about ten, I'm disappointed that our guests begin to leave. I've missed every one of them. I've missed our group and just hanging out. I'd like to do it more often, but if I move to Chicago with Hamilton, I'm not sure that will be possible.

———

Two days later, while Hamilton makes some calls, I shower, put on the appropriate black attire, fix my hair and apply my makeup. I'm nibbling on a granola bar and fresh fruit for a mid-morning breakfast, knowing I won't feel like eating at the meal provided by the church later. I even played blocks with Liberty until Amy arrived. Although she's still giving me the cold shoulder, she's nothing but kind to Liberty. I'm thankful she's able to stay here with her while we attend the funeral this afternoon.

I'm avoiding Amy's scowl and stares by hiding in the kitchen until Hamilton comes back inside or Memphis is done getting dressed. I've enough to cope with today; I don't need to verbally spar with her again. I know with time she'll work through her anger, and we will be friends again.

Unable to be alone any longer, I walk out to Hamilton in the driveway. He's explaining he needs one more day, then he will spend a few days in Chicago before heading back to Athens. It's clear they want him available for much more than he wants to commit to.

"I need to go; I have a funeral in an hour. I'll look at my calendar tonight and let you know which events I'll attend." Hamilton's tone further expresses his firm stand on this matter.

"Sorry." He pulls me into him, wrapping his long, strong arms around me tightly. "I'll be in Chicago two, maybe three, days next week. I need to make one more call. It should be quick; stay right here." He keeps one arm snug around my waist as he connects his next call.

"Sheridan," Hamilton greets. "Just got off the phone with Berkeley." He listens to the voice on the other end of the line.

"Yes, the funeral is today. I informed her I will be in Chicago for two, maybe three, days next week. Then, I will need to come back to Athens." During the pause, he places a peck on my forehead.

"Of course, she did. Anyway, I'm filling you in so that you can ensure the other members of the team cover for me as I have family matters to tend to. It's not like I'm at Disney World…" His agent must have interrupted him.

"I'm just wanting to make sure the club knows there was a death in the family, and that I am not on vacation. It's not too much to ask as I've jumped through every hoop up until this week." Again, he pauses to listen.

"Okay. Thanks." With that, he places his cell phone in his pants pocket.

Without a word, he guides us back into the house.

"There they are!" Memphis calls, and Liberty runs toward us.

"She thought you left already," Amy explains with a smile for me.

CHAPTER 20

Madison

We're at the church for lunch. Somehow, I made it through all of the hugs and kind words shared by most of the town of Athens at the funeral. I left the ceremony just as my mother had planned it. I would much rather have had a private burial and been done with it, but if this was her last wish, I granted it.

My mother hadn't been active in the church or community for many years. Visitors attended her funeral for the woman she used to be and to give me their support. Fortunately, there were only the minister, Hamilton, Memphis, and I at the graveside. A fitting goodbye to the mother that only yelled at me when she wasn't ignoring me these past years.

Memphis insisted I allow the ladies of the Lutheran

Church to serve a lunch for us. She reminded me that, once, my entire family was active in their church. I invited my girlfriends and Hamilton's family to join me here, since I have no other family to accompany me.

Hamilton and I are first in line to fix our plate. He scoops food onto mine for me. I'm not hungry, but I know he and Memphis will make me eat. The brisket and homemade mac and cheese look good; the rest of it I will pass on.

Memphis sits by Hamilton. Adrian, Salem, Savannah, and Bethany sit across the table from us. They do their best to distract me with their conversations while the quiet church ladies frequently refill our water and tea glasses.

I lay my fork down after a few bites. Hamilton squeezes my shoulders and whispers, "You should eat a bit more."

Reluctantly, I nibble some more. I don't taste the food; I only eat it so I'll have energy to play with Liberty tonight.

"Pardon me," a lady approaches. "Madison, your phone has been ringing nonstop in the kitchen."

I rise to take my phone from her. I must have left it in my purse–I hadn't even missed it. *Odd.* I've three missed calls from Trenton and one voicemail. I click on the voicemail then lift the phone to my ear.

"Madison, I know your mother's funeral is today. Crap! I thought it was over by now." The voice barely sounds like Trenton. "This can't wait any longer. Mom suffered another stroke this morning and passed away about nine. Call me when you get this so I can share the plans with you."

My legs buckle and the tile floor reaches up to slap me.

"Madison!"

It's all I hear as darkness engulfs me.

"Madison," Memphis firmly calls to me.

I struggle to open my eyes. They're too heavy as I try again. They open but a fraction. The bright lights burn; I close them quickly.

"Madison," Adrian calls this time. "Honey, we need you to sit up and open your eyes."

I use all my strength to raise my hand to shield my eyes before I slowly open them. I blink several times before they focus on everyone hovering above me.

"There you are," Memphis greets. "You gave us a scare. Here, sip some water."

No sooner do I swallow the water than I feel my stomach lurch. I crawl from the group, rise, and sprint to the restroom. At the toilet, I lose everything I just forced down. My stomach empty, I continue to dry heave for several more minutes. The pain in my abdomen does not compare to the pain in my heart.

I thought my world was falling apart before; now it has truly crumbled. Alma passed away, and I wasn't there. I didn't get to say goodbye.

A cold, wet cloth is placed on the back of my neck as I still bend over the stool. Hamilton's large hand warms my back. He doesn't say a word, just allows his nearness to comfort me.

In the hall, I hear Memphis direct Adrian to thank the church ladies, explain what has happened, and say goodbye for us.

When I attempt to rise, Hamilton scrambles to assist me. I

splash water on my face and pat it dry with the paper towel he hands me.

Memphis returns, pressing an ice pack to my scalp near my forehead. "Doc says to bring you right over. I think you need stitches."

I want to argue, but I don't have the strength. They help me to the car, buckle me in, and I watch as the town of Athens passes by the window. While Memphis drives, I hear Hamilton making calls in the back seat. I recognize the words "death", "Columbia", "not next week", and "make it happen". I don't even attempt to make out his meaning.

Memphis removes the ice pack from my forehead, claiming we'll ice again in an hour. Liberty stands from her cars on the floor to take a closer look. She didn't like that I was hurt. It took both Hamilton and Amy to distract her so I could rest nearby on the sofa.

"Mommy," she soothes, patting my shoulder. "Ow-wy." She points to my head. "Tiss?"

"Um, Hamilton." I call across the room to him for assistance.

He approaches, brows raised, unsure what she's said.

"Tiss, Daddy?" She asks him the same question.

"Honey, it hurts too much to kiss it," I explain.

"Libby, you can kiss Mommy somewhere else to make her feel better."

I smile. He's getting it. He's thinking like a Daddy now.

"Kiss me here." I point to my cheek.

My strong-willed daughter does me one better. She kisses both my cheeks and then my mouth before she blows a kiss at the five stitches along my scalp. I feel the tickle of her breath across the exposed stitches as Memphis returns to tape a fresh gauze over the wound.

I wince as I rise to a sitting position. Hamilton and Memphis hover closely, frowning at my movements. "I'm fine. I need to call Trenton then pack."

Hamilton shakes his head. I'm ready to fight when he speaks. "I've already talked to Trenton and Taylor." He sits beside me, and Liberty promptly climbs on his lap, wanting to care for me. "I told them we would text when we leave here at about 6."

Liberty reaches up to touch my cheek. I smile at her sweetness. "I'm okay."

"Taylor and Mom talked. We think it's best if Libby stays here with Grandma. There have been many changes for her this week, and Taylor worries returning to Columbia might confuse her even more."

I want to argue; I need her with me. I need her to help me. But I know they are right. I need to protect her more than I need to use her to calm me. I nod.

"If Mommy and Daddy go to a meeting, can you stay here with Grandma?" I search my daughter's face for any sign of fear. This will be her first time spending the night alone with Memphis.

"Na-Na!" She beckons toward the kitchen as she climbs off Hamilton's lap.

Memphis enters the room to face her.

"Ice-me?"

That little devil. She's not worried about spending the night without me. She's already plotting an ice cream celebration with Grandma. If Memphis isn't careful, Liberty will walk all over her kindness.

I laugh at her antics. It makes my head hurt, so I immediately stop. I look away from Hamilton's gaze as I don't want to be babied. I rise to pack and get on our way. I need to be with Alma's family.

CHAPTER 21

Hamilton

I feel as if my heart rips in half as I kiss my baby girl goodbye. In 48 hours, she's become everything to me. As one half of my heart remains at the farm with Liberty, the other half of it aches for Madison.

She slumps in the passenger seat beside me. The light that Liberty and Indie brought back to her face a day ago is nowhere to be found. The woman I love lethargically sits an arm's length away. I feel as though I'm losing her with each mile we drive.

I fiddle with the radio. "What would you like to listen to?"

She slowly turns toward me; her beautiful blue eyes are now empty pools. I caress her cheek with my free hand, but she doesn't lean into my touch. Glancing in her direction for a brief moment, I cringe at her haunting eyes and distant stare. I choose an oldies rock station, turning the volume down to be barely audible.

The entire family greets us on the porch as we pull into Alma's driveway. A wide, genuine smile hops upon her face. Gone is the haunted look. As I exit the driver's seat, Taylor's girls and Trenton's boys surround Madison in a group hug. Waves are exchanged, and Trenton assists me in carrying in our bags.

When the front door closes, McGee trots excitedly to Madison. She bends down to give him loves. In his excitement, on his hind legs, he knocks her onto her butt and slathers her with wet kisses. I wonder what will happen to him now that Alma is gone.

I bend to pet McGee, rescuing her from his love. She clutches her aching sides from her laughter.

"Everyone, this is Hamilton Armstrong." She swings her arm wide towards me.

McGee's magical kisses sparked more life into her.

"Duh!" one of the boys shouts.

"We all know who he is," another boy states.

Two girls whisper and blush near Taylor, who I met at my debut at Wrigley.

"Okay, well then," Madison acts offended. "Hamilton pay

attention. We will test you later." She prepares to introduce me to each family member.

"Let me," I interrupt, pointing. "Trenton, his sons Grant and Hale. Let's see, I think I remember hearing Grant is the oldest. So, you must be Hale, right?"

The boys nod in silent awe that I know who they are.

"And you must be Trenton's better half, Ava." She melts under my smile. Madison is shocked I've guessed correctly so far. She's talked of each of them often in our calls over the years I bet she didn't realize I paid attention. That with Libby's picture book told me all I needed to know.

"Taylor and her husband I met at Wrigley." I wave in their direction. "I assume those were your two giggling girls that ran from the room before I could get to them. And last but not least, you must be Madison's editor, Cameron."

Madison beams proudly at me. I've made a great impression with my knowledge of a family I've never met.

"Let's head to the kitchen," Taylor invites. "I'm sure you could use a drink and perhaps something to eat."

I place my hand in Madison's as we follow Alma's children to the kitchen. Madison's breath catches at the sheer volume of food on the counters and table.

"Mom's church family and neighbors have delivered food off and on all day," Cameron shares. "I hope you are hungry, because I can't eat another bite." She chuckles, rubbing her belly.

"We ate a sandwich before we left," Madison states. "I would like a snack, though." She skims her eyes from container to container, peeking under some lids, and groaning at the desserts.

"Check the fridge, too." Taylor orders.

The overwhelming amount of food is a true testament to Alma's love. Her activity in the community easily placed her dear to the hearts of many.

I slide a paper plate into Madison's hand. As I place odds and ends on my plate, I make suggestions for her to fill hers. We sit at two small spots cleared at the table while Trenton sits nearby, and his sisters lean on the counter.

"The funeral service begins at 10 at the church," Trenton shares while we nibble. "Burial will be in the church cemetery. Then, we will be served a meal inside the church."

In Trenton's eyes, I see the pain he attempts to hide.

"We've asked the praise band to play during lunch." Taylor smiles proudly. "Mom always liked the services they performed during." She shrugs.

Madison can't help the welling tears. She tries to bite them back, but they flow down her cheeks. I wrap my arm around her shoulders and squeeze. She lays her head on my shoulder as she wipes them away with her left hand.

"Oh! My! Gosh! Oh my gosh!" Cameron squeals, jumping up and down.

Everyone's eyes fly to her to see what is wrong. The thunder of the children running down the stairs fills the air with her continued squeals as she fans her face. The four kids freeze by their parents, afraid of what is affecting Aunt Cameron.

"I can't believe you!" She stares at Madison. "You little…"

I witness her search for an appropriate word in the mixed company. For the life of me, I don't know why she's squealing at her.

"I can't believe you didn't tell us," she brushes one index finger over the other in my direction. "Shame on you for holding out."

"What?" Taylor asks.

At the same time, Madison asks, "Cameron, what do you think I did?"

"Um…" She holds out her left hand, pretending to display a ring.

Crap! With her mother's death, my meeting Liberty, and the murder investigation, she forgot to tell them we got engaged.

"Oh!" She stands, walking toward Taylor and Cameron. "I'm sorry. Things were crazy the past couple of days."

"Oh." Cameron acts like her apology solved everything.

"So, how did it happen? When?" Taylor asks.

"What happened?" Grant asks still confused as to why his aunt screamed.

"Aunt Madison and Hamilton are engaged!" Cameron tells the kids.

The kitchen fills with cheers, high fives, and congratulations. Taylor awards the four kids a dessert to help us celebrate then sends them up to finish their movie before time for bed. It's easy to see she wants them out of the room to get all the details of my proposal.

Madison moves to the refrigerator for another water, bringing me one back with her. "I have to say, Memphis was the instigator."

I nod in agreement then kiss her temple. "You'll need to start from the day before, so they understand Mom's meddling."

"Okay." She sips her water to ease her dry throat. "I planned to drive to the motel in Athens. Suddenly, the thought of Liberty and I spending hours in a tiny, outdated motel room didn't appeal to me. When I pulled out of the driveway, I headed towards Memphis' farm. It only took a few minutes. She opened the door as I stepped from the van."

"I introduced her to Liberty and asked if I could stay with her. Of course, she was glad I was there." She looks to me for the next part.

Taking her cue, I continue. "Mom texted me after Madison and Liberty turned in for the night. She only typed that Madison was struggling with her mother's death, and I really needed to try to come to Athens." I smirk. "I wanted to be there; it's just the Cubs had me booked solid with World Series appearances day and night." I shrug.

"The next day, Memphis arranged for us to meet with the funeral home. The weird part was that she wanted to drive two separate vehicles." Madison shakes her head. "I figured she needed to run an errand, and she didn't want Liberty and I to be with her for it."

I jump in. "I had texted Mom when I left Chicago, stating I would be at the farm by dinner. I arrived, and no one was home. So, I texted her again. She claimed to be on her way home."

Patting my forearm, Madison shares, "Memphis sent me on home, stating she and Liberty needed to stop by the store. When I pulled in the driveway, I was shocked to see Hamilton there. Memphis had not told me he would be coming. We went inside and both our phones vibrated with texts."

I look to Madison before continuing. "Mom told me via text she would be home soon, and I needed to share the thing with Madison that Mom and I had talked about several times since last Christmas. I confessed to being lonely and to wanting her with me in Chicago. I shared that I spoke to Mom about it last winter and had been trying to find the perfect time."

"He fell to his knee and pulled out this ring." She wiggles her fingers, allowing the diamond to catch the light. "It was his grandmother's ring."

"But wait," I order over the oohs and ahs. "She didn't say yes."

"I wanted to say yes." Madison turns to face me. "You know I wanted to say yes."

I nod.

"I told him I needed to tell him something, and he might not want to marry me when I did," Madison explains.

"I promised her nothing she would share might change my wanting to marry her." I defend.

"That's when Memphis and Liberty walked in the kitchen," she announces.

"Yep," I agree. "This little girl bounds into the kitchen hollering, "Mommy" and climbs right into Madison's lap."

"He's still kneeling in front of me, staring at a younger version of his big sister," Madison adds.

"Long story short, when Mom calls Liberty over to put the ice cream in the freezer, I slide the ring on Madison's finger while asking her to marry me again." I look into her eyes and silently whisper, "I love you."

"I gave in," Madison finishes.

"No, you didn't!" Cameron argues. "You've wanted to be with him since the day we met you. You said yes because you're head over heels in love with him."

"And you're going to live happily ever after," Ava swoons.

"And raise a gaggle of future Cubs players," Taylor adds.

"Wrong." Trenton chimes in. "Cardinals players." He smiles, proud of himself.

"I forgive you for forgetting to share with us." Cameron is serious now. "You did have situations pulling you in several different directions, and I'm sorry I overreacted when I spotted the ring." She smiles shyly. "You've shared so much, and I was overwhelmed that something so big and so right finally happened for you."

CHAPTER 22

Madison

"I have a bit of business I'd like to go over with you before tomorrow." Trenton gestures for me to sit on the nearby sofa. "We want tomorrow to be a day of celebration and remembrance. Thus, I've already sat with my sisters regarding the will."

I look to Taylor and Cameron. Both smile and join us in the living room. Hamilton takes my hand in his as he sits beside me on the sofa.

"Mother, as you know, was very fond of Liberty and you." He clears his throat before continuing. "She amended her will with a clause that her house can't be sold until you and Liberty find a place to live. She wants you to have a place to stay while you make other arrangements. And the three of us agree. We all love you like a little sister; we want to make sure you are taken care of, and we hope you will allow us to continue to be in your life."

Tears fill my eyes. I want to speak, but words are caught in my throat. Hamilton's arm moves around my back and pulls me closer. I take a few moments to gather my thoughts and a couple of deep breaths.

"Liberty and I will be staying with Memphis while I take care of a few things in Athens. Then, we'll be moving to Chicago to live with Hamilton," I assure my adopted siblings and pause to fight the tears threatening to spill from my eyes.

"With all Madison has do deal with due to her mother's passing, we haven't had time to iron out all of the details," Hamilton jumps in for me. "She decided she'd move to Chicago; beyond that, we have much to discuss and plan."

"When I met with my parents' attorney," I explain, "I learned that I have a trust fund that I should have been given access to to pay for college, my parents' farm is paid off, and I also inherited my grandparents' farm that is doing quite well." I take in a deep breath while scanning the room. "Not knowing any of this before, I have several pressing financial decisions to make. The reason I'm sharing now is that I want you to know I don't need you to wait on me to make a decision about the house." I pin my gaze on Cameron. "Liberty and I will be taken care of and have a new home just waiting for us to move into."

"We will be neighbors!" Taylor claps and cheers. "You'll love Chicago. I'll show you all my favorite stores. And I'm sure the girls will want to babysit anytime you two want a day or night out."

"If we can return to business..." Trenton looks sternly at Taylor. "Mom made arrangements to leave her van for Liberty and you," he states, smiling.

"She detested your car," Taylor adds. "I can't tell you how many times she worried it would strand you on your way to or from campus. She even mentioned wanting to buy you a vehicle."

"I told her you were independent and would never allow her to purchase a vehicle for you," Trenton continues. "So, this is her way of making sure you have a safe vehicle to drive and leaving you no room to argue."

Alma's children chuckle.

A tiny smile graces my face. "It's rare that your mother doesn't get her way."

"I have all the documents you will need to transfer the title into your name." He motions to a file folder in his lap.

I didn't expect to be in Alma's will. We've only known each other for two years. Although I loved her like a mother, I had no intentions of being enveloped so deeply into her family.

"She also awards you her entire library."

"What?" I blurt. "No, I couldn't. Cameron, you work in the book industry; they should be yours."

Cameron shakes her head. "You've never seen it, but my library puts Mom's to shame."

"You should look through it; there may be something

each of you would want. You get first choice." My voice cracks the longer I speak.

"We can look through them when we are finished here," Taylor promises. "But Mom has given us books over the years."

"As I was saying," Trenton takes control of the conversation once again, "we can make arrangements with a moving company to box them up and ship them to you when we sell the house."

My eyes dart to Cameron. Previously, she shared her growing desire to move back to the area with me. She hates the thought of selling her parents house to strangers. She hasn't told her siblings she wants to buy the house. She shakes her head so only I notice. I need to help her open a dialogue soon.

Trenton passes a small, sealed envelope to me. I recognize the stationary as Alma's. "Mom left this for you, and she has one more item in her will for you." Trenton's eyes scan the room. "McGee!"

Thump-thump. Thump-thump. McGee trots down the staircase, sliding to a halt in the center of the hardwood floor.

"Mom wants Liberty to keep McGee," Trenton beams proudly.

With his statement, my shaky hold on my emotions crumbles. Tears swim steadily down my cheeks and a whimper escapes. Alma's really gone—we're parceling out her belongings and taking little pieces of her. Her thoughtfulness knows no bounds.

"Um," I look from Trenton to Hamilton. "I don't know if I can..."

Hamilton squeezes me as his lips graze my ear. "We can handle two dogs. I can't imagine keeping Liberty from her Me-Me."

He's so awesome. I don't know how I would have made it through meeting with my parents' lawyer or listening to Alma's will without him. I'm overwhelmed by the adult decisions thrown at me. In less than two weeks, I've lost my home, lost my mother, introduced Liberty to Hamilton, got engaged, learned I'm a millionaire, decided to move to Chicago, gained a puppy, lost my surrogate mother, and learned I get to keep McGee.

In Hamilton's gaze, my fears subside. "We can handle two dogs." His words play on repeat in my head. McGee is trained, and, thanks to Alma, I'll be able to train Indie. As the smile sweeps upon my face, I nod at Hamilton.

"I guess we will be a two-dog family!" I cheer. "McGee, come." Rubbing my hands under his chin, I murmur, "Liberty will be so glad to see you. Yes, she will."

McGee leans into my scratches. I've missed him the past few days.

"And with that, our business is done." Trenton passes me the folder, containing my copy of the will, before rising to put away his copy of the will. "Who needs a refill?"

While Taylor and Trenton fix drinks in the kitchen, I sidle up beside Cameron. "I think now is a good time to discuss you buying the house."

Her eyes grow wide, and she shakes her head.

"Trust me. They'll be okay with it."

Trenton hands a water to Hamilton before resuming his seat, interrupting my pep talk. Taylor hands a drink to Cameron, and I pounce.

"I have a potential buyer for the house," I announce.

All eyes pivot to me, and Cameron looks ready to flee.

"Are you open to all offers on the house?" I look from Taylor to Trenton. Both nod. I look to Cameron; she doesn't speak.

"Cameron has an interest in moving to Columbia." Bomb dropped, I move to Hamilton's side, smiling proudly.

Taylor cranes her neck around the men, looking at Cameron. "I didn't know that." She looks at me then back to Cameron. "Why didn't you mention it to me?"

I know why, but I'm not telling her–I hope Cameron doesn't tell her either. She needs to focus on buying the house, not start an argument with her older siblings.

"It's a recent idea. I just bounced it off Madison first." Cameron lies. "I spoke to my boss about transferring to the KC office and working from home as often as possible."

"Do they allow others to work from home?" Trenton inquires.

"It's becoming the norm to work from home and come to the office only for meetings." Cameron straightens her shoulders.

I see her preparing to stand up to her two older siblings. She's used to defending her decisions from their overprotective, been-there-done-that ways. "At first, I couldn't see anyone else living here. But then, I remembered last year looking at houses in Denver and New York City for a change of scenery. I'm tired of Dallas. It's just not my kind of place." She smiles at me before looking to Taylor. "And our talk last Thanksgiving with Mom telling me it's my turn to give her grandchildren got me thinking. I can't see myself raising a family in Dallas."

"Can you see yourself raising a family in Columbia?" Trenton teases.

"A family is a few years off, but I could see myself with a family here." She swings her arms wide. "I mean, it was good enough for us. It should be good for…"

Taylor interrupts, "You to find a man and have a brood of your own."

"Let's not get hung up on my future family." Cameron shakes her head. "I'm not sure what you plan to list it at, but I have a large chunk saved for a down payment. I figure my house payment should be less than the 2000 a month I pay in rent now." She shrugs. "So, let me have it. What do you think?"

Taylor wastes no time. "I love the thought of the house remaining in the family. You'll be closer to me, and, if you get to work from home, I think you should go for it." She winks at her little sister.

Cameron raises her eyebrows when she looks my way before facing Trenton.

"I have concerns," Trenton states. "I'd hate for you to suffer a setback at work by moving here. You've created a name for yourself in Dallas; you might have to start over in the Kansas City office, and, if you work from home, that might be difficult."

He pauses, allowing his worries to sink in. "This is a large, old house for one person. It will need maintenance and repairs. You won't have a super to call and fix everything like you do in the apartment."

Cameron nods with each point he makes.

"If this is something you've thought about and want, I will support your decision. Just be sure it's not just a decision you are making in grief. None of us want to sell this house; we want to hold on to the memories as long as we can." He clears his throat, taking a moment to collect himself. "I like the thought of you relocating to the Midwest, and I'm glad to hear you are thinking of a family." He chuckles. "I was beginning to worry that you would be the crazy, single, old lady with litters of cats and hordes of books."

Everyone laughs at the image he creates. I love that they supported Cameron and didn't just brush off her idea as an immature notion. They tend to struggle to see her as an adult instead of their baby sister. Cameron beams–any fear she had that they wouldn't support her has evaporated.

"The realtor is coming tomorrow night," Trenton states. "I'll call and cancel that appointment. We can take care of this transaction ourselves." The proud smile he wears is priceless–he likes the idea of Cameron living here.

CHAPTER 23

Hamilton

"Ham," Madison turns to face me as soon as I close the bedroom door, "we've got a lot to talk about."

"I know. It's been a busy week." I pull her towards the bed. "In a perfect world, my proposal would have led to us making decisions about our future immediately." I pull a knee between us on the bed. "Or at least discussions over the next couple of days. I felt like you needed to focus on other things, and we would get our time to chat later," I explain.

She nods. "It's been one thing after another, hasn't it?" She curls both legs between us and grasps my hand. "I'm exhausted, but we need to talk about some stuff."

"I've described the condo to you and the pet services we

have available. We can handle two dogs." I intertwine my fingers with hers in her lap. "I need to be in Chicago in three days. I'd like to take the two of you with me when I go back. I know you have stuff to arrange in Athens, but most of it can be taken care of over the internet and phone."

"Okay," She agrees, much to my surprise. "I'm ready. I'm ready to see where we will live. I'm ready to make us a home. From your description, I have an image in my mind. I'm sure it pales in comparison to reality."

I pull her tight against my chest, her head tucked under my chin. I kiss the top of her head. "I've waited so long to take you to Chicago with me. You have no idea how much I need you there." I lower my chin, so my lips graze her ear. "I love you." My husky voice breaks.

My heart jackhammers against the wall of my chest. With each passing day, our new life becomes more real to me. For so long, I wanted us to be a couple, and now we officially are. We are engaged! She's going to marry me!

Never taking my hands off her, I reposition her to an arm's length away. She looks up into my eyes, and I melt even more. This sexy-as-hell woman is mine.

"You've dealt with a lot this week. I've made some calls trying to prepare for your arrival in Chicago." I hesitate. I'm unsure how she will handle this news. "Berkeley, my publicist, found a four-bedroom condo upstairs from my current one. It's similar to mine only with two more bedrooms for us."

My eyes search her face. "I've asked her to get a

bedroom set similar to mine and a sectional for the living room. She rented them for us. We can return them and pick out our own or purchase them. I thought it might be an easier transition for Libby if we didn't live in my condo for a week then move to another one. This way, we can settle her in one time. We'll still need to buy furniture and decorate, but it will be ready for us to sleep in on our first night in Chicago."

Heat floods her cheeks. She pulls away from my touch to stand across the bedroom. Heavy stones sink to the pit of my stomach.

"Mady," I plead. "What did I say to upset you?" I make to stand.

She raises her palm, directing me to stay away. My breathing stops. *Talk. Talk to her.* We need to talk this out.

"Berkeley picked out our home?" she spits. "Berkeley bought our bedroom set? I'm not sure I like the idea of a strange woman making such intimate decisions for us. I want us to make these decisions together," she growls. "I'm sorry. Maybe I'm being irrational. My life is out of control. I need to reign it back in. I want to be in control and planning our life together can do that for me. I mean," she pauses to draw in a shaky breath, "I don't even know this Berkeley." She rolls her wrist, waving her hand in the air.

I stride toward her, not allowing any space between us. "I chose the condo, not her. I looked at the floor plans online. She only called the leasing agent to secure it. I love everything about my condo: the location, the layout, the design, the amenities, and the security." I run my thumb over her lower lip, eyes boring into hers. "You've seen the interior during our FaceTime calls. You seemed to like it, if I recall. I'm just trying to make it easier on the three of us."

She nods. It seems the red-hot rage cools slowly within her.

"We don't have to keep the bedroom set." I let out a frustrated sigh. "I'm so used to Berkeley arranging things for me, I didn't even think what it might be like for you. She's my publicist, my assistant. Nothing more. There has never been anything between us, not even a spark. We can sleep on the floor by the portable crib or on the sofa. We'll return the furniture and, together, select our own."

I don't want to say she blew this out of proportion. I'm not sure if she's jealous or what. I bet the fact that Berkeley was a part of my Chicago life when she wasn't hurts. I need to be more sensitive. I can't jump in, make a call, and decide everything.

"It's okay," she whispers. "One less move will be easier on Liberty. I want the three of us to be comfortable on our first night in our new place. I'm glad you arranged all of this. I am." She places her hand over my heart. "It's going to take some time for me to get used to you having money and people that work to make your life easier. I'm used to doing everything myself and making my own decisions."

"You have money, too," I smirk.

"It's surreal to me. I may never get used to it." She shakes her head.

"As my wife, my money is our money. You're the reason

I entered the draft in the first place. Liberty and you mean everything to me. I've already made arrangements. Soon, you'll have paperwork to sign that adds you to all my accounts. During the season, life is hectic. Much of what Berkeley did for me, you will be able to do for us. I leaned on her a lot while I was on the road. I'll lean on you from now on," I promise.

I press a kiss to the corner of her mouth. "I love you. We both need to get used to the changes. We're no longer single; we're a couple, a family. Forgive me?" I'm lost in her eyes.

"There's nothing to forgive," she whispers, fiddling with the envelope Trenton handed her earlier.

"Want me to read it to you?" I offer, feeling helpless.

She nods, extending it to me.

I carefully open the sealed envelope; I'm sure Madison will want to keep this forever. I pull the handwritten note from inside and unfold it.

"Madison, I need you to help keep my secret," I read, eyes peaking up to hers.

She shrugs, not knowing what secret Alma speaks of.

"In the garage, behind the red toolbox, are two boxes labeled 'cleaning supplies.' I need you to sneak them into your car without my children finding them. What you choose to do with them is up to you. I can't bear the thought of my three children finding them. They will not understand my addiction to steamy and erotic romance novels as you do. I feel it's best if we protect them from years of therapy if they were to envision me reading such books."

Through her tears, Madison laughs a real laugh. It seems her heavy heart grows light. Her eyes sparkle through her tears. I fold the note back into the envelope and tuck it in her bag.

"If you can stop laughing," I tease, "you can distract the family, while I go get the two boxes. If they ask, just tell them I forgot to bring in something."

She wipes her wet cheeks and squeezes the remaining tears from her eyes as she quells her laughter. Leave it to Alma to lighten her mood. She wouldn't want Madison to cry so much over her. She'd tell her to focus on her daughter and her recent reconnecting with me. She'd urge her to open one of those sultry romance stories and lose herself in it. Madison's going to miss her so much.

I can't fall asleep. I hold Madison snug against my body, her back against my front. I can't hold her close enough. *She's mine.*

I struggle to hide my body's reaction to her. With all she's dealing with, I can't act on my desires. She needs time to cope with the death of her mother and Alma and time to accept moving to Chicago. She needs time to help Libby adjust to our new life. There will be plenty of time for the two of us. We'll have a new home to christen. I adjust myself while trying not to wake her.

We haven't even been on a first date. I need to plan one. I can't expect her to marry me if we haven't even dated. One might argue that all the time we spent alone in high school were dates. I must plan a first date and a second; I owe her that much. I'll ask Berkeley to make us reservations. *No! I can't!* I need to do this myself. This is not a task to involve Berkeley in. It's important that Madison knows I planned our date, *every* part of it.

CHAPTER 24

Madison

On our drive back to Athens, I replay parts of Alma's service in my mind.

I smile as I remember Hamilton slipping his hand into mine as a silent symbol of support. It gave me strength and hope. As warmth encompassed me, I felt as though Alma was happy to see us together.

"I had a thought last night." Hamilton breaks into our quiet ride. "We need to find a farmer to rent your parents' land, someone we trust to make the improvements needed."

His eyes leave the road for only a moment, and I nod.

"We also need to find a reliable renter for the farmhouse. We don't want to constantly vet new renters." His words echo my recent thoughts on the matter. "I know one couple unhappy in their current situation. They would make great renters for both the house and the land."

Who could he mean? He's rarely in Athens. How does he know a reliable renter? A wide smile forms as I realize he's speaking of Latham and Salem. I've shared during our phone calls how Latham and Salem moved into the farmhouse when his parents retired to move into Athens. His brothers were not happy about it. Living on the family farm, they saw Latham as boss in their father's absence. They started arriving late and leaving early. They fight Latham at every turn if their father isn't around. Latham and Salem spend nights and weekends working their butts off while his brothers are in Athens with their wives.

I smile. Hamilton's idea sparks hope within me. "Do you think Latham would consider it?"

"I'm not sure how fed up he really is with his brothers. It's worth mentioning."

"I know Salem is unhappy," I state.

"I thought we might invite them to join us for dinner while we're in Athens. We could tell them we have an offer for them to consider. We still need to work out the logistics. Perhaps we don't charge them rent for the house–it could be part of Latham's salary. We could offer him a salary to fix the fences and outbuildings along with working the land. It's not a large acreage, but it needs a lot of work. I thought he might also be able to help at Mom's since the farms border each other. She works too hard, and I'd like her to be able to come to Chicago to visit anytime she wants to."

"I think it's worth discussing with them before we advertise for renters," I agree.

"In time, Latham could even oversee your grandparents' farm, too." Once again, he meets my eyes briefly. "I mean, if you choose to keep all that land, too. You should text Salem and see if they are free tonight or tomorrow night. We could discuss this before heading to Chicago."

"I'll text her now."

Me: What are you doing tonight?
Me: Hamilton & I want to go out to eat
Salem: I'm off today
Me: we could meet at Pizza Hut
Salem: I'll pull Latham in
Salem: to shower at 5
Me: meet at 6?
Salem: yes

"It's done," I inform him proudly. "We're meeting them at Pizza Hut at six."

I step from Memphis' truck; my feet feel like anvils as I approach the front door.

"One hour," Memphis' words soothe. "We just need you

to give us a few instructions. Then, once you give Salem a tour, you are free to take my truck and go." She squeezes my shoulders while she looks into my eyes. She attempts to share some of her strength with me.

I nod. *Why is it all of the happy memories hide deep behind the horrors of the past six years? Why can't I focus on the three of us happy here on the farm?*

Four of her church friends greet us on the small front doorstep. Memphis mentioned this ministry to me, and I clung to it like a lifeline–there's no way I could ever clean out my mother's house. I'm barely able to step inside without losing it. So, when Memphis described a group of ladies at her church that volunteer to box up, throw away, and donate households for families that lost a loved one, I gladly accepted the offer. I scan the empty boxes, crates, and trash bins littering the large, front yard.

"Madison, we understand this is difficult for you," a silver-haired woman much older than Memphis begins. "We only need a few directions from you, then we will begin."

"As you can see," a blue-haired, short, pleasantly plump woman explains, "we've labeled boxes for important papers and photos." She points to the two large stacks of labeled boxes. "We will remove all photos from their frames before boxing them up. We will place the frames in these tubs for donating."

My head swims as they continue to explain the process, just as Memphis had a few days earlier. Soon, we are walking through the entire house as I point to items I wish to keep. I'm not surprised there isn't much I want. I don't think any furniture was kept in our family for generations. My mother decorated with a modern theme in my early childhood, and nothing ever changed. I ask to keep my books, my favorite cereal bowl from my youth, and two wedding dresses hidden in a closet. I don't even know who they belonged to.

The women promise to keep anything of importance for me to look through at my convenience. They hope to finish by dinner tonight but state they might need a few hours tomorrow afternoon to clean after removing everything. I'm just grateful I don't have to stay here to see any of it.

Memphis guides me back to the front yard at the same time Salem and Latham pull into the driveway. I do my best to fake a smile for my excited friends.

CHAPTER 25

Hamilton

I excuse myself, claiming I need to work on the tractor in the barn. While the girls play in the front room with Mom, I sneak some supplies out the kitchen door with me. I load all the items I need on the four-wheeler, making two trips to the cemetery to deliver everything. I toss some of the items over the fence and carry the small grill over with me. Once set up, I step back to take in the scene. I try to see it from Madison's point of view for the first time.

It's our favorite spot. I figure it's the perfect location for our first date.

"Daddy!" Liberty squeals, running to my open arms. She jabbers on with all the stories of her day.

My smile grows as her animated chatter continues. I react to her words as if I understand. When her tales dwindle, she lays her head on my shoulder.

My heart bursts wide open with her love. I've waited so long for the day Madison and I could be together. Finally, our life together begins, and my daughter makes it even more special.

"Mommy and Daddy are going out." I tug on one of her springy curls. "Can you be a big girl for Grandma?"

Liberty lifts her head, frowning at me.

She wiggles her way down from my arms and runs over to Madison.

"Mommy, no," she whines with her arms in the air.

When Madison picks her up, Liberty clings tight to her mommy. Madison softly attempts to soothe our now crying girl.

Madison's eyes plead with me. I feel her pain. So much has changed for our little girl in the past week, it was only a matter of time before she began to show the effects. Suddenly, I have no desire to take Madison on a date. I want only to assure my girl that everything is alright.

Sitting on the sofa, Madison rubs her free hand up and down Liberty's back. She attempts to pull the tiny, clinging arms from around her neck.

"Libby, honey," she soothes. "Mommy and Daddy will only be gone for a little while." She kisses Liberty's hands. "We need you to be…"

Liberty squirms down from her mommy's lap and runs to me. "Daddy, no!"

The trails of tears on her chubby cheeks combined with her pouty lower lip are my undoing.

"It's okay, Mommy and Daddy won't…"

My words cease at Madison's glare and shaking head as she approaches.

Pulling Liberty's hands into her own, Madison whispers, "Grandma needs help with McGee and Indie. She knows how to take care of the kitties but doesn't know how to take care of the dogs." She purses her lips, pretending to contemplate the dilemma. "Can you be a big girl and help Grandma? You'll have to teach her how McGee does his tricks. Indie needs to go outside to potty and will need a treat before bed. Grandma doesn't know which treats to give him."

Liberty's sobs subside. Madison wipes her runny nose with a tissue. Sensing her persuasion working, she continues, "Grandma will need you to help her run your bath and put toys in the water."

I feel Liberty's nod against my shoulder. My heart still burns at the thought that my plans caused this.

"Maybe Grandma will read you three books tonight at bedtime," I suggest.

Liberty lifts her head. Her puffy, red eyes look into mine. Tears coat her dark lashes. Instead of a pout, a slight smile decorates her lips.

"How about it? Can you be a big girl and help Grandma for a little bit?" Madison asks.

Without a word, Liberty escapes my hold. She toddles

toward her grandma, extends her hand, then tugs her to the kitchen.

"I'm sorry." I meet Madison's gaze. "I didn't think she'd... I mean, she's seemed happy with Mom."

"She's tired, that's all." Madison wraps her arms around my waist. "She chased after two dogs and the kitties all day. This happens when she's too tired. She'll be fine with your mom tonight."

Her words should make me feel better. She has more parenting experience than I do. I'm reminded, again, that I'm playing catch up.

In the kitchen, Liberty stands on the counter, pulling mac and cheese from the cabinet for Mom. She smiles as she hops back into Grandma's arms. Mom whispers something before Liberty waves goodbye with a smile on her face.

"Get out of here," Mom orders. "We'll be fine."

It seems she's ready to start dinner now.

Madison smiles in my direction. "You take free time whenever and wherever you get it." She shrugs. "I don't remember making plans for tonight."

I move closer, taking her hand in mine. "We're going on our first date."

Madison freezes in shock. I drop the bomb, not giving any details. I'm sure she hadn't even thought about us dating. She's excited to marry me–I don't think she planned on the usual traditions that come before a wedding. I don't plan on waiting long, but I can allow us a few dates before we tie the knot.

"I should go change then," she offers, unable to keep the smile off her face.

"No," I say quickly, not letting go of her hand. "The only thing you need is a sweatshirt."

It's the first week of November in Missouri–the weather is mild.

I pull her towards the door, tossing a sweatshirt at her as we pass through the kitchen. We say goodbye to our daughter, and excitement builds at the knowledge of the evening I've planned for us.

I motion for Madison to climb on the four-wheeler. She hesitates for a moment before sliding on the back.

CHAPTER 26

Madison

"You drive," he urges. "We're going to the spot where we began."

The weight of his words warms me. We began the night I asked him for a favor; we met in the cemetery, and it changed my life forever.

Approaching the chain link fence surrounding the site, I notice twinkle lights hanging from the oak tree in the center. Beneath them, blankets and pillows cover the dead grass. A small grill holds flaming logs, a cooler and crockpot sit nearby. It seems Hamilton has been very sneaky this afternoon.

"Ham..." I choke on my words.

He pulls my back tight to his chest while wrapping his

arms snuggly around me as I take in the scene. "I've thought about a first date for a couple of days now. Movies, going out to eat, dancing, driving to Kansas City...none of those seemed perfect."

I spin in his arms, placing my hands on his cheeks. "This is perfect."

He chuckles. "You don't even know what I have planned."

"It doesn't matter. It's you. It's me. It's our special spot. That's all it needs to be perfect."

"Should we climb this fence so we can start our date?" Hamilton suggests.

We lay stretched out on the blankets and pillows, our bellies full of loaded grilled cheese sandwiches and tater tot nachos Hamilton prepared ahead of time for us. I could only groan when he offered to make s'mores for dessert. We decided to save those for later.

"Savannah called me today," I state as we stare up at the clear night sky. Of all our friends in Athens, she's the only one I haven't found the time to share a meal within the days I've been back.

"What's she up to, besides deer hunting?" He plays with my hair.

"Remember the donut guy I told you she's mentioned a couple of times?"

"The history teacher, right?"

"Yes, well," I cuddle a bit closer to his side, "he asked her out. She claims it's not a date, but it's a date. He asked her to be his plus-one to the faculty Christmas party the first weekend in December."

Hamilton smirks in my direction.

"She said he made it sound like she'd be doing him a huge favor by not making the new guy attend all by himself."

"So, she's going?" he asks, surprise in his tone.

"She told him she'd think about it," I smirk. "But she's going. I told her to call him tomorrow, claiming she shouldn't leave him hanging in the wind too long. It'll be a weird first date. She'll be attending with all of her teachers from school, every one she ever had. The principals, the coaches, and even the secretaries will be there. I mean, she's an adult now, but they all knew her as a kid in school. It will be weird, but he promised they would make an appearance and slip out early."

A silly smile covers my face as I stare at the sky. She wouldn't mention it to me or consider the date if she didn't like this guy. I like the idea of Savannah having the hots for someone. She's been on her own for so long, it's time she lets down her guard to let someone in. Several moments pass as I imagine her happy.

"So..." Hamilton rolls to face me, breaking the silence of a chilly evening.

"Okay." I roll to face him; my hand rests on his chest. "I want to elope. I don't see any reason to plan anything big. We don't have a lot of family, so we should keep it simple; we should plan it before you head to spring training in February."

"Uh, duh!" He laughs.

"Okay, Mr. Obvious. When?" I retort.

"The weekend after Thanksgiving," he deadpans without missing a beat.

Wow! He's thought about this more than I have. That's a couple of weeks away.

"I see the wheels turning in your mind." Hamilton taps my creased forehead. "What are you thinking?"

I only stare at him.

"Eloping means we have no planning to complete," he explains. "We just need to pick a date, arrange for a license, and bam!"

"Bam? Seriously? Like it's that easy." I release a breath I didn't know I was holding in. "We have to decide where. Like, in Missouri or Chicago? What are we going to wear? Who will be our two witnesses?"

"Easy," he chides. "I only meant you aren't a bridezilla. But I'm beginning to rethink that."

Lucky for him, he doesn't laugh at his own joke.

"If we pick a date, then we can pick where. The rest will fall into place. So, what do you think about after Thanksgiving? Mom and Amy will be in Chicago to help with Liberty."

I shrug noncommittally.

"C'mon," he urges. "Give me something to work with here."

I sigh deeply before engaging in the conversation. "In the next week, I'll be moving Liberty and me to Chicago with you." He smiles proudly at my words. "We'll be moving into a bigger condo, buying furniture, decorating, and stocking the cupboards. We're hosting 11 people for Thanksgiving, which is only two weeks away. That's a lot to do, and there's not much time to do it in. We have to make sure that with all the changes, we help Liberty adapt to her new world." I can't hold back the shrug that escapes.

"I see." Hamilton's thumb caresses my cheek, distracting me. "I think the keyword to remember there is 'we'. You're not alone anymore. I will be helping you. I only have a couple of appearances on the calendar. Taylor offered to help you shop, too. I know I've explained how the condo has delivery services. We'll pick out the furniture, and they will place it in the spot we tell them to. We'll also have Miss Alba, our housekeeper, to help with grocery shopping and keeping the place organized. I think you will find it much easier than it would be to start a new house in Athens. Trust me, we can do this."

"Besides, if you get stressed, I will run you a hot bubble bath and deliver glass after glass of wine for you to enjoy by candlelight."

I snort unladylike. "You've forgotten our daughter. There's no way she will leave me alone for a long, relaxing bath."

"Ah, but you forget, although I am new to the role of Daddy, I am quite adept at playing with Liberty. I will situate you in the bath then read her two stories, and she will fall asleep. You'll have plenty of peace and quiet while you soak." His sexy smirk makes an appearance. "Then, I'll lift you from your bubbly retreat, slowly dry every inch of you, and deliver a sensual massage in our bed. I'll have you relaxed in no time." He smiles proudly as his hands slip under the back of my sweatshirt.

"Perhaps you can rid me of stress," I admit. "We still have much to discuss, so don't try to distract me right now with your sexy smile and tantalizing touch."

Hamilton removes his fingers from my skin, returning one to the safety of my cheek. "When you envision eloping, what do you see?"

I quirk my mouth to the side while I think. "I see you in jeans and a nice shirt. I'm in a simple dress. And no flowers."

"Do you care where we do it?"

I shake my head.

"I'd like to fly to Vegas on the Friday after Thanksgiving. We could elope Friday night and stay until Sunday for a short honeymoon. Mom and Amy can stay at our place with Liberty."

"Ham, flying to Las Vegas over the holiday weekend is too expensive."

He doesn't respond with words. He simply smiles as his gaze wills me to get his message. I stare back until I remember I have money now.

"It's new to me," I defend. "You can't just expect me to stop worrying about money–I've counted every penny for so many years. I can't just shut that off and start spending your money."

"Our money," he corrects. "And you recall our meeting with your family's lawyer; you have plenty of money of your own now, too."

I hedge. He's right. It's still hard for me to process that

I'm a 20-year-old millionaire. It should comfort me that Liberty and I have plenty to live on, but I have no idea how to use it, save it, or get used to it.

"You deserve a mini-vacation." Hamilton interrupts my thoughts. "You've focused on your degree, raising Liberty, and caring for Alma…it's time you take a little 'me' time. No one will fault you for that. You've had a rough go of it these past few weeks. Two nights in Vegas, just the two of us, might be just what the doctor ordered."

I slowly nod as I imagine it.

Hamilton beams. "It's settled then, we'll elope in Vegas. I'll arrange everything."

"I'm going to need your help," I state. "I get so hyper-focused on tasks that I often forget to have fun."

"Evidently, you've forgotten my job has always been to drag you away and force you to have fun." He bops me on the nose playfully. "I realize we have a lot to do in the next couple of weeks. There are others willing to help, and I will make it my personal mission to make sure you have fun at least once a day."

My attempt to hide my yawn fails as it lasts several seconds.

"Okay, it's time I take you home and tuck you into bed. We have a long drive home tomorrow. I imagine we will need a ton of patience to drive six hours with a toddler."

"One: you have no idea." I raise a finger as I count off. "We will need to make frequent stops." I hold up another finger. "Two: It's awfully presumptuous of you to think I will sleep with you on our first date." I smile innocently.

"Ah, ah, ah." He wags his finger in front of my face. "I said tuck you into bed not have my wicked way with you by ravishing your body until the wee hours of the morning."

Another big yawn overpowers me.

"Let's go." He pulls me up and passes blankets for me to carry. "I've kept you out past your bedtime."

"It's barely 10 o'clock," I protest. "I don't know why I'm so tired all of the time."

Hamilton simply nods, causing me to wonder what he thinks. *Am I tired due to stress? Am I exhausted from the emotional upheaval in my life?* No matter the cause, Hamilton's support and understanding means a lot to me.

CHAPTER 27

Madison

"We're here!" Hamilton announces. "Our new home awaits."

When he exits the truck, fear floods my every cell. I sit frozen in the passenger seat; a sudden queasy feeling fills my belly.

Hamilton's voice talking to someone draws my attention. Turning my head, I find him speaking to a tall, gorgeous blonde in a see-through silk blouse and a tight, navy pencil skirt. He waves for me to join him. Reluctantly, I slide from my seat, leaning against the truck door.

"Hand me the dogs. The three of you head on up, and I'll have everything brought up for you," the blonde orders, pointing.

I stand slack-jawed as Hamilton obeys. He passes the two

dogs on leashes to her before returning to carry Liberty over to me.

"Let's go see the new place," he murmurs. "Berkeley will take care of our stuff."

She has a name. This is the infamous publicist, Berkeley. This is the person he allows to handle his personal affairs and make decisions about our new home, even about the bed we will sleep in tonight.

I want to release my inner rage. I want to scream and stomp my foot. I want to yell, but I don't want to embarrass Hamilton. I don't want him to feel he needs to hide his interactions with her from me. I don't want to teach Liberty that type of behavior is okay. So, instead, I wave to Berkeley as I allow Hamilton to lead me by the hand, across the parking garage to the waiting elevator.

My mind buzzes with the sheer size of this complex. It's not a city block; it's bigger. Hamilton had mentioned the center courtyard containing two dog parks as well as a playground for children. I imagined small spaces. Given the immense facade I witnessed upon pulling into the garage, the courtyard must be large.

I'm going to be living in these buildings of splendor with doormen. I'll have dog sitters, maid service, and nannies available at my beck and call. There's a pool, fitness center, gymnasium, and running track on site. This is now my home–this is now my life.

In a trance, I enter our condo while Hamilton holds the door for me. I scan the enormous space, void of decoration, void of all furniture but a sectional sofa and enormous television. I note a few toys strewn on the sofa; that's a nice touch. The kitchen counters are bare. There are no rugs on the dark, wood floors.

Hamilton owns no furniture–Berkeley rented a bed and sofa for us until we purchase our own. He has no dishes, no pans, no utensils, and I'm not even sure he owns any towels. Our shopping list looms large in my mind. Thanksgiving is only 10 days away. We'll need so much before our company arrives–my head swims.

I startle when warm, firm lips surround mine. Hamilton's strong hands secure me in place. I'm vaguely aware of Liberty trotting around the large open floor plan, cheering at the top of her little lungs. Hamilton's hot tongue slides across my lower lip, seeking entrance. I part my lips but a sliver. It's all the permission he needs–quickly our kiss heats. My mind plants itself firmly in the present.

Too soon, Liberty tugs on Hamilton's jeans, interrupting our kiss.

"Hey." Hamilton quickly lifts her between us. "What do you think of our new home?"

Liberty pats Daddy's cheek as if she understands.

I take a moment, spinning to take in my surroundings. It's a large, open floor plan. The kitchen area, with a large island, sits opposite the floor-to-ceiling windows. Outside, Chicago twinkles in the night, stretching out as far as the eye can see. A sunken living room area faces the windows. Opposite the kitchen, a dark wooden door promises a room behind it. Maybe it's a bedroom or an office.

Hamilton leans over my shoulder, whispering, "Welcome home."

Goosebumps cover my neck where his warm breath caressed. My belly flutters. "We're home." A large smile adorns my face. It's all I hoped for. It's better than I imagined. I am giddy with the possibilities this space provides for us, for our family.

The sound of a toilet flushing travels down the hallway. Hamilton's brows dart up, telling me he didn't expect a guest. I quickly take Liberty from him and stand behind his large body. The sounds of a giggling girl cause me to peek around his shoulder.

"Surprise," a female voice greets with little conviction.

"Hamilton!" a younger voice screams, and her little feet run to his outstretched arms.

"Aurora!" Hamilton spins her in a circle before placing her back on the floor.

"You're early," the female states, standing behind Aurora. "The guys just went down to get the food delivery. We planned to surprise you with a meal when you arrived. Sorry, our timing sucks."

Hamilton blows it off as no big deal.

Liberty squirms to escape my hold. Without a care, she approaches Aurora, and the two play with the toys on the sectional.

"Um, Hamilton..." the gorgeous female waves her index finger between herself and me. As he doesn't understand her, she prompts, "Why don't you introduce us?"

Before he can start introductions, the front door beeps as

the entry code is entered and swings open. I recognize Stan; he plays baseball with Hamilton. I assume the young man with Stan is his son, so the woman and girl must be Stan's wife and daughter.

"The gang is all here," Stan states, placing several plastic bags of takeout cartons on the kitchen island. The boy places two bags of beverages on the island, too.

"You must be Madison." Stan extends his right hand to shake mine.

"And you, Stan, are the reason my Cardinals didn't have any baserunners in the playoffs," I tease.

"My glove was on fire. What can I say?" Stan's chest puffs out, and he beams.

"This is his wife, Delta, his son, Webb, and daughter, Aurora." Hamilton motions to each of them as he speaks. He pulls me tight to his side. "This is Madison, and over there is Liberty."

"Your fiancé, Madison," Delta corrects. "Girl, let me see that ring." Her flawless, mocha hand, with an immaculate manicure, beckons mine.

"You've already seen the ring," Stan reminds his wife.

"Not on her finger," Delta informs, her tone clearly letting them know there is a difference. She *oohs* and *ahs* for a bit, remarking that it's a gorgeous heirloom.

"Let's eat," Stan demands, already filling a paper plate. "Hope you like Italian," he calls in my direction.

"What will Liberty eat?" Delta asks at my side.

"We stopped at five to stretch our legs and keep to her

schedule. She's already eaten." I smile. "Thanks for asking, though."

"Ours have already eaten, too," Delta confesses. "Aurora wanted to drop off a few toys for Liberty to play with until hers are unpacked, and we knew you'd be too tired from the drive to worry about dinner."

"This is so kind. Thank you." My words don't seem to be enough for their gestures. "I was so focused on getting here then settling Liberty in before bedtime that I didn't even think of our dinner."

"Thank you," Hamilton directs towards them both.

"How old are your kids?" I ask Delta while she follows me through the line of boxes. When my plate is full, I move to the other side of the island to eat.

"Webb just turned 13, and Aurora is 4," she beams as she occupies the empty countertop beside me. "Liberty is two, right?"

"Libby will be two in March," Hamilton corrects.

"She's got your height." Delta peeks over her shoulder at the two girls playing on the sofa.

"Along with his hair, his eyes, his dimples…" I add.

"She has her mother's smarts and stubbornness," Hamilton interrupts.

I want to argue, but he's right. When I look at our daughter, I only see the ways she looks like Amy and him—I don't see myself in her. So, I only smile at his words.

Stan's eyes dart between the two of us, looking for any sign I'll argue.

Aurora and Liberty play together as if they've done it a million times before. I love my daughter's ability to instantly accept others into her world without any hesitation. I dread the day she learns from anyone to prejudge others.

After dinner and the quick cleanup, the adults move to the sectional and the toddlers to the living room floor. Webb occupies the corner cushions between his mother and father; he's enthralled in his e-Reader. Although I participate in the adult conversation, I long to know the book he's reading. I catch a break when Stan and Hamilton begin to discuss tomorrow's public appearance.

"Webb," I call across the room, "what are you reading?"

He sits still, not acknowledging my question. If it weren't for his eyes looking from his mom's lap to his dad's and back, I might think he didn't hear me.

"Webb," Delta prompts, "Miss Madison asked you a question." She places her hand in the space between his face and the e-Reader.

Webb looks at his mom, sees her touch her finger to her nose, then looks in my general direction. The simple signal reminds him to make eye contact.

"It's a book by John Green," he states. His eyes quickly return to his mom's hand atop his e-Reader.

"I love his books," I reply. "Which is your favorite?"

As Delta hasn't withdrawn her hand, he looks to her before glancing back to me. "I'm reading *Paper Towns*," he states.

"I like *Looking for Alaska*, but *Will Grayson, Will Grayson* is my favorite book of his." I wait several moments for his response.

"This is the first John Green book for me." His eyes connect with mine for the first time.

Hamilton mentioned Stan's son was on the Autism spectrum during our phone calls last year. I know Webb's eye contact is a challenge and smile at his small connection with me, a total stranger, during our conversation.

"What other books do you enjoy reading?" I ask, wanting to continue our interaction.

His eyes return to the e-Reader. "I want to buy two books by a new author, but my parents are making me learn patience." He looks in Stan's direction. "I put my name on the waiting list in the school library. I'm never going to get to read it or the one that follows it. Two times they checked it back out before looking at the waiting list."

It's easy to see that he is frustrated with the long wait for his book and breaking the rules by not following the waiting list order probably caused an issue for him.

"What book is it?" Hamilton inquires, returning to the conversation as I head to the kitchen for another bottle of water.

I notice Webb looks to him without hesitation, making it clear the two have a connection. "She's a new author and has two books so far." His eyes never stray from Hamilton's. "It's M. Crocker."

Hamilton chokes on his laugh. Stan and Delta stare wide-eyed at him, eyebrows raised.

I quickly turn, staring into the fridge with my back to the group. I want to confess; I'm the author, and I want to hand him a book. I pretend to search the fridge for an item. His parents want to teach him patience.

"Webb," Hamilton's voice cuts into the room, "what do you know about that author?"

I pull a water bottle out, shutting the refrigerator door. Leaning against the island, I take a sip, facing the living room.

Webb rises from his seat, moving closer to Hamilton. He swipes a few times on the e-Reader then moves the device toward Hamilton. "She's a new author this year. So far, she's published two books. The publisher claims two more will release next year." Webb swipes one more time. "Here she is…" His voice trails off.

I watch as Webb's posture grows stiff. He grabs his e-Reader from Hamilton and returns to his corner of the sectional, safely between his parents. He doesn't look to Hamilton or me; he averts his eyes from everyone in the room.

Delta leans over, glancing at the author photo on the screen. "No way!" Her eyes are alight with excitement as she smiles in my direction. "Hamilton told me you were an author. I assumed it was Chick Lit or romance." I stand frozen as she approaches me.

"What am I missing?" Stan looks around the room, lost in the conversation.

Hamilton clues his friend in. "Madison is M. Crocker. She's the author Webb is waiting *patiently* to read."

Stan looks my way, slack-jawed.

Delta nudges my arm with her elbow, joining me at the breakfast bar. "So, not just an author. You're the hot, new, young adult author causing a buzz in middle schools everywhere."

I met her only an hour ago, and I already see the twinkle in her eye and pride on her face for my work. I'm going to like this woman.

"You should give Webb a book," Hamilton suggests. "I know you have a few copies in a box over there."

My wide eyes attempt to signal Hamilton that he is crossing a line. I chance a glance at Delta.

"You don't have to," Delta states, still smiling with excitement. "I mean…"

"I don't want to step on your toes," I explain. "I know it's important to follow through on the patience lesson."

"Oh, forget that." She lowers her voice for only the two of us to hear. "Webb has waited three weeks, and they keep checking out the book without following the waiting list. I think we've drawn enough patience from him. I mean, if you have a copy you can find easily, I'm sure he'd love it." She shrugs, attempting to make light of the situation.

"Ham," I call toward the guys, "would you mind finding the box labeled 'office' for us?"

He doesn't hesitate, heading straight for the boxes. Stan rises to assist him; a hesitant Webb joins them. Although no emotion graces his face, by approaching the boxes with the men, Webb shows he is interested in their task and my book.

"Ta Da!" Hamilton cheers. "Webb, come help me open the box."

I marvel as Webb hands his e-Reader to Stan and joins Hamilton at the box with "office" in large, black print on the sides. Hamilton lifts two flaps, and Webb immediately lifts a book from inside as if it's the Shroud of Turin or the Holy Grail. He shows no emotion, but his actions convey his excitement.

"Bring it over here, Webb," Delta motions towards him.

He slides beside his mother, my book cradled to his chest. She pulls it from his grasp, looking at the cover and then the back. Webb glances my way but averts his eyes quickly.

Delta taps his nose before prompting, "What do you say to Miss Madison?"

Webb directs his eyes to mine. "Thank you." His eyes return to the book.

"You need to wait until tomorrow to read it."

At his mother's words, Webb taps his wrist as if touching a watch. Stan immediately directs Webb to accompany him down the hall.

"Is that his tell?" I look to Delta. Hamilton smiles at me from her side.

"Yes. Tapping his wrist signals his teacher, his aide, and us that he needs a minute." She sighs. "I'm sure he's angry he can't open it now and hide in its pages until he finishes it in one sitting." She attempts a smile for me. "He's excited to read it but has school tomorrow. It's another lesson in patience."

I place my hand on her forearm. "I understand. He's

awesome. It's clear he is close to Hamilton, and he engaged with me, a total stranger in his first time seeing me." I smile at my new friend. "I know it's challenging."

She pats my arm and a genuine smile graces her face. "We have our moments. He's working so hard every day. It's all him."

Taking the book in hand, I find a pen in the kitchen. I sign my name on the title page. When Webb begins to read, I hope he'll find my signature.

I know Webb must work every day to fit into *normal* society. I also know his parents struggle with every decision, every event, every interaction he has outside his family. Webb's acceptance of Hamilton and even me tonight is a testament to the safety he feels with his parents, the skills they assist him with daily, and using his timeouts any time he requests one. I've learned a lot about Hamilton's friends, my new friends, tonight.

CHAPTER 28

Madison

With Liberty tucked safely in her portable crib in the room next to ours, I fall on our king-sized bed. Hamilton emerges, fresh from a shower, in his shorts as he snags a t-shirt from his bag. I admire the sculpted contours of his muscular abs and chest. My eyes delight in the sight of a new tattoo near his heart. I place my hand over my mouth to hide my shock when I realize he's going to flip when he finds my tattoo.

"I hope you aren't too upset they were here tonight," Hamilton states, sliding his shirt over his head.

"At first, I was," I confess honestly. "I wanted our first night to be the three of us. Delta was right though; we didn't plan for food or drinks. Besides, I had fun. They're easy to talk to." I yawn before continuing. "I'm nervous to meet your teammates and even more nervous about meeting their wives and girlfriends." I quirk my mouth to one side. "Stan and Delta seem normal, and I absolutely love their kids."

Hamilton nods in agreement, a large, lopsided smile on his face.

"You failed to mention Webb really likes you."

"I told you I hung out at their place quite a bit. I never know how he feels about me, but I keep treating him as I would any other kid. It seems to work." He shrugs.

He makes light of his connection to Webb. I know he understands the struggles that child and his parents face, and I decide to drop it.

"We have a big day tomorrow," he murmurs.

"Yeah, I'm exhausted just thinking about it."

"To sleep you go!" He swats me on my butt.

I giggle as he slides into bed and pulls me against his hot, solid body. I turn to face him and wrap my arms around his middle. I rest my head on his left shoulder.

"I love you," I whisper then yawn.

"Get some sleep," he whispers into my hair. "We have a big day of shopping tomorrow."

I nod.

He spins me in his arms before pulling my back snug to his front. "I love you, too. I can't tell you how good it feels to finally have you here with me." His hot breath tickles my ear.

In mere moments, I drift asleep.

Liberty leaps from my arms with the opening of our door. She jibber-jabbers as she walks into the space.

"Is that so?" Miss Alba responds as if understanding Liberty's every word, even though they only met this morning. "Would you like a snack?" She stands with hands on her hips a wide smile upon her face. Her brightly colored dress is protected by her apron. Hamilton assures me, I'll love her. So far it seems I will.

Liberty promptly nods and raises her arms towards Miss Alba. She lifts Liberty, and together, they browse, first in the pantry then in the refrigerator.

"Fresh fruit. That's the perfect snack after a busy day of shopping." Liberty nods to Miss Alba's statement and patiently waits as she's secured in her highchair. Once the bowl of diced fruit lies in front of my hungry daughter, Miss Alba addresses me. "What can I get for Momma?"

I shake my head. "I can get my own." I'm relieved to find a bottle of water in the door to the fridge as we don't have glasses yet. "Looks like you've had a busy day shopping today, too." The pantry is full, and the refrigerator contains many options as well. "I'm sure that took over an hour at the grocery store."

Miss Alba nods. "I love my job!" She smiles.

It's weird, allowing someone to shop for us.

"Let's set up your cell phone calendar to sync with the home calendar," Miss Alba suggests, pressing a few buttons on the refrigerator door.

A large screen within the stainless-steel door reveals a list of tabs across the top.

"I press the calendar tab like this," she instructs. "This calendar will show Hamilton's travel schedule, the dogs' schedule, Liberty's activities, my schedule, and your work schedule. With the individual tabs, we can view each separate calendar and make additions to them" She smiles while awaiting my show of understanding. When I nod, she continues, "Let's look at Liberty's calendar. In red are possible activities. Let's pretend she will be going to this tumbling activity tomorrow at three. When I press and hold it, the color changes to black. Black calendar events indicate her planned activities, and they show up over on the combined calendar, too."

I press a few tabs, viewing various calendars as Hamilton walks up behind me.

"Let's ask the dog walkers to take the dogs down at six tonight," he suggests over my shoulder. "Wanna put it on their schedule?"

I open their calendar, press today's date, and six o'clock, holding it until it turns black.

"Perfect," he praises.

"So, now what happens?" I ask, looking from him to Miss Alba.

"At six, one of the guys will ride the service elevator up and take both dogs down to run for a while at the dog park," Hamilton explains.

Miss Alba adds, "When the service elevator pings over here," she points to the elevator doors in the utility room off the kitchen, "they'll announce themselves before walking in. If no one is here, they'll still enter and get the dogs."

"Too easy," I reply.

"They make it all that easy for us," Hamilton states.

"The combined calendars will help me plan meals and clean areas of the condo," Miss Alba informs. "The list tab is where you place any special requests from the store. You can also leave me notes of meals you prefer or guests you'll be entertaining."

"Got it," I assure.

She presses a few buttons. "There. I've sent you a link to your phone, so you can schedule from it. If you enter a phone number for the iPad or email address right here," she points to a button for me, "you can send a link to connect it to all your devices to schedule from them."

"Very high tech," Hamilton assures me. "When we hire a nanny, her calendar will join the others."

I give Hamilton the look, to which he just glares back at me.

"We'll talk about it later," he smirks.

"Follow me," I demand, striding to my empty office.

"I guess we are talking about it now." Hamilton attempts to make light of this. "Open your calendar to the children's activities."

I do as he instructs. I'll humor him for a bit.

He leans in over my shoulder. "She'd love swimming lessons, tumbling, story time–she'd like all of these activities."

I nod in agreement.

"Even if we signed her up for only two of these, they meet three days a week." He moves to face me. "That would cut into your work time. If you were still teaching, Liberty would be in daycare or preschool from seven-thirty to four, five days a week. Writing is your job now; a nanny will give you more free time to write and allow Liberty to make new friends in the building."

"I guess we could look into it, but I'm not making any promises," I grumble. I've survived almost two years without a nanny. I leaned on Alma to care for Liberty while I attended classes. My mind tries to calculate the hours Alma cared for Liberty each week.

"I love you, stubborn woman," he states prior to kissing my forehead.

After dinner, the long day begins to take its toll on me. I long to prop myself up on a few pillows in the corner of the sectional.

"This way," Hamilton urges as we walk down the hallway.

I hear the sound of running water in the master bathroom. "What's up?" I pause, looking up at Hamilton.

"Liberty and I have a surprise for you." He continues to maneuver me towards our bedroom with his hand firmly at the small of my back.

"Sup-pize!" Liberty jumps up and down on our bed as I enter my room. "Sup-pize, Mommy!"

I climb onto the bed and begin jumping with her. Liberty wraps her little arms around my legs, and together, we fall to the mattress, giggling. She wiggles her way up my body.

She points to the master bath. "Sup-pize, Mommy!"

I crane my neck. Hamilton bends over the sunken tub, turning off the faucet. He dips his hand in, testing the temperature.

"Perfect," he declares, looking my way. "Your bath awaits." His long arm gestures above the tub.

"What's all this?" I lift Liberty, walking towards him.

"Libby and I want some Daddy-Daughter time, so we thought you could relax in here for a bit." He extends his arms, and Liberty quickly climbs into them. "Let's light the candles for Mommy."

I stand in the doorway as the two position six candles around the tub, counting out loud as they light each one. The faint scent of vanilla wafts in my direction. My eyes shift from my daughter; Hamilton's sexy smirk says it all. He loves when I use vanilla body wash and body spray. His eyes stare hungrily at my lips. It's clear he has plans for after my bath.

"Bye-bye," Liberty announces as they vacate the room, turning off the light as they pass.

I dip my fingers through the bubbles, testing the water. I'm pleased to find it hot and deep. I remove my clothes, placing them in the hamper. I lift one foot over the edge into the tub then the other. I slowly lower my body below the bubbles into the blissful heat. I don't move while it acclimates. Goosebumps prick upon my shoulders despite the heated air. The hot bath causes the warm air to seem chilly.

I extend my legs, placing my toes near the waterline. With arms braced on the edge where cream bathtub meets oatmeal and chocolate tiles, I gradually lean back, my eyes closing, submerging myself to my chin in the divine warmth. Tiny bubbles pop near my ears as I swirl my arms beneath the water.

Opening my eyes, I notice a hand towel, cradling earbuds, next to a glass of white wine. Condensation on the glass signals me that the wine is cold. Raising the glass to my lips, the chilled liquid starkly contrasts the heated water. The refreshing, fruity wine is another point scored by Hamilton. I realize Miss Alba must have helped purchase the wine. But Hamilton thought ahead to place it in the refrigerator for tonight. He remembers I like wine in the evening from time to time.

Curious, I lift one ear bud gently, placing it in my right ear. A 1980's power ballad plays as I scan the bathroom for a device it's connected to. I find nothing. While Warrant sings "Heaven", a deep calm slides over me. The wine, the bubbles, the warmth, the candlelight, and the melody coaxes the last month's stress from every bone in my body.

I rest my head against the tub and close my eyes. I lift one foot, letting my toes peek out from the water. I lift it higher and higher to rest it on the spout. Slowly, the foam glides down my shin and over my exposed calf. As the bubbles pop, the sensation prickles my heated skin. I immerse the foot beneath the tranquil water.

Opening my eyes, I reach for my wine again, taking a deep sip. I savor the blend of apples, citrus, and peaches as it refreshes my mouth and throat. I return the glass to the tile tub edge and raise my other foot to enjoy the tiny bubbles popping, releasing even more tension.

My muscles loosen and my thoughts evaporate as the alcohol affects my head. I stir the remaining bubbles by gliding my hands just below the surface. I further unwind by removing one earbud to enjoy the sloshing my waves create.

I notice my empty glass is full again. My sneaky man must have tiptoed in. As I consume more wine, I sit up, allowing the bubbles to explode on my back and shoulders. Goosebumps form, chilling my skin. In three long gulps, I down the wine before exiting the warm, soapy haven to rinse in the shower.

I choose a warm temperature from the dials before I step under the spray. I allow the stream to pelt my scalp, spinning for the water to fall on my face, my back, and my chest.

I wipe the water from my eyes before I open them to find the vanity lights on and Hamilton leaning against the counter. I wipe a large circle of water drops from the shower door. Hamilton smirks, arms crossed over his chest. My nipples come to full attention as warmth sinks past my belly.

He strides towards the shower door, snagging a heavy, terrycloth robe from a nearby hook. I turn the water off, anxious for what he plans next. He opens the glass door, robe opened for me to easily slip my arms into it. The soft, fluffy material engulfs me.

"I told myself to give you a few nights to settle in, but I can't resist you any longer," he growls into my neck. His humid breath taunts my sensitive skin.

I tilt my head, exposing my neck. He nips and sucks playfully. He palms my chin, turning me into his kiss. His mouth devours mine. I pivot, positioning myself tight to his chest. My hands tug at his belt, exposing my urgent need.

He carries me to our bed, laying me out before him. His jaw ticks as his hands deftly open the robe. I watch through hooded eyes as he scans down my body.

When his brows raise and lips part, I know he's spotted my tattoo. I expect his eyes to find mine or for him to speak—he does neither.

"Do you like it?" I whisper. It's almost identical to the one he has over his heart. Although we never planned it, we chose similar tattoos.

He crawls onto the bed, his fingers tracing the lines. I watch his eyes fill with lust, rubbing my upper thighs together slowly to ease my growing need. After several moments, I attempt to sit up, needing to touch him.

With one forceful hand, he prevents my movement. He climbs up my body, a feral look in his dark eyes.

"Do you like it?" I whisper again before wetting my suddenly dry lips.

His eyes track the motion of my tongue. "It's the sexiest tat I've ever seen," he growls before attacking my lips and tongue with his.

He pulls his mouth from mine. "I imagined a design placed here." He licks the area behind my ear.

Lowering himself, he nips my collarbone on his descent. "I fanaticized of script along here." His thumbs graze under the curve of my breasts before he nips and sucks each nipple.

He tugs my arms from the robe I forgot I was wearing and flips me over as if I weigh nothing at all.

I flinch as his warm mouth licks down my spine. "I imagined a delicate, vining floral design here."

He palms one ass cheek and bites the other. After my squeal, he informs, "The thought of one here haunted me for hours at night."

He plants kisses on the back of each knee before lifting one foot into the air. "I imagined an animal or four-leaf clover here." He lightly runs a calloused fingertip over my ankle.

With both ankles in hand, he twists my legs, prompting me to roll over. Like a large cat, he prowls up my legs to my waist.

"I spent countless hours and too many sleepless nights fantasizing about your secret tattoo and its location." He licks the perimeter of the baseball then kisses its center. "This is the sexiest gift you could ever give me."

I pull his mouth to mine. As our mouths collide and tongues dance, I feel him squirm as he removes his pants. I fist the hem of his shirt and tug it up and over his head, breaking our kiss only when necessary.

"We match," I state.

That's where our tattoo exploration and conversation end. Hamilton carries out his plan for our bodies to reconnect.

CHAPTER 29

Madison

When my alarm sounds, my body aches in protest as I stretch. It's the delicious reminder of a long rendezvous with Hamilton last night. My muscles crave a long, hot soak in the tub, but I'll have to settle for a long, hot shower.

I groan, remembering the hours of shopping planned for me today.

"It won't be that bad," Hamilton calls from our bathroom.

I crawl down the bed, excited at the prospect of ogling my naked man. I groan again when I find him already dressed with Liberty sitting next to him on the vanity.

I want nothing more than to crawl under the covers for a few more hours of sleep. But my day awaits.

Only 40 minutes after I kiss Hamilton goodbye, our doorbell rings. Since the doorman didn't call ahead, it must be a resident or someone on Hamilton's pre-approved list. *I need to see who he has on that list.*

With Liberty behind my legs, I hesitantly open the door.

"Oh, hello." I greet the last person in the world I want to see at our door.

"Hello," the super-peppy Berkeley greets and enters without my invitation.

"Um..." I'm not shocked she's here but shocked by her boldness. "Hamilton's already left."

"Oh, I know," she states, squatting carefully in her heels and pencil skirt. "Hi, Liberty. How are you today?"

My daughter looks to me for direction. I smile and nod, anxious to see her reaction.

Not one to disappoint, she barely lifts her hand in a half-wave then darts back to her toys without a word.

Gracefully rising to stand, Berkeley seats herself on the sectional she secured for us. I follow her lead and take a seat.

"What brings you by today?" I ask, wanting to hurry this awkward visit along.

"I didn't want to intrude on your first night in Chicago," she begins. "So, I thought I'd drop by today and introduce myself."

I'm at a loss for words. *What do I say to that?* She's Hamilton's employee, not mine. I have no reason to talk to her.

The service elevator beeps, signaling Miss Alba's arrival. Liberty takes off running to greet her.

"Good morning," I call from the sofa.

Miss Alba returns my greeting, Liberty in her arms. "Oh, hello, Berkeley," she adds.

I can't read the tone with which Miss Alba greets Berkeley. It seems flat; *maybe she's not a Berkeley fan.*

"What brings you by?" Miss Alba inquires.

"I needed to officially introduce myself, and I hope I have a solution for Hamilton's family," Berkeley proudly replies.

Miss Alba raises her brows at me before releasing Liberty to the floor.

"What problem do you have a solution for?" I ask, dying to know the real reason for Berkeley dropping by when her boss is not present.

"First, let me share my card with you," she offers, flustered by my forwardness. "I work for the Cubs and Hamilton, but if you ever need anything, feel free to reach out. I was new to Chicago four years ago. I know what it's like to be all alone in a new city." She quickly corrects herself, "I mean, you're not alone, but I'll help if I can."

Whoa. So, she's really here to be nice and help me? I won't let my guard down that easily, but, given that Hamilton trusts her, I'll keep an open mind. I thank her for the card.

"I wanted to talk to you in person about a nanny for Liberty," Berkeley states, looking toward my daughter playing with blocks near my feet.

"I'm not convinced we need a nanny." I tell her the same thing I've told Hamilton several times in the past week.

She moves beside me and pats my knee like we've known each other for more than 48 hours. "Nonsense. You'll need time to write and a sitter to watch her while you attend the Cubs functions. Anyway, I have the perfect nanny for you."

My eyes widen as she ignores my protest and continues.

"Slater is a trainer for the Cubs and lives here in your building. His fiancé, Fallon, just graduated with a degree in Psychology and moved in with him. She's filled out the paperwork and plans to nanny as she slowly works on a master's degree. She knows the ins and outs of the Cubs life, and who's better than a psych major to care for a child?"

I nod. She sounds too good to be true.

"I've met Fallon a couple of times over the past two years. I've been talking to Slater the past two weeks, and this just seems like a perfect fit."

My head swims. I recall the information Hamilton shared about the services the condos offer. They keep a large staff of screened nannies and back-ups available for tenants.

"I thought we could invite Fallon over this morning, just to see if she might be a good fit for your family." Berkeley's timid smile lets me know she's really not trying to force me to make a choice. "Can I text her? The two of you could chat, and she could play with Liberty a bit."

"Would you like a drink?" I need a moment to mull this over.

"No, thank you," Berkeley responds.

As I approach the refrigerator, Miss Alba moves to my side.

"Nannies don't usually live in the building," she whispers so only I can hear. "It might be worth meeting her before another family grabs her up."

Every part of me trusts Miss Alba's advice. Maybe Berkeley isn't as bad as I imagined.

I sip from my water as I return to the sofa. "Text her. I'd love to meet her." I smile genuinely at Berkeley. "I'm still not convinced we need one, but it can't hurt to meet her. If she's free before one, she can come on over."

I move to the floor with Liberty and her block towers.

Berkeley welcomes our guest, motioning to the sectional.

"Madison," she introduces, "this is Fallon."

I wave at our new guest.

"And this little princess is Liberty." Berkeley squats, accidentally knocking over two of her block towers.

"No!" Liberty points at Berkeley and stands, hands on hips. "No, pin-thess. Me Batman." Finished with the conversation, she marches to her room.

"Umm, excuse us." I follow my headstrong daughter down the hall. I'm sure she's looking for her costumes, and we haven't unpacked them yet.

"Follow me," I instruct her, continuing to my room.

From my large suitcase, I pull out her Batman costume. I hold it up, and Liberty grasps my arms as she steps into the pant legs before sliding her arms into each sleeve. I tie it behind her neck.

"I'm gonna go back out to talk to Fallon," I inform her. "I hope you'll come out and play with us."

As I walk down the hallway, I hear her tiny feet following behind me. I seat myself on the sofa, smiling proudly as Liberty stands in the center of the sectional, her hands on her hips, shoulders thrown back, and chin up.

"Batman," she states.

"I love your costume," Fallon says, moving to sit on the floor. "What does Batman do?"

Liberty wastes no time demonstrating as she speaks. "Wun, jump, fwy..."

"Careful," I remind her as she climbs upon the sectional and hops to the floor.

Liberty takes Fallon on a tour of the house, points out her toys and books, and even demonstrates McGee's tricks for her. The two are fast friends. When they return from Liberty's room, Fallon prompts her to tell me what she's learned.

"Hola, Mommy!" My pretty girl waves proudly.

"Hola!" I wave back.

"She's bright," Fallon informs. "I'm fluent in Spanish and thought I'd teach her a word." She waits for my reaction.

"I love it. She's a sponge; she'll soak it up quickly." I smile.

Fallon stays for an hour, during which Liberty and I fall in love with her. We're still visiting when Taylor arrives to escort us shopping. We plan for her to nanny four days each week with other hours as needed.

Shopping with Taylor is as bad as I expected. We have much to buy, and shopping is my least favorite thing. I'm thankful Liberty sleeps through most of it, and, in the end, I'm glad Taylor is along. She proves to be a great help. However, once we climb off the elevator back at the condo, I can feel the exhaustion already setting in. "I'm hungry," Taylor tells me as we open the door. "Lucky for you, I've already prepped snacks!" Miss Alba chuckles from the kitchen. "Go get washed up while I set it out."

―――――

As we fill our plates with mini sandwiches, chips, and items from a relish tray, we share our shopping adventures with Miss Alba.

"Just before you returned, maintenance phoned to state your furniture arrived. They'll be bringing it up the service elevators soon." She looks to me for approval.

"Libby, did you hear that?" I lean towards her highchair. "Your new bed is here!" I clap my hands excitedly, and Liberty joins me.

"Wow, you've got a busy day," Taylor states.

"I'm sure I'll be exhausted tonight," I reply.

"Nonsense," Miss Alba tisks. "The guys will place it all where you want it and even assemble the beds for you. You only need to instruct them where to put it all."

"Hamilton will be home soon," Taylor reminds me,

patting my forearm on the marble island. "He can help direct them for you."

As if summoned by her, Hamilton emerges through the front door at that moment.

"Daddy!" Liberty cheers with a cheese cube in her hand.

"What have we here?" He smiles at the four of us around the kitchen island.

"Take a stool," Miss Alba offers Hamilton. "Furniture is on the way up. You need to eat quickly."

Without argument, Hamilton tosses his coat on the sectional and strides to the empty barstool near Taylor. Our conversation returns to shopping and plans for the furniture while we enjoy our meal.

"Thank you." Hamilton shakes the three maintenance men's hands as they board the service elevator off the back of the kitchen.

When the doors close, he maneuvers himself through the waist-high stacks of boxes bordering the walls of the kitchen and dining room. All of our purchases from this afternoon have been delivered, too.

"Why don't the two of you take a break?" Miss Alba offers. "I've got dinner ready. The furniture is all in place. You can relax a bit before you begin opening all the boxes."

Hamilton hedges, but I am ready to eat and sit for a spell. "The new sheets will be done soon in the dryer, and most of the new dishes are now clean and dry." I wrap my arms around his waist. "I need to sit and eat."

He looks down into my eyes, assessing me. "Then we will eat. You know, the rest of this can all wait until tomorrow."

I shake my head–the thought of waking to so many full boxes tomorrow doesn't sound enticing. "Eat, rest for a minute, and then we will open the rest of the boxes."

He holds out a barstool for me, and I slide upon it. Miss Alba places Liberty into her chair while I begin cutting up a tender chicken breast for her plate.

"I can stay if you'd like." Miss Alba looks to me.

Hamilton shakes his head as I quickly respond. "Thank you for offering, but there's no need. We will work a little more before we call it a night." I smile. "There will be plenty left for you to help with tomorrow morning."

We work for just over an hour. Hamilton opens each box, and I wipe a cloth over each item before finding a location for it to grace in our new home.

I admire our work. Furniture now fills each room while the walls and ledges hold decorative frames, vases, and artwork. This recently vast, empty space now looks like a home.

Hamilton wraps his arms around my waist from behind. As I melt in his warm embrace, he whispers in my ear, "Once the trash and recycling are removed, our home will be ready for company."

I turn my lips to his cheek, placing a warm peck upon them. "They arrive tomorrow."

"You're exhausted," he murmurs softly into my messy hair. "Let's tuck Libby into bed before we wash off all of this day and rest for our company."

Hamilton

I turn on the shower, allowing the spray to warm up before we enter. Madison attempts to run her brush through her tangled hair. I stand, frozen in awe of this gorgeous woman of mine. Her life has been uprooted and her world completely changed. She's taken every blow with her chin high, always looking for a solution.

In the past two days, she and Liberty have moved with me to Chicago and helped me create a new home. She shows no fear, although I know she feels it just as I do. She's determined to start her new life here with me, and I love her even more for agreeing to do so.

Her eyes lock onto mine in the large mirror. She tilts her head to the side and quirks a smile at me. Unable to abstain any longer, I close the short distance between us. I place my hands upon her jaws and press my lips to hers. Our kiss begins slow but quickly becomes feverish. When she gasps, I slip my tongue into her mouth. My left hand entwines in her long locks, insisting she remain tight against me. My other fingers trace along her jaw, down her delicate neck and collarbone. I need her, but not here.

"Let's shower," I whisper as I begin to tug her t-shirt off of her.

We make quick work of our clothes, and I guide her ahead of me into the steam-filled stall. My hands remain on her hips while she leans her head back into the spray, wetting her hair. I fight the urge to run my hands up her abdomen to her breasts that lunge towards me while her back arches.

She pulls her head from under the spray, opening her eyes. In them, I see her desire, and my control crumbles. My lips seek hers in a punishing kiss while my hands knead her breasts and pluck her nipples into tight buds. She moans into my mouth. causing me to press myself against her soft flesh from thigh to chest. The water slickens our skin, and my erection continues to grow for her.

Behind her back, I pour shower gel into my hand. Starting at her shoulders, I slowly slide my hands up and down her arms then glide them over her chest. Again, her head falls back as her lips part. I allow one hand to trail down her breastbone, over her navel, to the soft mound above her entrance. I love that she waxes but leaves the landing strip. I gently tug on the short hair.

Madison

I jump back to life, turning in his arms, quickly lathering my hands with soap, while he massages my back. I spin, my hands flying to his cock between us. Gently at first, I glide my slick hands over him then slowly increase my grip with each stroke.

His hands press against the glass wall behind me to steady himself while he pumps into my fists. I've never showered with anyone. I've seen my share of sexy shower scenes in movies and read them in erotic romance books, but this is more than I ever imagined.

A low growl climbs from Hamilton's chest moments before he grasps my wrists, removing my touch from his erection. He holds my wrists above my head with one hand as we allow the spray to wipe all soap from our bodies. His eyes are liquid pools, staring into mine, reaching to my soul. My lips part, and my tongue darts out to moisten them.

He pounces–his lips on mine inform me playtime is over. I'm spun around, and he places my hands on the glass. He lifts one of my knees, allowing my foot to rest on the shower seat, opening me up to him.

My back arches when he glides his bulging cock between my cheeks, down toward my entrance. He growls in my ear to keep my hands on the wall just before he slides into me in one swift motion. He's still, allowing me to stretch over him after his intrusion. I lean myself back into him, craving the contact of his chest against me, needing more of him, all of him.

He begins pounding in and out of me in a hard, steady rhythm. The sounds of our wet bodies slapping together fill the shower enclosure. I grind myself by swiveling my hips while he remains deep within me.

I feel the pelting water move from my backside. I'm so in the moment, into the sensations and momentum, that I didn't notice his hand leave my hip and move the shower head, adjusting the stream of water. I squeal when the spray connects with my sex while he's deep within me. Thank goodness for handheld shower heads.

Hamilton slows his pistoning as he begins swirling the shower jets over my sensitive lips and swollen clit.

"Oh, oh... Ham," I groan as my body speeds from 60 miles per hour to over 100. "Hamilton..." I gasp for small breaths as the sensations overwhelm me. "So close."

Hamilton leans his torso onto my back, his mouth suckling at the nape of my neck. He stills the circular motions of the spray, now targeting it directly on the center of all my nerve endings.

"Yes!" I scream, feeling my release near. My core clenches, my muscles strain, and the tight coil prepares to release.

Hamilton nips my neck, and I fall apart. Wave upon wave racks through me. He doesn't still; instead, he continues to drive into me, the showerhead tormenting me.

My orgasm doesn't wane; my forehead hits the wall as tremors overtake me. Feeling me quake, Hamilton drops the showerhead to the tile below. His hands plant on my hips as he drives into me hard once, twice, and I feel him shutter as he grinds his release deep in me. While he trembles and sputters within my channel, my body turns to gelatin. My knees bend; my hands and head slide down the wet glass as I start to fall.

Hamilton withdraws, increases his grip on my hips, and steadies me. His arm around my waist tugs me to him, and he wraps another around my chest, gripping his hand over my bicep. My head falls back upon him.

Our rapid breaths begin to sync with each other as we fall deeper into each other.

CHAPTER 30

Madison

Delta: What are you up to today?
Me: Prepping for company
Me: Some writing
Delta: I'm on my way to pick you up
Delta: We're taking Liberty shopping
Me: okay?
Me: I'll have doorman send you up

I only met her a week ago; I'm not sure what to make of this spur of the moment shopping trip. I let Fallon know she may have the rest of the day off. Liberty exudes more enthusiasm than I for our impromptu outing. She greets Delta at the door with cheers.

"What is all of this about?" I ask while we stand in the kitchen.

"Hamilton didn't tell you about today, did he?"

I recall our conversation last evening. He mentioned two events today: a public appearance and a meeting with his team. I shake my head.

"I figured as much." she smiles. "They had to R.S.V.P. a month ago. I knew he wouldn't remember this is a family event."

My eyes bulge. *Family event with the team? I'm not ready for this.*

"We've got this," she states. "It's a pre-holiday party for the Cubs organization and their families. We shake a few hands, gossip, eat a meal, take a few photos, and slip away at the first moment we can."

She must sense my fear. "I promise that I will not leave your side, unless Hamilton is with you."

"I..." My hand covers my lips. "I have nothing to wear."

"Duh," she laughs. "I knew you needed something new to wear. Thus, our shopping trip, silly." She wraps her arm around my shoulders. "Don't be upset with Hamilton. I'm sure if the R.S.V.P. came through now, he'd include you in all of it."

I shrug. I don't blame him, but I don't really know how I feel about it. Perhaps scared is the best way of explaining it.

———

Upon entering the department store of Delta's choosing, we are whisked to a large, private dressing room area. Beverages and snacks appear along with three saleswomen.

"Did you see what Hamilton took to wear?" she asks.

"A blue dress shirt with a Cubs-colored tie," I inform.

"We're looking for royal blue party dresses for Madison and Liberty," Delta points as she instructs. "Not cocktail, though."

Liberty toddles from mirror to mirror, enjoying the view as she giggles and waves.

The saleswomen nod before setting out on their task. I marvel at the large area–I've never seen a dressing room quite like this. I've never shopped in a store like this.

Delta places her hands upon my shoulders as she bends to make eye contact. "It's my treat today. Let's have fun." She mistakes my shock for worry.

"Delta," I murmur, "it's not that. I mean, it is, but it isn't." I look toward the ceiling as I struggle to compile my words. "Money isn't an issue. I'm just new to it. That's all." I smile, not wanting to ruin her gesture. I lower my voice near a whisper. "Since my father's death, I've struggled for every penny. My mother fell into depression and sought to ease her pain in bottle after bottle. She didn't reveal that I had a college fund, didn't share that the farm was paid off or that I had inherited my grandparents' farm. Weeks ago, I learned I should never have worried about money. I spent years scraping every penny I could from part-time jobs. When not at school or work, I studied. I took several college classes while in high school and took the CLEP test to earn others.

My grades earned me a full ride. I lived with a charitable woman who provided free room and board for Liberty and me." I lift my eyes toward Delta's. "I have money. Hamilton has money. I'm just not accustomed to it. I shop at Target." I laugh.

"We are not that different, you and me." Delta places her hand upon mine. "I didn't inherit money, but marrying Stan rescued me from a shanty in Louisiana." A small smile climbs upon her face. "I understand it's hard to spend more money on things, but you deserve nice things and to attend these events."

I nod as racks of dresses roll into the room.

"Now for the fun part!" Delta stands, extending an arm to me. "You try on yours, and I'll help Liberty into hers. We'll meet out here by the mirrors with each outfit."

I enter the changing room as several dresses are placed over the door for me. I revel in the bright blue fabrics, some solid, some floral. I slowly inspect each as I place the hanger on a hook. I draw in a deep breath, vowing not to glance at the price tags. I need a dress worthy of being at Hamilton's side.

I wait at the three-way mirror. I turn this way and that, admiring the solid wrap dress, its length falling just above my knees.

"Mommy!" Liberty calls as she runs excitedly toward me. She sways side to side, enjoying the full skirt with layer upon layer of wavy tulle. The bodice is a simple tank ornamented with large, threaded flowers with rhinestones in the center. A large bow decorates her waist, a large rhinestone adorning it as well. "Wook, Mommy!"

The royal blue suits her dark curls and twinkling, brown eyes. The matching lace-top anklets and patent leather Mary Janes perfectly finish the look. I love it; it's fancy, yet appropriate for a little girl. Her excitement is contagious. While she admires herself in the mirrors, I look to Delta.

"I think I found my dress." I shrug, embarrassed. I feel I am trying on clothes, waiting for my mother's approval.

"Uh-huh," she shakes her head. "You must try them all on."

I cross my arms across, tapping my toe. "This is the perfect dress. There's no need to try on the others."

I slowly spin with outstretched arms for her inspection. I love the simple structure, the flow of the fabric, and the fit at the waist. It's blue screams Chicago Cubs. It's a dress I will happily wear again.

"Why don't you go look at the rack of dresses and tell me if you see one you like more than this one," I suggest to my friend. "I'll assist Liberty in trying on her next dress."

We return a few minutes later with Liberty proudly swirling in a long, blue satin dress with lace tulle and an ostrich feather adorning the flower broach at her right hip. Although she looks lovely, I dislike this choice. My daughter looks five instead of nearly two. I humor her as she parades into the common room, posing for Delta and the sales staff.

Delta agrees with my initial dress selection. After modeling two more dresses, we decide on Liberty's first dress. She squeals with glee when I inform her that she gets to wear it out of the store. I've remained in my new dress and adorned it with the matching heels and jewelry they offer.

I shakily hand over Hamilton's Amex to cover our bill. I remind myself we now have money to afford such things. I attempt to focus on how the two of us look and Hamilton's surprise when we arrive rather than the large amount we spend.

After picking up the kids from school and quickly changing at home, Delta delivers us to the event. I try to hide my nerves as we ascend in the elevator. I should have texted Hamilton to let him know we'd meet him. I fear what it might look like when we arrive separately.

With a ping, the elevator doors announce our arrival. I prompt Delta and her family to lead the way. Liberty proudly walks at my side as the hem of her dress sways down the long hallway toward the party.

"Delta," Stan's deep voice calls as he exits the elevator.

Turning, I find Hamilton standing bewildered beside him.

The two girls run towards their fathers; Webb remains at our sides. With daughters dancing at their feet, the men quickly join us. Hamilton opens his mouth, but Delta stops him with an extended palm.

"I thought you might forget this is a family event, so I delivered your family for you." She smiles proudly.

His eyes dart to mine, apology clear on his face. "I didn't know. I promise," he pleads.

I nod. "Delta said you had to RSVP last month; it's no big deal."

Hamilton's gaze sweeps over my entire body. My skin prickles at his attention and the lust I see in his gaze.

"It's new." My nerves are evident in my voice.

"I like it."

"Daddy!" Liberty interrupts, drawing Hamilton's attention from me. "Daddy, wook!" She spins in a circle, causing her dress to billow out further.

"You look very pretty." Hamilton smiles proudly at her. "Both you and Mommy are very pretty."

Liberty lifts her arms; Hamilton scoops her up. She places a kiss upon his cheek while wrapping her arms tightly around his neck.

"Shall we?" Stan gestures toward the nearby entrance.

I observe Delta closely and follow her lead. Hamilton removes his hand from the small of my back, securing the backpack on his free shoulder.

"I'd like to introduce Madison and our daughter, Liberty," he proudly announces before returning his hand to my back.

I smile and shake hands with the team's owners and management each time Hamilton introduces the two of us. Liberty even extends her little hand to shake.

"Mommy," her little voice calls to me as she points to the small backpack Hamilton holds. "Cubbie Bear?"

I assume she's feeling overwhelmed in this crowd of strangers and wants her bear to hold. I easily pull it from the backpack still on Hamilton's shoulder. When I extend it, she quickly cuddles it to her chest.

"I recognize this pretty face," a gruff voice announces from our right. "This is Hamilton's number one fan. I told you about her; she's from his Des Moines debut."

Hamilton allows the three men to enjoy a chuckle prior to continuing his introductions to the coaches.

"I hope this means you've joined him in Chicago," the pitching coach states. "We could use an extra set of eyes to keep Hamilton in tip-top shape."

Over the loud chuckles, Hamilton informs, "Madison has finished college, and we've just moved into our new place." His hand on my hip pulls me snug to his side.

It doesn't escape me that the way Hamilton has introduced us tonight implies we've been a couple. It's no one's business; I'm glad he isn't drawing attention to the fact we aren't wed, and he didn't know he had a daughter a week ago.

"Daddy, wook!" Liberty squeals, pointing across the large room. "Cubbie Bear!" She animatedly points with one extended finger before using her hand pressed to his jaw to turn his head.

"Excuse us," Hamilton begs of the coaches. "She's a huge fan."

His hand slips from my hip before he lowers Liberty to the floor. Quickly, his hand grasps mine as we hurry to follow our daughter who is running towards the Cubs Mascot, calling loudly to Cubbie Bear.

I now regret not teaching her that the Chicago Cubs mascot is Clark. The plush toy she clutches in her tiny hand now is the Iowa Cubs Mascot, Cubbie Bear. Although it's their minor league team, the two mascots are different.

She freezes five feet from the oversized bear. Her little head cranes upward to marvel at the life-size version of her plush friend. She extends her tiny free hand and waves.

Clark quickly returns her greeting before kneeling to her level. Liberty extends her Cubbie Bear, proudly showing it. The mascot places his large, furry hand over his mouth and bounces to mimic laughter.

Liberty grabs Hamilton's hand and pulls him closer with her. Many one-and-a-half-year-olds enjoy mascots from safe distances but fear them up close. Not our daughter–I marvel at her inquisitive nature and fearlessness. Clark stands as she draws near, so Hamilton lifts her into his arms. The mascot pats her on the head. Liberty leans forward to kiss his cheek.

A female photographer wearing three large cameras, urges us to pose as a family with the mascot. While I stand on the right of Clark, Hamilton holds Liberty on the left side. With one camera and then a second, she rapidly snaps several photos then excuses herself.

"Libby is kissing him in half of the photos," Hamilton whispers when I return to his side. I shake my head as we approach Stan's family.

"That was adorable," Delta states. "Libby, who was that?" She points at the mascot.

"Cubbie Bear," Liberty replies, extending her stuffed toy.

"His name is Clark," Webb states matter-of-factly, staring at his hands. Beneath them is the copy of my book.

"Cubbie Bear!" Liberty argues, wiggling her stuffed bear towards him.

"In Des Moines, the I-Cubs mascot is named Cubbie Bear," I tell Webb, hoping he'll drop the argument without drawing more attention to us.

"Hamilton pitched for the Cubs minor league team there for a month before he moved to Chicago," Stan informs Webb.

"Can I see your Cubbie Bear?" Webb inquires, looking toward Liberty.

Leaning forward from Hamilton's grasp, she places her beloved bear in Webb's hand for inspection. He turns it over then looks to Clark and back.

"They aren't the same." He passes the toy back to Liberty. "I like your Cubbie Bear better."

Happy with his approval, Liberty nods firmly.

Hamilton leaves me with Delta to speak with teammates, and Stan follows. Aurora invites Liberty to join her and a few other girls near the windows. They have dolls spread out everywhere as the sun sets in the background. "You may read for 30 minutes," Delta tells Webb.

He quickly rises, book in hand, and escapes to read by himself on the floor.

"I feel like a million eyes are burning my back," I confess.

"Oh, everyone is looking and speculating why you are

here with Hamilton." She leans closer and lowers her voice. "Can you blame them? Hamilton keeps to himself. The team and fans know very little about him. Now, suddenly, he arrives with a hot woman and little girl in tow." She purses her lips. "It will wear off. Hamilton and Stan are probably setting the guys straight as we speak."

I sneak a peek. Hamilton stands, facing a group of guys with his back towards me. The men are hanging on his every word. I turn around, searching for Liberty. She's not with Aurora or Hamilton. I scan the room. She's seated near Webb while he reads. She doesn't seem to be bothering him, so I leave her be.

"Would you mind keeping an eye on Libby while I join Hamilton for a bit?"

Delta nods as I rise. When I approach, undetected by him, I slip my arm under his and lean in close.

"Hello," I greet the group of wide-eyed men as Stan simply chuckles. "I'm Madison."

"Oh, we know who you are," a tall, muscular, blonde states.

He is promptly slapped on the back of the head by the pitcher next to him.

"What he should have said is, 'we're the idiots you've heard cat-calling in the background as Hamilton attempted to speak to you on the phone.'" I quickly recognize him as a closing pitcher.

"Hamilton's not a chatty soul, but he has spoken of you." This comes from the third baseman.

"I haven't witnessed Hamilton smiling so much; it's clear

you're good for our ace," the tall, muscular blonde states. I finally realize he is the backup catcher.

Glancing to my left, I find the gaggle of women staring daggers in my direction. Not wanting to insight a riot, I excuse myself, claiming I need to check on our daughter. I don't need anyone to think I'm flirting with their man.

Liberty still sits beside Webb as I return to Delta at the nearby table.

"If your goal was fewer eyes upon you, you failed." Delta stares back at the group of ladies across the room.

"I only wanted to meet the team. They can inform their women."

I refuse to peek at the women. Instead, I look toward Hamilton. A wide smile graces my face as he approaches. At the last moment, he swerves toward Liberty and Webb.

"I miss that," Delta states longingly.

"Miss what?" I ask, still watching as Hamilton kneels by the children.

"The whole can't-stand-to-spend-a-minute-away-from-each-other, beginning-of-a-relationship feeling."

I peel my eyes from Hamilton. "If you ever want Hamilton and me to watch the kids so the two of you can go out for adult time, you only need to ask." I love the smile I bring to her face.

"That's very generous of you." Her smile morphs into a smirk with wiggling eyebrows. "Maybe in a few weeks, after you learn to hold the honeymoon hormones in check between the two of you, at least while others are around."

I shake my head as Delta giggles and my cheeks pink. I

do attempt to keep my hands and lips to myself while in the company of others. Apparently, I have not succeeded while in her presence.

"Here comes Hamilton," she announces. "I'm sure all of five minutes have passed since you last made contact with one another."

"What are the two of you smiling about?" Hamilton teases. "Wait. I don't want to know."

Liberty climbs upon my lap, Cubbie Bear in one arm and her other hand twirling a curl. It's a clear sign she is tired.

"We should go soon," I inform Hamilton. Turning to Delta, I continue. "She gets whiney as she gets tired. It's not the type of thing I want anyone here to see."

"Mommy, poddy," Liberty whines.

"We'll be right back," I inform the group before quickly escorting my daughter to the hallway.

"I'll go, too." Delta rises and joins us, keeping her promise not to leave me alone this evening. She takes a seat in the hall near the restroom door while Liberty and I enter.

CHAPTER 31

Hamilton

Incessant vibrations from Liberty's backpack interrupt my conversation with Stan. I pull Madison's cell phone from the outside pocket. Cameron's name lights the screen.

"Hello," I answer.

"Hamilton?" Cameron's voice greets. "Is Madison there?"

I excuse myself from Stan and head toward the hall. "She's with Libby in the restroom. We're at a function. Can I have her call you back on our way home?"

As I emerge from the room, Cameron replies. "It's pretty important. Can I speak to her for just a minute?"

"Hold on," I instruct. "Delta, please tell Madison she has an important call."

Delta rises without delay, entering the restroom. She holds the door wide; I see Madison and Liberty at the sinks. Delta helps wash Liberty's hands as Madison returns to me.

"Who is it?" She pulls the phone from my hand as I mouth, "Cameron."

"Hello?" Madison can't hide the apprehension in her voice.

I watch as concern fades from her face, replaced by excitement.

"Daddy!" Liberty screams, running in my direction.

I catch her as she hops into my arms, quickly pulling her to my chest. My eyes remain on Madison as I hug my daughter.

"Daddy." Liberty's hands clasp the sides of my face, directing my eyes to hers–she assesses me for a moment. A wide smile graces her face just before she places a kiss on my lips.

I smile down at her as she scans my face once again. This perfect little angel holds my heart in the palm of her hands. I never knew such a love could exist. I thought nothing would ever compare to the love Madison blindsided me with, but, when Liberty bolted into my mother's house mere weeks ago, my heart swelled. Instantly, I knew an even greater love.

I toss my daughter skyward–she squeals with glee. I spin us in circles, enjoying the carefree happiness it brings. When we stop, I direct her attention to Madison.

"Mommy's talking to Aunt Cameron." From the corner of my eye, I notice Liberty's nod. "Mommy's pretty when she smiles. Isn't she?"

Liberty pulls her eyes from her mom to mine, nodding in agreement. She begins to wiggle, so I allow her down to the floor. She scurries over near the floor to ceiling windows. Her hands and nose press upon the glass; she marvels at the spectacle that is Chicago at night.

Delta passes by, placing a hand to my forearm. "I'll watch her."

I nod then return my attention to Madison as she ends her phone call. Her free hand fans her face. Her eyes are wide and sparkling, her smile, broad and radiant. Moments pass before her eyes focus on me mere feet in front of her.

"Cameron..." she attempts to speak through excited breaths.

"What did Cameron have to say?" For the life of me, I can't imagine what could be so important to interrupt our evening and draw such an excited reaction from my fiancé.

"I..." Madison fans her face again as she swallows hard between her shallow breaths.

"Through your nose," I urge. "In and out, in and out."

A moment passes.

"I'm a USA Today Bestselling Author!" Her voice cracks as she smiles, tears welling in her eyes.

I whisk her up, placing kisses upon her lips while we spin in circle after circle. She pulls her mouth from mine to squeal. I hear Liberty's laughter and clapping nearby. I slow our spin and place one long, soulful kiss upon her lips. The kiss grows deeper, and soon, we're lost in one another. I feel her warm tears as her cheeks press to mine. Liberty interrupts our inappropriate celebration.

"Daddy, me turn! Me turn!" She demands.

Madison's palms push away from my chest, so I gradually release my hold upon her hips. She remains close while I scoop up our daughter.

"Mommy's famous!" I share.

The three of us cheer as we share a group hug.

Several long moments pass with our family in own little world. Faint murmurs draw my attention to the nearby seating area. Delta and the photographer croon over the display screen on her bulky camera.

Madison is the first to investigate; Liberty urges me to follow. As the camera turns for our inspection, I catch a glance of our family celebration captured for eternity.

Madison

"You took these?" My voice fills with concern. "For what purpose?"

"These will be only for you," the female photographer quickly explains. As she rambles, it is easy to sense her need to defend her actions. "I didn't mean to intrude. I just happened upon a sweet moment between father and daughter." She deftly scrolls to the photos of Liberty and I while Madison took her call. "I'm hired to take promotional photos for the organization, but these won't be included. The scene called to me—I couldn't resist. The excitement continued to grow, and I had to record it for you."

She gulps in a breath before continuing. "I wasn't close enough to hear anything; my zoom allowed me to capture the image without intruding. Please scroll through all of them." She passes the camera to me, while Hamilton peers over my shoulder.

"I ask her to get a pic of the four of us each year at this event, so I can use it in our Christmas cards," Delta adds. "Give Madison your card," she urges the photographer.

"Here. If you contact me, I'll send you all of the files." She pauses, drawing in a nervous breath while Hamilton takes the extended card. "I've started my own business. If you'd like, I could play with some of the images. You know, so you could blow them up or stretch them on a canvas."

I can't tear my eyes from the images. Shakily, I nod. "Yes, please."

"Madison received very exciting news during her phone call. I'm grateful you caught the moment for us." Hamilton's smile eases her mind.

"You have quite an eye," I compliment. "We'd love to have these images. Thank you." I pass the camera back. "Don't lose that business card."

Hamilton bites his lip as he makes exaggerated motions tucking it into the outside pocket of our backpack.

"I'm dying to know," Delta blurts. "What are you celebrating?" Her eyes ping pong from mine to Hamilton's and back.

The photographer attempts to excuse herself, giving us

privacy. Hamilton holds his arm blocking her escape. "M. Crocker," he gestures toward me, "is officially a USA Today Bestselling Author." His chest swells with pride. "She's worked hard for this honor; she should be proud and shouting it from the rooftops."

"Oh. My. God." Delta rises, wrapping herself around me tightly, rocking back and forth.

"Congratulations!" The photographer shakes my hand when Delta finally releases me.

"My editor called to let me know it will be announced this week. We can't publicize it until the paper officially prints the updated list. So, no social media posts." I point my finger sternly at Delta.

With hands defensively between us, Delta promises her lips are sealed.

"We should say our goodbyes. Libby needs her bed," I tell Hamilton.

At my words, he notices the weight of our daughter's head upon his shoulder. Her eyes are half-mast, Cubbie Bear is tight to her chest, and her fingers spin in her curls. She's sweet in her relaxed state.

"Would you mind snapping a picture of her?" he whispers over Liberty's head to our photographer friend.

While photos are captured, Delta gathers her family.

———

Hamilton presses the elevator call button as Stan, Delta, and kids approach.

"Congratulations," Stan whispers.

I assume Delta spilled the beans and instructed him to keep it a secret. I smile back. The elevator pings, and we all climb aboard. I notice Webb standing beside me, holding my book. A bookmark marks his place midway through the story.

"What's your favorite part of the story so far?" I ask him.

Webb's eyes remain downward, and he holds the book tighter.

"The main character," he answers without explanation.

My eyes widen, my breath catches, and I will my body not to react further when he slides his hand in mine between us.

"She's like you, but you aren't alone. I am your friend, Madison." He entwines his fingers with mine.

I lick my lips, eyes darting toward Delta's. I witness the same revelations there. I was a stranger to Webb a week ago. Social interactions with others, especially new acquaintances, are difficult for him. Personal space and contact with others are learned, not a natural reaction. His understanding of the similarities between the character in my book and me along with his empathy and proclamation of friendship are a huge achievement for him. I do my best not to make a scene.

"Thank you, Webb," I whisper as my voice feels trapped in my throat. "I can't wait to discuss it with you when you finish the book."

He pulls his hand back to his side, inches from mine. "I'd be done if Mom didn't only let me read it for an hour a day."

Again, I bite my lip. This time, it prevents my smile. I

keep my eyes from the other adults. I'm sure they are fighting the same battle as me.

While exiting the elevator, we say our goodbyes, promising to talk tomorrow. Hamilton escorts me to his vehicle within the parking garage. While he secures Liberty in her car seat, I slip into the front passenger seat, tears rolling down my cheeks. Strong in the elevator, I no longer win my battle holding the emotions back, and I don't try to hide them.

Hamilton pulls onto the street before he notices. "Honey, what's wrong?"

Guys can be so oblivious sometimes.

"Webb." I sob. "That was huge, you know?"

Hamilton nods.

I wipe my tears, realizing he doesn't understand it all. I raise my cell phone and FaceTime Cameron.

"Hello." she greets as her face lights my screen. "How was your first Cubs Event?"

I do my best to keep my tears from sounding in my voice. "We had fun. The photographer took amazing photos of the three of us. I can't wait to show them to everyone."

"Are you in a car?" Her face scrunches as she moves closer to her screen to see clearly.

"We are on our way home," I respond. "I had an interaction with a young fan tonight that I couldn't wait to share with you."

Cameron's face lights up. In the small inset, I see the streetlights flash light upon my face occasionally.

"One of Hamilton's teammates has a son that I gave a book to last week," I begin.

"Stan's boy. I remember you telling me about the night you met him and found he longed to read your books," Cameron shares. "He's on the spectrum, right?"

"Yes," I reply. "This evening, our two families shared an elevator as we were leaving the event. The elevator car was full, but not so crowded we were touching." I smile and goosebumps prickle my skin at the memory. "I noticed Webb held my book, so I asked him what his favorite part of the book was so far."

"He kept his eyes turned down and simply stated that he liked the main character. I loved his answer. It was his true thoughts, and I imagined the confused feelings someone with autism might feel as they read of such a lonely girl, struggling through high school." I raise my hand as I recall his next actions. "I felt his palm slide next to mine. He touched me, and that's huge for him. Still not looking at me, he stated 'She's like you, but you aren't alone. I'm your friend.' Then, he clutched my hand in his for a moment before pulling away again."

"Wow!" In the well-lit kitchen that I once lived in with Alma, I see the tears forming in Cameron's eyes. "He understood it all. That's so cool."

"Right?" This is why I needed to call her. I needed someone else to understand what Webb's words meant for him, as well as for my writing. "Even with his social challenges, he understood the pain I wrote about. Having met me, he assumed I wrote about a real part of my life, and he demonstrated empathy in a manner he's been working on with his parents and his teacher."

"It's your validation as an author," Cameron states.

"Exactly! It means more than the online reviews. They mean the world to me, but they are anonymous. I know this boy; I know the constant struggles he faces in his daily interactions." My tears have dried; I'm overcome with happiness. "If I've reached Webb, then I'm reaching other readers as well. They understand my story."

"I'm glad you now believe what I and many others have stated about your work for months now. You may be the only author that being named to the *USA Today Bestselling Authors' List* wasn't validation enough. You had to hear directly from a young reader." She chuckles. "I'm glad that you finally see. I'm happy you called to share with me, because I need to ask a favor of you."

"You know I'd do anything for you," I remind my adopted sister.

"Um..." Cameron fidgets. "What time does your flight leave for Las Vegas?" Wide-eyed, she clenches her teeth.

I glance at Hamilton. We fly to Las Vegas on Black Friday to elope. Surely, she won't mess with my wedding for a favor.

"We fly out at 11," Hamilton answers for me. "What do you need?"

"Our world-renowned author backed out of his book signing today," she groans, fisting her fingers in her hair. "He was to be at a Chicago bookstore all day Friday." She bites her lip, hesitant to continue. "I know it's a busy and exciting day for you, but I thought maybe we could squeeze in an hour or two with you signing books to appease the store owner." With hands on either side of her head and palms toward the camera, Cameron proceeds, "I realize you're not a morning person, so I'll majorly owe you for this. Maybe we could schedule the book signing from seven to nine that morning. This could start the buzz for your new book, releasing in January. What do you think?"

I look to Hamilton for guidance. It's a busy day, a busy weekend.

Removing his eyes from the road for only a moment, Hamilton smiles and nods.

"I think we can make it work," I tell Cameron. "Will you make all the arrangements?"

"Of course," she quickly replies. "I'll email you all of the details, and I'll owe you big. So big."

"I'll make sure you make good on it, too. Cameron, who's there?" For only a moment, I spot a man without a shirt walk behind her.

She quickly turns the phone and herself so my view will be obstructed from any further visions.

"Oh." Her eyes seem to search for an explanation. "I have a dripping pipe in the basement. I asked the neighbor to check it out for me."

"That didn't look like Mr. Edwards," I inform her.

She rises. In the background, I see she moves through the kitchen then down the steps into the basement. Her finger covers her face in my view before the camera angle switches to show the basement.

"Dalton, is that you?" I recognize him immediately; it's Mr. Edwards' son. He works with his father in the family construction business. Alma told me he left college many years ago to help his dad through a cancer battle and to take over the family business.

"Hey, Madison. How's Chicago?" Dalton waves, a smile on his face, dimples and all.

"What happened to your shirt?" I tease.

Dalton points to the pipes overhead. "Fixing pipes is wet work."

I nearly choke at his words.

Cameron returns the camera to her face view. "Behave," she scolds. "I'm lucky he lives next door. I planned to duct tape the area until I returned from Thanksgiving with you."

Dalton's voice interrupts from across the room. "I'm glad she mentioned the drips to my father. If I hadn't checked on it, she would have returned to a flooded basement."

Cameron rolls her eyes. "I think he exaggerates, but I am glad he had time to fix it tonight for me."

Hamilton

"I'll tuck her in," I offer.

Madison nods, fixing a water in the kitchen while chatting with Indie and McGee at her feet.

"The guys let the dogs out an hour ago, so they are ready

for bed," I inform as I carry my sleeping daughter to her room.

I turn on the small bedside lamp then pull back the blankets. Liberty barely stirs as I lay her on the bed. I contemplate waking her for the bathroom or covering her up as is. I decide her dress wouldn't be comfortable sleepwear, so I gently lower the zipper and remove it. I unbuckle her black shoes and tug off her frilly socks. Pulling up the sheet and comforter, I tuck her in. My little girl looked like a princess tonight.

I was proud to introduce Madison and Liberty to my teammates and coaches tonight. While Madison encourages Liberty to ignore gender norms, it pleases me she chose such a pretty dress for this evening. I place a kiss on her chubby cheek as McGee assumes his position at the end of her bed. I pat his head before heading out; I pull her door closed until only inches remain open then go in search of my fiancé.

"I love this dress," I state, my eyes locking on her reflection in our bathroom mirror.

Madison stands at the vanity, removing first her earrings and then her necklace. She turns towards me, smiling.

"Why this dress?" she asks coyly.

I spin her around to face the mirror as I stand behind her. My hands at her hips, I press into her back. The softness of her bottom surrounds the hardness of my erection. I stifle the groan rising in my throat. I slide my hands to her shoulders, keeping my eyes on hers in the mirror.

"Blue is definitely your color," I whisper, my lips near her ear. My fingers trace the edge of the fabric as I continue.

"The neckline taunted me all evening. This hint of cleavage continually called to me, wanting me to uncover the body hidden beneath."

Madison's lips part, and a tiny gasp escapes. I tease the skin exposed at the top of her breasts. My hands slide over her shoulders and then just under her arms. As I trail them slowly down her ribs, Madison's head falls back on my shoulder while her heavy-lidded eyes remain on my reflection.

"It falls just above your knees, revealing only a hint of thigh," I confess. "When you sit," I sigh deeply and return my fingers to grip her hips, "it slides up to expose more, and my mind wants your thighs wrapped around my waist while I bury myself deep inside your warmth."

"This tie at your hip..." I allow my groan to escape as my fingers play with the thin fabric. "My mind wondered if I tugged on it, would the dress allow me access to all that lies beneath?" I pinch the free end of the tie, preparing to tug and find out.

She places her hand on my wrist, applying pressure, causing me to pull the strings apart. Her free hand quickly unties a smaller tie on the opposite hip when the front of the dress falls open.

My lips play at her ear and exposed neck as my hands slide the dress from her shoulders. While nibbling at her collarbone, my eyes take in the silky blue dress circling her feet in the bright blue heels. My gaze trails up her long legs, past her red lacy panties, over her bare stomach. It lingers on her tattoo before continuing to her heaving breasts peeking out of her red lace bra.

She pulls away, spins in my arms, and our mouths collide feverishly. Tongues tangle as her hands make quick work of my tie and front shirt buttons. Her soft fingers slide up my chest, over my shoulders, and down my arms until they are stalled in the attempt to remove my dress shirt.

I chuckle before pulling away. As I unbutton my cuffs, she deftly removes my belt and unfastens my pants. My head falls back, and I bite my lip when her long fingers snake below my boxers and clutch my cock. Already, I am close. This woman affects me in every way.

Madison

"I need you now," I beg through a whisper. My nipples threaten to slice through my bra, and my panties are soaked. "I can't wait. Here," I demand.

Hamilton slides my panties quickly down my thighs. My hands steady on his shoulders while I step out of one side then the other. Suddenly, he lifts me to sit on the vanity; I squeal as the cold tile connects with my heated backside. He steps back, slipping off his shoes and making quick work of removing his boxer briefs and dress pants in one swift motion. I giggle as he places his hand on the counter after nearly losing his balance attempting to remove his socks.

"Find that funny?" he growls, pulling me to the edge and spreading my thighs.

I shake my head, no longer in the mood to play. *I want release, and I need it now.*

His large hand cups the nape of my neck, pulling my mouth to his. His free hand unlatches my bra; I moan into him at its release. My pert nipples pebble further in the chilled air. My teeth lock on his plump lower lip while the pads of his thumbs graze each nipple. The sensitive buds become rock hard–his contact now on the precipice of pleasure and pain.

"Ham, please," I whimper, digging my nails into his back.

Wearing his trademark crooked smile, he continues teasing me. I need him; I need our connection, now. I quickly slide my hands down the taut planes of his chest and abdomen. His smattering of dark hair guides my fingertips further south toward the treasure I seek.

I wrap one hand around the velvety skin covering his steely girth. When my other hand joins the first, I begin stroking him from base to tip. I see his smirk has disappeared. His eyes are half-mast, his lips parted, and his head falls back. Now, he will give me what I need. While I pump, I pull him toward my eager center.

When his sensitive, mushroom-shaped tip meets my wet entrance, Hamilton takes control. One of his hands replace mine on his shaft while the other secures my hip. Looking at him, I witness the carnal desire grow on his face as he watches his cock slowly impale me. Seated entirely within me, both hands on my hips, his forehead now pressed to mine, he whispers, "I love you."

My hands fly from his shoulders to his jaws. "I love you, too." My voice is a needy plea as I rotate my hips.

Taking my cue, he finds a slow, constant rhythm, gradually raising each of us toward climax. He lowers his mouth to my shoulder, gently biting down on my muscle. It's primal–it only hurts a minute before it turns to pleasure. As he gradually increases his bite, I not only reach my peak, but I tumble from its cliff.

"Yes!" I cheer in a drawn-out growl as my thighs grip his waist like a vise. My core spasms, my internal muscles gripping his cock.

He curses, pumping into me three more times before he shudders, his forehead on my shoulder. We hold each other tightly while we regain our breath and float back down to earth.

"That was…" I'm the first to speak.

Hamilton interrupts, "I'm not done with you yet." His smirk is back.

I moan as he disengages our joined bodies and giggle when he scoops me up, carrying me to our bed.

CHAPTER 32

Madison

I groan when my alarm summons me from slumber before eight. I stretch and remind myself family begins to arrive for the holiday today. The flashing lights on the monitor signal Liberty is awake in her room, too. I slide one foot towards the floor then another. I shiver as the warm comforter no longer protects me from the chilly air.

As I approach the door to our master suite, I call down the hall, "Libby, Mommy's up."

She squeals, and I hear her speak to the dogs as I await her arrival.

"Hola, Mommy," she greets. I groan internally that she's a morning person.

"Come shower with me," I invite, and she runs past me

towards my bathroom. She enjoys standing on the shower seat while I use the hand-held nozzle to clean her. I'm nervous to leave her unsupervised and usually speed through my showers. Today, I need to enjoy the warm shower spray before my busy day begins. I turn on the water to heat while I place my robe and towels just outside the shower for us.

"We get to go to the airport to see Nana and Amy today," I inform Liberty.

Her face lights up. "Nana!"

"And Aunt Amy," I remind her.

"Nana and Amy, my house," she cheers, and I join her.

"You can show them your big-girl bed and your books," I explain. "We will take our shower, eat breakfast with Miss Alba, then drive to the airport to pick them up and bring them to your house."

Liberty nods as I speak.

I'm verifying everything I might need is in Liberty's backpack when my cell rings on the kitchen island, and Delta's name appears on the screen.

"Good morning," I answer.

"I'm downstairs. Can you tell them to let me come up?" Her voice sounds both desperate and excited.

"Yes. See ya soon."

"Delta's coming up," I inform Miss Alba before calling down to the lobby.

"Deltha!" Liberty yells from her highchair.

"You need to hurry. Finish your breakfast so we can go get Nana and Aunt Amy," I remind her.

I barely have time to contemplate why my friend showed up unplanned before she raps on the door. Miss Alba answers while I tuck a fresh bottle of water into the side pocket of the bag then secure it over my shoulders.

"Hi," I greet as I clean Liberty's face and let her down from the chair.

"I realize you are busy today," Delta begins. "I stayed up half the night and finished your book."

I slip Liberty's coat on while glancing up at Delta.

"I have questions, so we need to talk," she states. "I'll drive you to the airport so we can chat."

I smile, shaking my head at my new friend. "You're welcome to ride to O'Hare with us, but I need to practice driving in Chicago."

We say goodbye to Miss Alba, and Delta helps me load Liberty into Hamilton's SUV. *Well, I guess it's my SUV now, too.*

I type our destination into the navigation before we pull from our spot and exit the parking garage.

"Are you sure you can talk while you drive?" Delta teases. "Relax. I'm sure you've driven on interstates before."

"Yes, but interstates weren't six lanes or bumper to bumper," I defend my nervousness.

"So, the prank on the middle school principal in your book," Delta begins her interrogation. "Did that really happen and were you involved?"

"Yes and no," I answer.

"Okay, so was Webb correct to assume you and the main character are one in the same?"

"No character is solely based on someone in real life," I state as I merge lanes, preparing for the upcoming turn on the navigation screen.

"Uh-uh," Delta shakes her head in my periphery. "You're not getting away with any official statements given to you by the publisher. I'm your friend, and I deserve answers."

I glance in my rearview mirror, glance at Delta, then return my eyes to the traffic in front of me. I clear my throat before I answer. "There are many similarities between the character and me," I confirm.

"Okay. Thanks for not spilling your guts," she deadpans.

Silence falls upon the vehicle as I ponder an honest answer to share.

"Let's not compare me to the character." I turn my blinker on as prompted by the voice in navigation. "I'd much rather spill my guts on a sofa with drinks in hand," I confess.

"Okay, so let's just focus on the Madison now living in Chicago." Delta glances over her right shoulder. "You can merge if you hurry."

I do so, anticipating the next turn on the screen.

Delta sits quietly for a bit.

"I realize Stan and I threw ourselves in your face on your first night in town. I hope you know that we think the world of Hamilton and want you to know we are here for anything, so don't hesitate to call, text, or drop by."

Several quiet moments pass.

"Delta," I begin, but the navigation interrupts, stating we

have reached our destination. After driving around a bit, I find a parking spot and quickly claim it before someone steals it.

I place my hand on Delta's forearm before she can exit the vehicle. "I promise we will find a time, just the two of us, to share our pasts. And you didn't throw yourselves at me. I've enjoyed the time we've spent together. Things are moving fast, what with prepping the house and Thanksgiving this week, so we haven't had a lot of laid-back, get-to-know-you time."

She nods, smiling at me.

"We don't have time right now, so here is the *Cliff Notes* version. My characters are a mosaic of the students I went to school with. My father died before my eighth-grade year; my mother, in her depression, became an alcoholic. The only family I had was my mother, and she was rarely sober. I often felt alone in the world. I had a few friends, but as I couldn't drive anywhere and they all lived 15 minutes away in town, I spent much of my time alone in my room or on the farm. I bumped into Hamilton, literally, and he lived on the farm beside ours. We began hanging out, and, with his help, I had friends around me and felt less alone." I sigh deeply in preparation for her reaction and extricate myself from the driver's seat.

Delta walks over to my side. "I just need to know," Delta fidgets, "do you feel isolated or alone now?"

I shake my head as I zip the front of Liberty's coat and place her in the stroller. "I haven't felt that type of loneliness in years. I'm actually excited about the new life we're building in Chicago. And I'm glad to have you as my friend."

"Sounds like a Hallmark movie. Enter the cheesy, up-beat instrumental music," Delta razzes and pulls me in for a quick, tight hug. "Okay, so we got that cleared up. Let's go get the family."

I scan the crowd of holiday travelers scrambling around the airport–meeting Memphis and Amy may be harder than I anticipated. Delta and I maneuver the stroller as best we can towards the baggage claim where we planned to meet and anchor ourselves by a large pole to wait.

After a few moments, Liberty begins waving animatedly. My eyes follow hers. Leave it to my baby girl to spot Memphis before the two adults.

"Na-na!" She yells, wiggling against the seatbelt restraint of her stroller.

Memphis strides toward us, still waving at her granddaughter. I unbuckle and lift Liberty. "Just a minute, Grandma will be here in just a minute." My words do little to soothe her.

"There's my girl," Memphis croons with outstretched arms.

Liberty leans towards her with arms extended. I release my hold, allowing the two to celebrate their reunion. Memphis peppers kisses over her cheeks, nose, forehead, and chin, causing her to giggle.

When the two settle down, I scan the nearby crowd and ask, "Where is Amy?"

"Hamilton asked her to pick up something from an airport shop," Memphis informs, shrugging. "She'll be here in a minute. We're supposed to grab our bags."

I guide our group toward the moving conveyor belt. Memphis describes the bags, and we anxiously wait for them to appear.

"Excuse me," a loud, female voice rudely calls from behind. "What's an aunt have to do to get a hug from her favorite niece?"

Amy stands behind our group with hands on hips in faux annoyance, three large, brown, paper bags on her arms. Beside her, we find the two large suitcases we were waiting for.

"Amy!" Liberty squeals, stretching out her arms.

Amy places her bags on the nearby luggage handles before hugging her mini-me.

"Let's move toward the car," Memphis encourages our group. "I'm ready to escape this crowd."

Madison

"Liberty..." I free her from her car seat in the parking garage. "Take Grandma's hand and show her how to use the elevator." I wink at Memphis.

I assist Delta and Amy with the luggage, and we follow Liberty's lead. She pushes the elevator call button then smiles proudly at our guests. Inside the elevator, I lift my daughter to press number 14. Liberty cheers when the elevator stops on our floor. This time, she takes Memphis and Amy by the hand as we walk into the hallway. At our door, Liberty releases her holds and knocks on the door.

Miss Alba opens, anticipating our arrival. "Hola," she greets. "Miss Liberty, who are your guests?" I love that she supports us in encouraging Liberty's independence.

"Na-na," Liberty points. "Amy."

Miss Alba holds the door as our guests and their luggage enter the condo. I bend down next to my little girl, removing her coat.

"Why don't you show Grandma and Amy your room?" I suggest, knowing they want a tour of the entire place.

Liberty takes their hands once again and guides them down the hallway.

"I should get out of your way," Delta offers.

"You're welcome to stay as long as you want," I invite. "If the kids are at school and Stan is out, stay and visit with us."

She looks from me to Alba and back. "You sure you aren't too busy preparing for the meal and company tomorrow?"

"I think Miss Alba has already bought everything we need. We're gonna sit around and visit." I make pouty lips. "Please?"

"For goodness sakes!" Delta swats at me playfully. "Stop acting like a 2-year-old."

"Then it's settled," I state. "Can you find us something fun to drink while I go check on them?" I motion down the hallway.

As conversation begins between Miss Alba and Delta, I follow the sound of Liberty's squeals to the master bedroom. Memphis and Amy laugh as Liberty jumps up and down on my bed, her arms swinging as she points to my attached bathroom.

"What is going on in here?" I pretend that I don't like what I am seeing.

Memphis rescues her granddaughter from the mattress. "Libby was just telling us about your shower. She says she likes taking a shower."

"Would you like to see the rest of the condo?" I ask, motioning towards the hallway. "Liberty, show Grandma and Aunt Amy where they will sleep and then to Mommy's office."

Liberty nods, smiling and clapping her hands. She wiggles down and trots to the hall. "Nana here. Amy here." Liberty points to the spare rooms as she continues on to the front room.

"Maybe she'll let you actually look in the rooms before bedtime," I tease as they follow my daughter.

"Toys," Liberty points. "Food. Office." Done with her tour, she enters the kitchen and asks Miss Alba for water.

"We're making margaritas," Delta announces, throwing

her hands into the air. "Well, actually Miss Alba is making her famous margaritas." She claps her hands.

"Keep an eye on Libby. I'm going to give a much slower tour to my guests." Delta nods.

I usher Memphis and Amy into my office. "It's still a work in progress." I explain the unorganized shelves and boxes still in the corner. "I've actually found a few hours to write."

"When?" Memphis asks as she takes in the view from the windows behind my desk.

"Are you taking some poor neighbor kid's Adderall?" Amy asks, straight-faced. "There is no way a normal human can furnish a place this size, buy all the little things to make it livable, attend functions, care for a toddler, and find time to write in a week."

Memphis admonishes her daughter.

"Hamilton insisted on keeping Miss Alba fulltime as well as a nanny," I admit, embarrassed. I chance a glance at Memphis, worried how she will react. It's Amy that surprises me.

"I'm glad he did," Amy states. "He leads a busy life. You deserve time to work as much as he does. There's nothing wrong with hiring help."

Now, I feel bad that I forgot that Amy's a nanny. She works for a young woman that now has guardianship of her twin nephews who are a little older than Liberty.

"I didn't mean…"

Memphis interrupts, placing her hand on my shoulder. "It's important to ask for help when you need it. You're an amazing author, and Hamilton knows it's important that you continue to write." She hugs me tight to her side. "It took me a while to understand the crazy life and schedule Hamilton keeps. It may seem unnecessary now, but come baseball season, you'll be glad you have 2 extra pairs of hands."

Uncomfortable with the serious tone our conversation has taken, I finish showing them the rest of the condo, and we end the tour by dropping off luggage in each of their bedrooms.

"I'm ready for one of your famous margaritas," I call to Miss Alba as we return to the kitchen island.

"Be warned: she has a heavy pour," Delta states before taking a tiny sip from her margarita glass. "I'm glad I talked you into adding these to your shopping list." She clinks her manicured nail, complete with rhinestones, against the glass.

Miss Alba doesn't apologize for her recipe. Instead, she fills a salt-rimmed glass for Memphis, Amy, and me.

"Is there anything else you would like me to help with before I leave?" Miss Alba murmurs, leaning closer.

"No. You've helped so much already," I look at my Fitbit, noting the time is now one p.m. "What are your plans for this afternoon? Do you have a lot of baking to start on?"

She hedges for a moment before speaking. "I'll wait on my husband in his office. He plans to leave early today. I'll begin my baking in the morning. We eat late tomorrow afternoon and evening."

"You should stay and visit with us until he's done," I invite, taking her by the hand and squeezing. "You'll be more comfortable here than in his tiny office for hours."

"I'll just watch my telenovelas…"

"Stay with us," Memphis pleads. "You've made margaritas; stay and enjoy them with us."

With Memphis' words, I believe Miss Alba begins to consider the invitation.

"Peaz," Liberty begs from the hem of Miss Alba's dress.

She scoops her up in her arms, spinning her once. "Of course, I will stay with you, Miss Libby."

Yes! Thank you, Liberty. My heart warms; I enjoy spending time with my new family and friends. We move our festivities from the kitchen island into the living room.

"We seem to have lost Memphis," I inform the crowd.

"It was all of 10 steps," Delta muses.

"Libby, I have a present for you," Memphis calls as she emerges from the hallway. She chooses the empty cushion next to me, places her glass on the nearby sofa table, and waves a book at her granddaughter.

Liberty loves books. She springs from her blocks on the floor to climb on her grandma's lap. Her little hands caress the hard cover as her eyes take in the boy, girl, and dog on the weathered exterior.

"This was my favorite book when I was a little girl," Memphis informs her. "Can I read it to you?"

"Me read," Liberty states with attitude.

She's everything I'm not. She's confident and goes for what she wants with reckless abandon. I love her independence and attitude. That is, when she's not throwing it back at me.

Her little fingers gently open the cover, turning to the first page. She glances up at Memphis, points her index finger, then begins. "This is..." She pauses for Memphis' help.

Memphis looks to me, surprised. When Liberty repeats herself, she supplies in a shaky voice, "Jack."

Liberty nods and continues, "This is..."

"Kim," Memphis says, short of breath. She can't take her eyes off of Liberty, but she can't help looking at me. I'm no help, however. I'm just as shocked as she is.

"See Jack. See Kim," Liberty's little voice continues.

While Liberty turns the page, my mind explodes. She's never seen this book before—no one has read it to her before. She points to each word as she reads each sentence. They are choppy, but she reads them. She won't be two for four more months, and she's reading. *I didn't just imagine it, right?* When I return my focus to the guests in the room, I find every pair of eyes on me—they seem as shocked as me.

"Did that just happen?" I ask the room.

Everyone nods, wide-eyed.

"Miss Libby," Miss Alba calls. "Come help me take the towels to your bathroom, please."

Liberty gently passes the book back to Memphis before climbing down to shadow Miss Alba. I'm grateful for the distraction she offers so we may discuss the situation.

"That's not normal." Amy simply states what we all struggle to comprehend.

"Have you read that story to her before?" Delta asks Memphis.

When Memphis shakes her head, she looks to me. I also shake mine.

"Reading starts at about age five. For some, as early as four," I recall from my education classes.

"Webb told me Libby read to him last night. I assumed she pointed to an 'a' or 'I', so I didn't ask him for the details," Delta shares.

"Read what?" My mind reels.

Delta only shrugs; she's no help. *Why does my chest feel so heavy? She read a couple sentences. It's not like she's sick or hurt. Why does this feel like a bad thing, and why am I fighting tears?* Memphis pats my thigh as Liberty storms back into the room.

"Libby," my voice cracks nervously, "what book did you read to Webb last night?" I hold my breath, waiting for her answer, for any answer, for any idea how to handle this.

"Mommy's book," she proudly answers. Her little hands are now poised on her hips.

"Mommy's book?" I parrot. "You read from my book?" I rise from the sofa, approaching her in the center of the floor.

Liberty nods once, still smiling. In a trance, I walk into my office, snag a book from the shelf, and hold it near her.

"This book?"

Liberty points at the cover as I hold it out. "Mommy's book."

"What did you read?" I can't believe I am asking my baby girl this. Of all the things I worried about as a mother, this was not even on my radar.

"Ten." Liberty pulls the book from my hands, slowly turning page after page.

I help her turn to page ten. Liberty shakes her head at me.

I quickly flip to chapter ten.

Liberty points to the large, bold numbers at the top of the page. "Ten."

"Can you read this to me?" I'm not sure what I want to witness. *Do I want her to read it word for word? Or do I want her to point to one word and be done?*

Liberty sits on the wood floor, the book in her lap. She points to the first word of chapter 10 and begins. "The sun..."

She's reading. Again. She is actually reading. Really reading. *Now what? Do I encourage this new skill? Do I start teaching her?* I'm lost. I wish Hamilton were here. I know he wouldn't know any better than I do, but at least he could hold me.

Liberty has closed my book and moved back to her building blocks. I remain sitting on the floor but spin to face the women. My face must say it all.

"Ladies," Miss Alba stands, "bring your glasses to the kitchen. It's time for more margaritas."

We follow her directions. In the kitchen, we may discuss without tiny ears listening.

"It's important not to panic," Memphis states.

At least I knew that much. I've kept my panic hidden on the inside. So far, that is. *More. I need more. What's next?*

"We shouldn't make it seem unusual. We don't want her to be ashamed. She should be proud."

I stare at Amy–her words shock me. She's right. I just thought it would come from Memphis or Delta. They are mothers; Amy isn't.

"Taylor will be here later this afternoon. She might have contacts to talk to about it," Memphis mentions.

She's right. Of course, she is right.

I nod, words eluding me at the moment. Inside, I have hope. We're making a plan. I need to find a specialist to discuss this with. Hamilton and I will find one.

I slap my palm to my forehead.

"What was that for?" Amy chuckles while Delta pulls my forearm back to the table.

I am such an idiot. *Why didn't I think of it before? She should have been the first person I reached for.* I raise my cell to my ear.

"Hello," Fallon greets.

"Fallon, I'm sorry to bother you on your day off," I begin while still trying to find what I want to say. "Would you have a few minutes to stop by? Something important just happened with Liberty, and I'd like your input."

Fallon promises to arrive in a few minutes. This is good. Fallon studies these types of things–she'll have resources for us.

"Who's Fallon?" Amy blurts the minute my phone disconnects from the call.

"Fallon is our nanny. She lives in the building." I turn to Delta. "You've met her; she's the trainer's fiancé." Turning back, I explain, "Slater is a trainer for the Cubs, and Hamilton's publicist introduced us."

"She's a sweetheart," Miss Alba informs the group. "On her first visit with Libby, she taught her to say hello in Spanish."

My cell phone vibrates loudly on the counter in the silence of the kitchen.

Hamilton: Call me when you get a chance (heart emoji)
Me: (thumbs up emoji)

I sip the last of my drink, wiping away the salt from the corner of my lip. Liberty still plays with her blocks. I ask the group to keep an eye on her while I make a quick call.

"Hello." Hamilton's deep, cheerful voice causes me to smile.

"What's up?"

"Hold on," he instructs as I hear rustling on his end of the line. "I didn't know what you girls were up to, so I thought it might be best to have you call me when it was convenient for you," he explains, his heavy footsteps echoing in the background.

I can't tell him about today's events over the phone–I need to do that in person.

"Liberty's playing blocks while we are visiting, so it was a good time." I sink into my leather office chair and swivel to look out the floor to ceiling windows at the lively city of Chicago. "Taylor and the girls should be here in an hour. Your mom and Amy are relaxing after their early flights this morning. Where are you? It sounds like you are in a cave."

"I'm in the stairwell," he chuckles. "We are in between

events here, and I wanted some privacy. This was the nearest door I found."

Privacy? Is this bad?

"The P.R. lady stopped me in the hall this morning. She met with the photographer from the function last night and loved the photos of the three of us with the mascot and the one we posed for. They are working on a holiday promo and asked our permission to use the images for the Thanksgiving and holiday season message." He pauses to catch his breath.

My mind races. *Publicity for the Cubs. Photos of our family. Do I want Liberty in the public eye?*

"I've emailed you the three images they would like to use. I also attached the release we must sign if we agree to give permission."

I sense the hesitation in his voice.

"You've mentioned keeping Liberty off social media posts and stuff to protect her; I'm okay with it either way."

"I'm opening the email right now," I state as my fingers maneuver the mouse over the attachments. "Ahh, I love the mascot shot."

"Which one?"

"Both, but where she's kissing the mascot is my favorite." I continue on to the image of the three of us in front of the Cubs logo. "These are good. I can't wait to see the others she took for us."

"P.R. stated the commercial would just say, 'Happy Thanksgiving' or 'Happy Holidays to your family from our Cubs family.' They have photos of a couple more families. I think Stan and Delta are in one," Hamilton concludes.

"I guess they can," I begin. "I don't see anything wrong with the photos. Has Delta allowed them to use pictures in the past?"

"Yes," Hamilton quickly replies. "I remember Stan complaining about Delta forcing him to pose for photos of the four of them so she could use them in holiday cards and the Cubs using the same photo, causing her to take a different picture. He hates posing for pictures. Action shots don't bother him; it's the standing still and posing that he detests."

"Do we both have to sign this release?" I ask as my finger hovers over the print icon.

"Yes, but we can sign it digitally," he explains. "If you place your mouse over the signature line, she says it's easy."

"I see. Okay. I've signed it," I announce. "Can you sign it while you are there today?"

"Yes." His voice echoes in the stairwell. "I'll swing by the P.R. office and do it before my next meet and greet. I should be done about two today."

The echo disappears, and I can tell by his breathing that he is walking again.

"Text me if you need me to pick up anything on my way home," he offers.

"Okay. I love you." It still makes me smile, knowing I get to profess my love for him publicly now. It's taken us so long to get to this place–I'll never take it for granted.

"I love you, too, babe," Hamilton whispers before disconnecting our call.

I jump when Memphis' voice calls to me from my office door.

"Here you are! I asked Libby where you were, and she just shrugged. She loves playing with those blocks, doesn't she?" Memphis hovers near the corner of my desk. "What are you working on?"

I pivot my laptop screen toward her, displaying the mascot photo first. "Hamilton called. The P.R. Department needs our permission to use three shots of our family in upcoming ads." I scroll through the three photos.

Memphis' face lights up at the images.

"That is so sweet!" She points to Liberty kissing Clark, the mascot. "I love how her hands hold his face so he can't pull away from her." She turns her face from the screen to me. "Are these by the same photographer that you were telling me about?"

"Yes. I can't wait to see the other photos," I state.

When the doorbell rings, Liberty sprints from her toys, excited to see her cousins.

"It's probably Fallon," I inform my daughter, raising her into my arms. "Let's see."

Fallon smiles as we open the door.

"Hola!" Liberty immediately reaches for her. She plants a noisy kiss on Fallon's cheek. "Pway?"

Fallon lowers Liberty to the floor. "I need to talk to your mommy for a bit, then I will come play with you."

Happy with the promise, Liberty scurries back to her blocks on the wooden floor across the room.

"What's up?" Fallon asks, voice lowered.

"Let's move over here." I return to the barstools and my friends. "This is Hamilton's mother, Memphis, and his sister, Amy." I motion in their direction. "And you've met Delta, right?"

"Yes. We've met a few times," Delta answers.

Fallon says hello to my guests, nervously climbing onto an empty barstool.

"I've called you here to help with something new we've noticed with Libby. I want you to have some time to help us research strategies moving forward to assist her the best we can." I'm rambling.

I sip from my glass. Before I can offer one to Fallon, Miss Alba slides a freshly made margarita in her direction.

"Okay," Fallon begins after her first drink. "You've gotten ahead of yourself. I'm happy to help, but I need to know what we are talking about. What have you witnessed?" Fallon pivots on her seat to gaze at Liberty across the room.

"She can read," Delta stage whispers, not wanting the little one to hear.

Fallon looks from Delta to me, brows raised.

"Let's start with the details," I direct the group. "Memphis brought her favorite book to share with Liberty. Liberty has never seen the book before today. She demanded to read instead of Memphis. We thought she would tell a story from looking at the pictures only."

A tear forms in my eye. *This is not something to cry about. Why am I getting so upset over it?*

"Liberty used her index finger to point to each word as she read it."

"Here," Memphis interrupts, sliding the book to Fallon. "She read the first two pages."

Fallon opens the book, flipping through the first several pages. She closes the book, sliding it back to Memphis.

"Delta's son, Webb, told Delta last night that Libby read to him. Of course, we didn't think anything of it. But, after reading for us, we asked questions." I pause as Amy opens my book to chapter 10. "She told us this is the part of the book she read to Webb last night." I give Fallon time to read the passage. A few silent moments pass.

"What do you think?" Delta asks, breaking the silence.

"First, understand that although I majored in psychology, I am still working on my graduate degree." Fallon scans the group for understanding. "I do have many resources I can look to for assistance, but we may need help from more than one source.

"As you are close family and friends, I'm sure you already know that Libby demonstrates advanced linguistic levels for a 2-year-old. This might be because she spends much of her time in the company of adults, but when I asked for background information from Madison, I found Liberty, like her peers, has spent three days per week with children her own age."

Fallon pauses for another drink. My mind is dying to hear what she thinks, and mentally, I will her to hurry up.

"Two days a week at Mom's Day Out and time in the church nursery on Sundays is comparable to other children's interactions outside the home for her age. As Libby and I began attending playgroups and tumbling this week, I've noticed she interacts appropriately with children near her age. The ways she interacts with adults varies greatly from the way she interacts with young children. She's learned to speak at the level of the company she keeps."

Fallon smiles sheepishly. "I've already spoken to a professor about this, and I've started seeking other studies on children with her linguistic abilities. I'm not going to focus on this topic now as it's not what has you concerned today. It is, however, important that you understand most children that are advanced linguistically do not interact well with peers and often prefer to stay with the adults at playtime."

A wide smile forms upon Fallon's face, and she lays her hand on mine. "She's a bright child. I'm sure we've all witnessed this. We need to understand her talents and encourage her in the areas she prefers." Looking straight at me, she continues. "You've mentioned noticing Libby quietly observing certain situations. You stated it was as if she was taking in all that was going on around her. Perhaps she was learning. Children are little sponges, soaking up everything they see and hear."

"I need to interrupt." I lift my hands in the air in front of me. "I'm sorry." I stand; I can no longer sit still. "My mind has been racing since I heard her read. I've been playing over events from the past year. I may be overanalyzing everything, but prior to the end of October, Libby spoke a few words and sounded more baby-like. She did often sit quietly, taking in all going on around her." I chuckle. It sounds fake. "I don't know why it didn't faze me at the moment, but she started talking more, said more words correctly starting right around Halloween. 'Ma-ma' became 'Mommy,' 'Da-da' became 'Daddy,' and so on."

Memphis rises, pulling me into a hug. "You have had so much on your mind with the passing of your mother and Alma–It's been a stressful time."

She's trying to make me feel better, but I don't want excuses. Liberty is my daughter. I should have celebrated a new milestone in my daughter's life. I should have documented it in her baby book. Regardless of the events in my life, she is my daughter, and I am her mother; I should have recognized each change.

Fallon encourages me to resume my seat beside her. "Children can sense moods around them. Libby knew her mommy was upset. She knew changes were occurring around her. Her home changed, she met new people, she visited new places, and she was around adults during this time."

She pauses, letting us process her words. "Perhaps, during the changes around her, Libby began her transition. She began communicating at a higher level to cope with her new surroundings."

Fallon turns, facing me. She places her hands on my shoulders and stares into my eyes. I fear what she plans to say next.

"I hope I don't overstep my boundaries or upset you, but I need to state the obvious."

I nod for her to continue.

"In the past 30 days, Alma moved from the only home

Liberty knew. You drove to Athens, to a different home for a few weeks. Although she had seen photos, she met Memphis and Hamilton for the first time. She watched her mom cope with the death of two women and then moved into a new home in Chicago, meeting new people at every turn." Fallon lifts my chin, directing my eyes back to hers. "Children are resilient. Libby seems to be adapting well to all of the changes. We need to adapt to changes in her, too." She places her arm across my shoulder as we turn back to the group. "Libby can read three years before her peers. She speaks better than other 2-year-olds. She's also much taller than kids her age. As her family, we need to be aware of all of these things and any others that appear. She doesn't now, but she may struggle to fit in with other children if they notice her abilities. We shouldn't shelter her—we need to nurture her talents and foster relationships with other children. I'm going to speak with all of my professors and conduct research on my end. You should continue to read to her and allow her to read when she volunteers."

We all agree with Fallon's assessments. I feel a bit better knowing we have a plan and someone training to be a professional guiding us. I struggle to rejoin the group conversation as my mind swirls.

Fallon leans into me, adding as an afterthought, "The next time you see Taylor, you should talk to her. She can guide you to professionals in the medical field with much more training and experience than me."

"She'll be here." I look to my wrist. *It's four. She should already be here.* I glance at my cell phone screen to see if I missed anything from Taylor. *Nothing. That's odd.* "She should be here any minute." I raise my voice for the entire group to hear. "It's about to get much louder and more crowded. Taylor and the gang are due anytime."

Proving that children are sponges, taking in their entire surroundings, Liberty rises from across the room. She hops up and down while clapping and cheering. Taylor's twins dote on her; she's excited to see her cousins.

"I should get out of your way," Fallon states.

"No, stay. I mean, if you're not busy, we'd love for you to stay and chat." I smile at my new friend and nanny. "What are you and Slater doing today?"

"He's working until dinner," Fallon admits. "I've just been reading."

"What book are your reading?" Memphis asks, always looking for her next great book.

Fallon blushes. "I'm reading a published paper on 'Social Media Behavior, Toxic Masculinity, and Depression'."

Memphis laughs. "I won't be adding that to my 'To Be Read Shelf.'"

We join in her laughter.

"Well, I believe you need rescued from so much excitement," I state. "Stay with us for a bit. Drink margaritas, gossip, cook, or sit with me and watch these fabulous women cook." I motion to the group.

"Maybe we should give Madison lessons while we cook this afternoon," Amy suggests, teasing.

"Amy, behave," Memphis scolds.

"No way am I cooking today or tomorrow," I state

emphatically. "Thanksgiving is a major meal, and I don't want to go down in history for ruining any part of it." I wave my hands back and forth in front of me. "When I set off the fire alarms..." I look up. *Do we have fire alarms? I'm sure we do.* I search for the nearest one while I keep talking. "The dogs would go nuts, the kids would scream, the guys would never let me live it down...it's just not going to happen."

Miss Alba looks directly at me. "I will give you cooking lessons once a week, starting next week. No pressure, just easy dishes."

Her tone leads me to understand there is no room for debate on this topic. I half-smile and nod.

Turning back to Fallon, I insist she stay. "Surely this group is more interesting than your fun reading at home."

Fallon agrees to stay. We celebrate by filling everyone's margarita glasses.

"Delta, what are your plans for tomorrow?" Memphis asks.

She sips from her margarita. "We don't have traditional Thanksgiving dinner."

"Wow," Miss Alba jumps in. "So, what do you serve instead?"

Delta looks down at her hands, fiddling with her glass. It's clear she does not want to answer.

My eyes dart from Miss Alba to Memphis to Fallon.

"Last year, we fixed Mexican," Delta murmurs. "Tomorrow, we're fixing pizza."

"Why do you do that?" Amy pries.

Delta chuckles, "It's just the four of us, so it's silly to fix a huge dinner."

"So, it's not because you can't cook or avoid the holiday?" Amy pries further.

Delta simply shakes her head.

"So, join us," Memphis offers. "We have too much food and plenty of room. The kids can play together, too."

"I don't know," Delta hedges.

"You're eating with us," I state. "If I have to, I'll call Hamilton to get Stan to agree."

Delta smiles.

"Good. That's settled." I squeeze her hand before turning my attention to Fallon. "Would Slater and you like to join us?"

Fallon chews on her lower lip for a moment. "I don't think your table will hold us."

Miss Alba answers for me, "They're bringing up tables and chairs from the meeting rooms."

"Please. Say you'll join us," I beg with a smile.

"Unless the paper you're reading is more exciting," Amy adds sarcastically.

Fallon's eyes float around our group. When she looks back to me, she nods.

"Yay!" I clap. "My new Chicago family will all be here!"

The doorbell echoes through the space. *It's about to get louder. Let the holiday begin.*

Taylor, her twin daughters, Trenton, his wife, Ava, and their sons, Hale and Grant, spill into the front room. Their arms are full of groceries, pots and pans, board games, and electronics. One of the delivery staff wheels a metal cart full of more goodies. Silly me. I thought we had most of the stuff we needed for tomorrow.

"Everything to the dining room table, please," Taylor instructs her minions.

I approach my new guests as Liberty leads McGee and Indie from her bedroom. I begin passing out hugs, and they take turns petting the dogs and kissing Liberty.

Trenton murmurs before releasing our hug, "I'm ready for adult time. Can you help your big brother out?"

"Okay." I raise my voice above the crowd. "Kids grab your electronics and follow me. Trenton, I'll need your help for just a sec, please." I draw out the word while making a praying gesture.

The troops follow me down the hallway. "This is Libby's room. You are welcome to play in here." I point as I walk, "This is now the game room. Trenton, will you make sure the game system is hooked up right for me? I moved it this morning after Hamilton left; I thought it would be simple, but the two TVs are different. There are so many cables."

"I've got it," Trenton states.

I elbow him before I exit the room. "I'll have a special drink waiting for you in the adult room when you're done."

He returns to the kitchen moments after me. I slide him the beer Ava stated he would enjoy.

"Make yourself at home." I motion to the front room.

"You can have the entire living room to yourself. We will try not to be too loud over here baking and stuff."

"And stuff?" Trenton teases.

"I have no idea what all of this needs." I swirl my hands at the dining table, the island, and the counters. "I'm just here to…"

"Look pretty," Trenton teases, messing up my hair.

"You," Taylor uses her mother tone, "to the living room. Find some boring guy show to watch. Summon one of us when you need a beer; otherwise, don't bug us."

Trenton does his best to pretend he's being punished as he settles himself on the sectional in front of the large flat screen.

I assume a bar stool at the island and enjoy chatting with the ladies while they scurry around, prepping relish trays, bread, noodles and desserts for tomorrow's meal. I do my best to keep beverages full for everyone and monitor the kids in the playrooms.

———

"What do we have here?" Hamilton shouts when he returns home.

Memphis and Amy swarm him with hugs.

"Hello, beautiful." Hamilton snatches me from the group, placing a long, somewhat inappropriate kiss upon me.

"Hamilton," Taylor chides. "There are children in the house."

His thumb wipes the corner of my mouth as he displays

his crooked smile. He looks around. "No kids in the area." He pulls me back into his chest.

I place my palms flat against him. "Why don't you go say hi to the kiddos then entertain Trenton? He's been the only dude in the chick zone for over an hour now."

"Hey," Hamilton greets Trenton. "Can I get you another beer?" When he nods, Hamilton pulls two beers from the fridge. "Hey Amy, where are you hiding the popcorn?"

"What popcorn?" I ask him.

"I asked Amy to buy some Garrett's popcorn for us to munch on. You haven't tried it yet; you're going to love the Chicago Mix."

Amy pulls the three large, brown bags from her guestroom. Miss Alba makes quick work of producing three large bowls and filling them with cheese, caramel, and a mixture. I watch as she quickly scoops smaller bowls and delivers them to the children's rooms with waters for everyone.

"You're off the clock," I remind her. "Sit down and have another drink."

She attempts to argue, but Hamilton speaks up. "You're a guest; enjoy yourself."

With a wide grin, she sips from her glass.

Taylor plops in the seat next to me with a big sigh. I wrap my arm around her shoulders, laying my head on her.

"I can't believe Cameron changed her flight. Did she give you a reason?" Taylor shakes her head. "I bet it was work."

I shake my head, fighting the urge to smile.

"I see that." She points at the twitching corner of my mouth. "You know something. Spill it," Taylor demands.

"She's dealing with the plumber," Hamilton answers, unaware of his slip up.

"What plumber?" Trenton asks, joining us in the kitchen, a fresh beer in hand.

"Is something wrong with the house?" Taylor prods, rising to stand by Trenton.

I bet they don't realize they gravitated to each other to become a united front to interrogate. I suddenly realize how Cameron must have felt every time they badgered their baby sister. "First of all, I called her about my book last night–that's how I know. She didn't call me," I explain. "I saw someone walk by while we were Face Timing. She carried the phone down into the basement to let me see the neighbor, Dalton, fixing the pipe. I guess it was only a drip, but he said it might have flooded if she hadn't called him," I shrug. It doesn't seem like the big deal they make it out to be.

"Dalton Edwards?" Taylor smirks. "So, is she staying while he makes repairs or…" She wiggles her eyebrows suggestively.

"I mean, he was shirtless, but that's because it was wet from the drip," I continue sharing what I was told. "Just because he's cute and she's single doesn't mean they hooked up."

"Yes, it does," Trenton states, and Taylor laughs.

"What am I missing?" I stand with hands on my hips.

"They were high school sweethearts," Taylor smiles slyly. "They dated from ninth grade until college."

"I never should have let her move back to Columbia," Trenton spits, shaking his head. "I forgot he lives with his dad next door."

"Just because they have history…" I start being the voice of reason.

"Oh, trust me. They'll hook-up," Taylor sighs.

"Please," Trenton pleads. "Can we not discuss my little sister's sex life?"

We all laugh at his discomfort, and I scramble to change the subject.

"All done?" I ask, a bit ashamed that I'm not more involved in the baking process.

"All set until we start the turkey in the morning," Memphis states from across the island. She takes the margarita Amy hands her.

"That's the last of the margaritas," Amy announces to the room before sticking her head into the fridge.

She emerges with a bottle of water. She looks from the glass water bottle to me with raised eyebrows before she takes a sip.

Sitting back down, Taylor confides, "Fallon spoke to me about Liberty reading. I texted a friend from work; she's a child psychologist. She'd like to meet with you. She'll look at her calendar on Monday and set something up for the two of you."

I lift my head. "Thank you."

"It's a good 'problem' to have." She makes air quotes. "I dealt with a biter and a five-year-old that wet the bed every night."

I raise an eyebrow in her direction.

"The joys of parenting," Taylor shrugs. "We work with whatever pops up."

"I'm exhausted," I confess, falling onto our bed after 10 o'clock.

"I'm glad Mom suggested turning in early," Hamilton smirks, leaning his body over mine.

"We do need to be up for Taylor by seven in the morning," I remind him.

"Some of us are always up by seven," Hamilton teases as his nose gently guides along my neck.

"Ham," I half moan, half protest.

He presses himself up on his straightened arms as if doing a push up. "Let's place a bookmark in my intentions. What's had you distracted all day?"

I bite my lip. I should have known I couldn't hide this from him. I roll my eyes before I begin.

"It's that bad?" he asks.

"No. I rolled my eyes because I hoped to keep it from you until we were alone. I thought I did a better job hiding it," I admit. "It's nothing bad, just a parenting challenge for us."

His eyes morph from full of desire to concern for our daughter. He sits up on the bed, pulling a folded leg between us. I prop myself up, crossing my legs in front of me.

"Webb told you that Libby read to him last night, remember?" When he nods, brows furrowed, I continue, not wanting to worry him any longer. "Well, it turns out that Liberty really did read to him. Libby can read."

He tilts his head to the side. "Read?"

"Let me back up. Your mom brought a book she liked as a child to read to Libby. She brought it into the living room, and Libby hopped onto her lap. When your mom offered to read it to her, Libby demanded to read it. We all watched, expecting her to pretend to read." I shake my head at the memory.

"Ham, she pointed her little finger and read every single word as if she were in kindergarten or first grade." I rub my tired eyes while I wait for him to respond.

His lips pull to one corner of his mouth while his eyes roam around the room, unfocused. He's thinking.

"Delta mentioned Libby reading to Webb last night. So, we asked Liberty what book it was. It was my book." I smile proudly. "She stated she read number 10. When we turned to page 10, she said that wasn't it. I turned to chapter 10, and she again pointed her index finger and began reading from *my young adult book*."

"So, it's not..." he pauses. "She really can read?"

"It seems so," I reply. "I called Fallon to come over. I figured she could provide some help and research for us. And Taylor is arranging a meeting with a friend of hers that's a child psychologist."

"Can I go with you?" Hamilton asks.

"Of course," I quickly answer. "We need to work together, learn together, and help her."

Tears well in my eyes and proceed to flow down my cheeks.

"Honey, what's wrong?" Hamilton brushes his thumbs to wipe my tears away. "Did something else happen?"

I shake my head adamantly, but inside, I know there is.

"Madison, something has you upset, and I have a feeling it's not that our little girl can read." Concern engulfs his features. His eyes dart over my face, reading my emotions.

"I'm her mom," I cry. "I'm her mom, and I missed signs. I was too caught up in my own drama and didn't even notice…"

Hamilton squeezes me to his chest and lets me sob. He doesn't pry; he doesn't interrupt. He lets me work through my overwhelming emotions in my own time. After several long moments, my bawling subsides.

"She changed," I share. "While I was dealing with Alma's fall then stroke, my mother's death, and then Alma's death, our little girl reached milestones, and I didn't even notice. She started using more words. She changed from baby talk to that of a big girl, and I didn't notice until today. It took me a month, and if she hadn't read to us today, I still wouldn't notice."

Hamilton doesn't speak. He offers no words to contradict mine. He places one warm peck to the corner of my lips. Then, another on the other corner. His next kiss is followed by a sweep of his tongue along my lower lip. Without conscious thought, my body opens for him. He doesn't rush, and he doesn't dominate. He slowly caresses my tongue with his.

As my tongue begins to dance with his, his hands move from my back to my hips. My chest, no longer squeezed to his, begins to heave. The repetition of my nipples grazing his firm muscles triggers another response from me—one deeper and lower on my body. My blood hums, pulsing heavily through my veins.

Hamilton pulls away from my mouth, resting his forehead against mine, our heavy breaths between us. Slowly, we calm. He opens his eyes. We stare deep into each other.

"You are an awesome mom," Hamilton states and squints as his eyes drill his statement home.

I pinch my lips between my teeth. "Fallon and the girls reminded me of everything I had on my plate in the last month. Fallon thinks with all of the changes in her surroundings and in reaction to my emotions at the time, Liberty began using her advanced language skills to better communicate with all of us. She doesn't do it at playgroup."

"So, what kind of changes are you talking about?" Hamilton inquires.

"Before Alma's fall, she used words like Ma-ma and Da-da; they changed to Mommy and Daddy. A pretty big difference," I admit.

"I never got to hear her say Da-da."

"Ham, I'm sorry. I should never…"

He places two fingers over my open lips to silence me. "I'm just realizing out loud that what I hear now, what I think is baby talk, isn't." He hugs me tight. "Promise you won't laugh?" When I nod, he continues. "I freaked out," Hamilton confesses. "The night I met Liberty, I freaked out. I couldn't fall asleep, even with the two of you lying in bed next to me. I got up, woke my mom up, and we talked for a few hours."

His eyes search my face for my reaction. I give him my warmest smile. *I'm not sure what this has to do with our current situation.*

"She told me that all parents make mistakes." He taps the end of my nose with his index finger. "She admitted Dad and she made many mistakes. She stated that the two of us would make them, too. We just have to do our best as parents and learn from our mistakes."

It hurts a little that he didn't talk to me. I'm glad he talked to Memphis and that she helped him, but I long to be the one he leans on. *Did he go to her because I kept my secret from him?*

"What's going on in that pretty little head of yours?"

I paste a smile that I don't mean upon my face.

"Promise me you won't dwell on this," Hamilton pleads.

I fight it internally. I know I need to let this go so I can focus on Liberty moving forward.

"I'll promise if you'll do something for me," I counter.

Hamilton

. . .

Is she giving me an ultimatum? This woman. She's everything to me. They are everything to me. There is nothing I wouldn't do to be near her. I'd even give up baseball if it meant I could live the rest of my life holding her, loving her, being near her.

I nod, anxious to hear what she wants.

"Can you ask your mom if she would consider traveling to Vegas with Liberty?" She smiles sweetly, a glint in her eyes. "I want Liberty there when we elope."

How did she find out? Did I leave anything out for her to see? Maybe she overheard a phone call with Berkeley. But I was careful, very careful. I didn't text or talk on the phone in the condo for fear she might hear. One of her friends must have spilled the beans.

"I wanted to elope so my side of the church wouldn't be empty at the wedding," she explains. "I've thought about it, and I need Liberty with us; she's my family."

Madison seems nervous. *Or is she afraid of my reaction?*

"And I'm feeling guilty for not allowing your family to attend the wedding. I want Memphis and Amy with us." She shrugs sheepishly.

My smile widens–*my surprise is safe.* I'm not the only one hesitant to leave our little one this weekend. I've wanted to ask her a million times.

"Why are you smiling?" she inquires.

"I want them there, too. I'll speak with them first thing in the morning," I promise.

"Now, let's get you showered." I smirk as my eyes scan her head to toe. There's no way I'm letting her shower alone.

CHAPTER 33

Madison

What is that incessant noise? I roll over, covering my ears with my pillow. As I still hear the noise, I groan out loud. Suddenly, it stops. Hamilton pulls my pillow off my ear. I open one eye in his direction with another groan.

Hamilton chuckles. "Taylor will be here in 15 minutes."

When I groan and cover my head with his pillow, he full on laughs at me.

"Maybe a shower will help wake you up," he suggests. "I know you took one last night, but it might make this morning easier for you. I'll go get you coffee. You get up."

I peek from under his pillow as he leaves our bedroom. Part of me wants to grab him by his belt loop and tug his jean covered ass back into bed and have my way with him–

morning sex would help me wake up. Maybe I should mention that to him for future reference.

As I approach the kitchen, Hamilton extends a large travel mug of coffee to me. I accept it, not convinced it will perk me up the way he intends it to. I hold the cup at my side, cozy up nice and close to him, and whisper, "thank you," while batting my eyes up at him.

I find solace in the warm, sensual kiss he gifts to me. I wrap my arms snuggly around his waist, even with my coffee in hand. His warm heat and his hard, muscular body soothe my soul. I melt in his touch, enjoying the hot friction our tongues produce, longing for that friction to continue between my thighs.

A throat clearing behind my back pulls our mouths from one another. I don't need to turn. Hamilton pulls his smile from me towards his sister.

"Good morning, Amy." He laces his words with sarcasm.

"You two need to learn some self-control," Amy spits, passing on her way to the coffee pot. "Some things should not be seen first thing in the morning."

"Bacon will be ready in five minutes," Memphis interrupts, changing the subject.

Hamilton ushers me to a kitchen stool with his hand on my lower back. Memphis pulls yogurt and fresh fruit from the refrigerator, placing them on the island.

"I brought donuts!" Delta motions to the large box of pastries before sliding a stack of paper plates our way.

Hamilton fixes a plate of yogurt with fruit and another with a glazed donut, yogurt, and fruit. It's easy to know which plate mine will be; Hamilton rarely indulges–he strives to keep his body a lean, powerful machine.

While I chew my first, sweet bite of the donut, I watch Liberty eat her banana slices with her fingers. I pinch a bite of my donut and place it on her tray; her little eyes light up.

"Your cell is vibrating." Hamilton slides it towards me.

Taylor: We're here, be up in a minute
Me: I'll open the front door

"Taylor and Cameron are on their way up," I notify everyone.

With guests beginning to arrive to help with the cooking, our Thanksgiving Day officially begins. Excitement builds in my belly despite the early hour. I open the front door, anxiously watching the elevator. When it opens, Cameron exits, followed by Taylor.

"Good morning," Cameron sings, briskly approaching me. She wraps me in a tight hug, rocking me back and forth. "I'm so ready for a weekend off. Let's start this party!" She proudly pulls orange juice and vodka from her large purse.

"She's got a four-day weekend. You'd think she won a

Powerball jackpot," Taylor teases as I guide them into the condo.

"I hate to be Debbie-Downer," I tell Cameron, "but you are working tomorrow morning. Remember? You asked me to do a book signing on Black Friday."

"Of course! I didn't forget." She rubs my upper arms. While keeping her arms upon my shoulders, she locks eyes with me. "I owe you big for saving my behind tomorrow. I realize it complicates your day of travel, and I can't thank you enough for squeezing it in for a couple of hours."

"You promised it would be fun," I remind her. "I don't get up before six a.m. for just anyone."

"I realize that. That's why I owe you *big*." Cameron turns to the small crowd in the kitchen. "Let it be known that I, Cameron, will owe Madison Crocker big for an entire year."

The group brushes off Cameron's words. Memphis and Delta fill Taylor in on what's presently cooking and what's next and show her the list for the day. Hamilton helps Liberty sort her blocks by colors in the living room while the two dogs look on from nearby.

Cameron finds champagne flutes in the kitchen to create her screwdrivers. She passes them out then joins me on the stools at the island.

"I should pour your screwdriver over your head," Cameron murmurs from my side. "Trenton and Taylor spent an hour last night discussing Dalton. Seems someone mentioned he was helping me in the basement." She pretends to be angry.

"Sorry," I whisper. "I swear I didn't know that the two of

you had a history. I'm sorry they grilled you about it. How bad was it?"

Taylor interrupts, "We didn't grill her. Trenton expressed some concerns about repairs on the house. And the two of us simply cautioned her to take things slow this time with Dalton."

Cameron rolls her eyes at me, expressing her frustration with her older siblings' interference. In our past conversations, she's shared their constant attempts to over-analyze her decisions, guide her career, and mention that she needs to start a family. It has to be hard being the baby of the family.

———

My cell phone vibrates on the kitchen island. I rise from the hallway floor where I've been playing with race cars with Liberty.

Webb: I'm ready to come work with your books?
Me: you may come anytime
Me: tell your dad

Two hours later, I peek into my office and watch Webb put two more books on the shelf. He was mesmerized by my empty office shelves and box after box of books to populate them. Delta mentioned he loves to sort and organize items and offered to let him help me.

I'm happy to see him loving the work. "Webb, do you need anything?" I ask.

"No," he answers without interrupting his task. He pulls out another book and slides it onto the shelf. "No, thank you," he corrects himself.

I slip from the room, leaving him to his preferred task.

"I wish I could do that," his mother states from beside me. "Imagine what I could accomplish in a day with his laser focus," she teases on her way to resume helping the cooks in the kitchen.

Was she checking on Webb, or was she checking on me? Oh well. No big deal. I'm just glad her family is joining us today and that she is helping cook in my place.

I'm so happy that I can't stop smiling. The gang is all here. Hamilton and Stan return from working out and finish their showers prior to Fallon and Slater arriving. A few minutes later, Taylor's husband and girls arrive with Trenton's brood.

The kids play in Liberty's room or with electronics in our room, occasionally popping out for a nibble or a drink. The men flip back and forth between college and NFL football games in the living room. They even agree to lower the volume when Delta hollers in from the kitchen area.

When the service elevator pings open and the dog walkers peek in, I'm surprised it is already 11. I round up the dogs and make the guys promise to fix a plate and stay a bit when they return at one with McGee and Indie.

Delta, Taylor, Memphis, and Amy buzz around the kitchen. Their intensity increases as we are nearing our one o'clock meal time. I rise from my stool, sliding the eight-foot folding table and small card table into place. Ava and Fallon join me in placing the autumn orange table cloths on each. The three of us make quick work of setting the table, taking care to put out the centerpieces that Taylor's daughters made. Once we finish, I stand back and admire our work. The fall colors work well together.

I know better than to offer to help with the final cooking preparations. Tensions in the kitchen rise—the last thing they need is for me to burn something.

"Can we place anything on the tables yet?" I ask the three cooks. "We could put condiments on the tables and set the rest up in a buffet line," I suggest.

A look of horror from Taylor leads me to believe it's a stupid idea.

"With eight at the long folding table and four at the card table, things are tight," I explain.

Memphis crooks her head to the side, considering my idea. Delta stays out of it.

"I guess it would work," Taylor admits.

"The whole point of today is to enjoy our company," Memphis reminds us. "It'll be nice to have some space at the tables."

"Then it's settled." Taylor claps her hands together. "We

can place the butter, jelly, salt, and pepper on the tables. The rest we'll spread out on the island."

Ava, Fallon, and I begin following Taylor's directions. We leave space for the large turkey platter and ham plate then place the green bean casserole, mashed potatoes, and other sides on the island. Ava moves the bar stools against the wall while I organize the desserts at the other end of the island. Pecan pie, cherry pie, pumpkin pie...

"Time to eat," Memphis announces from the kitchen.

Delta fetches Webb from the office while Amy collects the children from the playrooms. Memphis and I help direct the younger kids to the smaller tables. Amy, Cameron, and Delta offer to sit with the children while the rest of the adults take seats around our dining table. All conversation ends when we are seated.

I look around at my guests and squeeze Hamilton's hand which rests on my thigh under the table. When I stand, all eyes focus on me.

"We don't want our meal to get cold, so I'll keep this short." My guests chuckle at my words. "Thank you for coming and sharing Thanksgiving with us. I've felt alone for so long. You'll never know..." I struggle to clear my throat before continuing. "You mean more to me than you will ever know. In the past month, my family and friends have grown exponentially. My life is full and so is my heart. Thank you for accepting Liberty and me in your lives. We may not be blood relatives, but I consider each of you my family."

My throat closes tight as tears threaten. I return to my seat, ready for all attention to be off of me. I didn't expect to spill my heart today. I'm not prepared for the overwhelming feelings of acceptance and belonging that blindside me.

Hamilton's hand rubs up and down my thigh. He knows it's not easy for me, and I love that he's trying to soothe me secretly under the table.

"Let's say grace; please bow your heads," Memphis suggests.

After her lovely blessing, we assist the children in filling plates then take turns as couples filling ours. Light conversations circle each table. I love my family. I hope it is always this easy.

―――――

We excuse the children as soon as they finish eating. Amy, Fallon, and Delta pull their chairs to the large table, and we enjoy staying, nibbling on dessert, and chatting for another hour.

Eventually, the guys begin to hint that there are football games to watch. Memphis, as the matriarch in attendance, releases the men as the elevator pings, and the dogs sprint inside.

I usher the guys in to fill a plate and allow them to eat in the living room with the men and the football games. Luckily, they don't argue and fit right in. I thought we'd have to deliver a plate to them; I'm glad they felt welcome enough to come up as we suggested.

We round up the dishes. Delta places silverware, glasses, and as many serving bowls as she can into the dishwasher. I realize now how smart it was of Ava to load the dishwasher twice during the day. We only have a few large bowls and platters to hand wash. I scrub, Fallon dries, and Memphis puts them away. It takes little time to finish the task.

"I'm having a second piece of pie," I announce, snagging a paper plate and plastic fork.

Delta, Memphis, and Fallon join me in a second serving of dessert. While we snack around the island, I lean towards Taylor. "What's going on in there?" I ask, tilting my head toward my office.

Taylor's daughters' giggles can be heard clearly in the kitchen. I believe the only other person in the office is Webb, and I'm worried we might need to rescue him.

"They've entered the 'into boys stage,'" Taylor states, smiling. "They flirt every chance they get. I think my husband is going to go insane before they even reach 16."

"You can't blame him." I bump my shoulder against hers and admit, "It can't get any easier as they get older. I'm already dreading how fast Liberty is growing."

We both turn as the girls wave bye to Webb from the office door then walk to the fridge for a water. They attempt to tell secrets, but we can hear them.

"Who are the guys sitting with Dad?"

"What guys?"

"Look!" She turns her twin's head to the sectional in the living room.

Then, their eyes meet ours and they race down the hall, giggling the entire way.

Taylor rolls her eyes, sighing dramatically. "I see nothing but drama in my future."

"I hear ya," I agree; she has her hands full. The twins are only 13 years old. I can only imagine what they'll be like at age 16 or 18. My mind imagines Liberty at age 16, driving and dating boys. I bite my lip while imagining Hamilton's stress as boys show interest in his little girl. He seems easy-going, but I imagine he won't be when our daughter's dating phase comes into our lives.

"I'd like to bite that lip," Hamilton whispers hot against my ear.

Surprised, I jump. I was so lost in my daydreaming that I didn't hear him come up behind me. He looks quizzically at me.

"I was daydreaming about Liberty," I murmur.

He rubs his hand up and down my back. "She's not dating until she's 30."

Apparently, Hamilton paid attention to Taylor's daughters, too.

When our last Thanksgiving Day guest leaves, Memphis directs Hamilton and me to go pack while she and Amy pick up. We only agree because there isn't much left to clean.

"Can you believe we fly to Vegas tomorrow, and in two days, we'll be married?" I ask Hamilton as we lay our toiletries out to pack in the morning.

"I'm ready," he quickly replies. "We're still getting married in t-shirts, right?"

I nod–I love the idea of us wearing our favorite baseball shirts. I'm not a traditional girl. I want to elope. It'll be quick and we'll be comfortable.

CHAPTER 34

Hamilton

I wiggle the tinkle bell on the end of the elf cap then allow it to touch Madison's cheek. Her eyes squeeze tight, her nose wrinkles, and her lips purse.

"Stop," she gripes. "Make it stop!"

"I would, but Cameron is counting on you. You promised her, so you need to get up," I remind her, safely out of arms' reach.

"Fine," she spits, sitting up. "What the…"

Her eyes look to me. They struggle to focus then process the sight of her husband. I'm prepared for this reaction. I give it five minutes, then she'll spring up and join in the fun.

"Oh my gosh!" She covers her open mouth with her hand. "What are you doing?" She laughs.

"It's Black Friday," I begin to explain. "You usually decorate your bedroom and car today."

Her eyes grow wide with the realization of holiday fun to come.

"You start playing Christmas music on Black Friday," I add. "I thought since you had a book event and couldn't decorate at home, I'd find a way to let you celebrate your favorite holiday."

"You're wearing that to my book signing?"

"Umm, no. *We* are wearing this to your book event." I wave her costume. "I ran the idea by Cameron, so we are all set."

She looks from the costume to me.

"Seriously?" she asks again. "You are really going to wear that in public with me?"

She said 'with me;' I knew she'd like this idea. She's even perking up–I might just make a morning person out of her after all.

I wiggle the costume in hopes she hops up soon, and she does. She takes the hanger from me then leans in close.

"I'm kinda diggin' the tights," she murmurs. "Can I lift the hem of your jacket and check out your package?" She flutters her eyes at me while making duck lips.

"If you get any closer to my package, we will be late, and Cameron will kill you," I say through gritted teeth. This woman tests my restraint constantly.

"Okay. I'll leave your package alone for now." She turns, shaking her beautiful behind into our bathroom.

Think about Grandma, puppies, and ice cream. I attempt

to prevent the tenting of my tights. These tights show everything. I didn't think this through when I picked out these costumes.

I sit on the bed and open my social media to distract me from the fact that Madison is naked mere feet away from me right now. I scroll through all of the Thanksgiving posts I ignored for the last 24 hours. I haven't posted for over a week; I should post something today.

I walk over to our full-length mirror, hold my phone in front of me, and snap a photo of everything from my elf hat to booties. I open Instagram and post the picture. I type, "Elfin' around Chicago today. Stop by Lake Street Books 7-10am. #LakeStBooks #BlackFriday #ArmAndHammer" Next, I tweet the same post on my Twitter account.

"We need to leave in the next 10 minutes," I call towards the bathroom as I wheel the two suitcases to the hall, and I park them at the front door.

Madison

He bought us elf costumes to wear on Black Friday. He must really love me. I absolutely love the costume. The dopey grin I'm wearing in the mirror matches it perfectly. *I better not grin like this all day, or my fans will think I'm a weirdo.*

I look one more time front and back in the mirror. Liking what I see, I enter the bedroom. *Where'd he go?* I peek in on

Liberty before I head to the kitchen for coffee and a protein bar.

"I've got your breakfast." Hamilton waves a bar and travel mug my way. "You can eat in the car."

I nod and follow—we have a tight schedule today. I can't fault him for hustling me along. In fact, I'm grateful he's helping me this morning.

"Our car is waiting downstairs," he mentions as the elevator plummets to the ground floor.

We pause for a photo with the doorman prior to joining Cameron in the back of the car. She's laughing and explaining how the crowd will love our holiday themed attire. Seems we will enter through an employee entrance, meet the owner, arrange the signing table, then open the door to shoppers and fans.

"I'll have to go around a few blocks to get access to the back of the store," Our driver informs us. "Looks like you have a lot of fans."

His words puzzle me. I peek out the window of the car to see a line from the front doors of the bookstore, down the block, around the corner, and blocking the alley entrance.

"Is there another author appearing today?" I ask Cameron.

"No." She pats my thigh. "These are your fans, silly."

"There's no way they're all here to see me," I state.

I did notice the crowd seemed to be a mix of teens and adults. They are the right demographic for my genre, but at a book signing this early on Black Friday, they can't all be for me.

I look at Hamilton. "What's up with your phone?" It won't stop buzzing. His phone never buzzes this much prior to seven.

He tugs his phone out of his elf jacket pocket. "I posted a pic on social media this morning," he confesses. "I guess I make a great elf. Everyone's sharing and commenting."

"Oh my gosh," I laugh. "Your teammates are going to save the picture and use it against you. You know that, right?"

He nods. "It's worth it. I wanted to promote your book signing."

"Wait. What?" Cameron leans forward to see Hamilton. "What exactly did you post?"

Hamilton opens Instagram before passing his phone over for us to read.

"I knew the fans weren't all here for me." I breathe a sigh of relief.

"Trust me, they're here for you." Hamilton squeezes my shoulders. "I promoted your book signing."

"I love you," I whisper.

He believes they are here to see me, but many are coming under the guise of my signing to see him in the elf costume. If it helps me sell a few books, I'm glad he posted it. I'm actually a bit relieved that I don't draw this big of a crowd. I want readers, but I'm not looking for mobs to stalk me everywhere I go.

When the driver parks the car, we quickly hop out and slip in through the back door.

"Hello! I'm Cameron with D.C. Bland Publishing." Cameron extends her hand to shake.

"I'm Mr. Richmond." He shakes Cameron's hand.

"I thought I'd be meeting with…"

He interrupts Cameron, "I'm the assistant manager; the owner had a family emergency yesterday, so I'm filling in." He motions for us to follow him through the backroom and out onto the sales floor. "We've placed a table for you here to the side. I noticed a line formed outside, so I arranged these felt ropes to guide those interested in your book signing to line up over here. This way, they won't interfere with our Black Friday shoppers."

It might just be my nerves, but I feel like Mr. Richmond doesn't want me here today. Cameron made it sound like the owner was elated that I was filling in for the true crime author that baled. Mr. Richmond acts like my signing event will be small and in the way of the regular business.

I will not let him ruin my signing. I will not let him ruin my signing. I chant inside my brain. My nerves ratchet up another notch. This is my first, big city signing. I've been to a few small, independent bookstores. I've never signed at a store of this size, and this is Chicago for goodness sake.

With Hamilton's help, Cameron and I cover the table, stack books, set up the backdrop and my banner, and place a sign at the end of the velvet ropes so guests know what the line is for and where to line up.

"The books you pre-signed are in these two boxes." Cameron motions to the opened boxes at my feet. "If the line is long and a fan doesn't fill out a card for a personalized autograph, you can hand them one of these as you speak to them for a minute."

I nod my understanding.

"Hamilton, will you help me offer these to guests in the line," Cameron points to a stack of cards and ink pens. "If they would like a personal message with the autograph, they should fill one of these out to hand to Madison when it's their turn. Encourage them to print legibly."

"Yep! Let me know if there's anything else I can do to help," Hamilton answers. He tucks a handful of pens and a stack of cards into the pocket of his elf jacket. He leans across the table to me. "Can I get a kiss before the public enters, and there can be no elf PDA?"

Cameron excuses herself. It's a good thing there is a table between us. Our kiss, while hot, remains PG-13.

"The doors will be opening in five minutes," Mr. Richmond announces without looking in our direction. He peeks out the giant windows, trying to gauge the length of the line formed outside.

I open and close my right hand a few times in an attempt to stretch out my fingers for the three hours of autographs that lay before me.

"Stop worrying," Hamilton murmurs. "They already love your book. They're going to love its author, too. And with that cute little elf costume, they'll love you even more."

I love his words, his enthusiasm, and his support for me. It's weird having him as my number one fan. I've always been his fan; now the tables have turned. I guess I'm not surprised he supports me. It's just new. For that matter, being a published author and holding my own book signings is also new to me.

Hamilton

It's been a busy first hour–time truly does fly when you're having fun. And I am having fun. I wish I could spend more time with Madison, but I'm enjoying my interactions up and down the line of anxious fans waiting for her autograph.

I had no idea my two social media posts would spark so much interest. Lucky for me, the Cubs fans that arrive today also seem to truly be interested in Madison's books, too. The only people here to see me and not the books are my teammates. I didn't expect any of the guys to be up this early, let alone dress and come find me.

I'm sure one of them saw the post and called the others to wake them up. I can handle it. Let them save the picture and try to embarrass me with it in the future. I'm doing this for my girl. A successful signing and a happy Madison will make it worth their teasing in the future. I would not have posted the pic of me in the costume if I didn't expect it to be seen.

The guys have even started posing for pictures for people still in line outside. The fans chat about the Cubs, and my teammates find a way to bring up Madison's books with each of them. I'm going to owe them big for this. They've helped me hand out free copies of Madison's two books to lucky fans. We've signed Cubs gear, posed for individual and group pics with fans, and even posted a few on our social media platforms.

"Excuse me." A deep, male voice demands my attention. "Who's in charge here?"

I turn around to find a group of eight police officers scowling. I don't think we are breaking any laws here, but it's not my place to decide.

"The bookstore assistant manager, Mr. Richmond, and an agent from the publishing company are inside," I promptly inform them. "If you'd like, I can take you to them." I motion toward the bookstore doors.

"Hamilton Armstrong?" one officer asks, squinting at me.

I extend my hand to shake his.

"Are the Cubs to blame for this crowd?" another officer asks.

I notice their scowls have morphed into smiles.

"Maybe," I reply. "My girl is signing copies of her book until 10 today. I decided to dress up and join her. Some of my teammates had come down to razz me, and they stayed to entertain the crowd while the fans wait. We didn't mean to cause any traffic issues," I apologize.

"We'll spread out along the blocks to ensure traffic continues to flow and no one stands in the crosswalks," an officer offers. "Beats working the strip malls with crowd control today."

All the officers chuckle and agree.

"Thank you." I shake his hand. "Let me know if you'd

like to meet the author or snap a photo with some of the team."

Madison

As I speak to a teenage girl and her mother, I sneak a glance at the long line that seems to have no end.

"Look who I found!" Cameron's cheery voice draws my attention behind me.

"Hola, Mommy!" Liberty calls from her stroller.

"Hi, guys" I greet Memphis and Liberty. "Can you believe the turnout? Isn't this crazy?"

"One hour left," Cameron murmurs near my ear. "I'm showing these two around before our driver takes them to the airport."

"Wish I could visit," I apologize to Memphis.

"No, you don't. Don't apologize for working. Being busy means talking to fans and selling books." Memphis hugs me before returning to Liberty's stroller. "We just wanted a peek."

I wave to them then quickly return to the next female in line.

"I apologize. My family dropped in for a second," I tell the 20-something woman as I shake her hand.

"Your daughter is adorable," she states. "My students are raving about your books. I planned to snag a copy for my classroom. When I saw on social media that you would be signing today, I couldn't miss it."

"What grade do you teach?"

"I'm an eighth-grade literacy teacher," she informs me.

I raise my arm, signaling for Cameron to return to me. I ask her to get two unsigned books to donate to the middle school. She quickly pulls them from behind a partition.

"Here are two copies for your classroom or the school library," I explain, handing them to the teacher. "This way the autographed copy can remain in your personal library."

"You are so kind." She blushes.

"I love to encourage young readers whenever I can. I'm also a former teacher, so I know about funding shortages and the price you pay to create your classroom."

"Thanks again. My students will be thrilled."

Hamilton and his teammates gather around my signing table. Cameron lets me know we are in the final 10 minutes of the signing.

The line still expands out the door and down the block. I feel bad for those that waited in line so long and won't get to meet me. Part of me wishes I could stay.

As if she's reading my mind, Cameron murmurs, "The owner called me, excited about the turn out. He's offering coupons for 10 percent off a purchase to everyone still in line as we leave. Hamilton and the guys are going to go pass those out right now." She quickly hands little cards to the men who quickly start passing them out to everyone.

"Can I walk down the line and thank them all for coming?" I ask her. "I feel like they should at least see me after waiting so long."

I sign the next book then rise. I utilize my teacher voice to thank everyone for coming and apologize that I can't stay. I encourage them to make sure they get a coupon then move farther down the line to repeat the process.

Several fans snap photos of me with their phones as I wave and talk. When Hamilton approaches, more cameras pop out. Everyone cheers for us to pose together as the two elves. We continue to work our way down the line and even pose with the men in blue. Hamilton posts that photo on his social media and tags the Chicago PD.

Before I know it, Cameron approaches to whisk us inside, through the back room, and to our waiting car. The assistant bookstore manager thanks us and informs Hamilton that if the Cubs or his charity ever need donations or books to be sure to contact the store. It seems the large crowd softened his heart towards having me there today.

Cameron shares some sales numbers and stories with us as we travel to the airport. Then, she passes us our duffle bag. While she and the driver focus on the road ahead, Hamilton raises the partition, and we change into our travel attire for the flight. I would have loved flying in the costumes, but Hamilton doesn't want to draw attention to himself. I hadn't thought about it, but he wants to disguise himself so we can enjoy our weekend without cameras or fans.

"It's clear you don't change on the go very often," I chuckle as I am finished, and Hamilton still struggles.

"I'm a bit bigger than you," he states. His long legs stretch to the floor board in front of me while he remains in his seat, attempting to pull up his jeans and fasten them.

"Excuses. Excuses."

When he finishes, he lowers the divider. Cameron informs us we are pulling into the airport. My nerves ratchet up a notch. I'm not afraid to fly. It's just that this is the first time I'll be flying with Liberty. Hamilton purchased stand-by tickets for Memphis and Liberty on our flight. He claims someone won't show up, and they'll fly with us. Although I've researched flying with toddlers online, I'm still very nervous about it. *What if they don't get on our flight?* Memphis will be stuck in a busy airport with her for who knows how long.

Taking in the multiple lanes of bumper to bumper traffic and airplanes taking off, I worry we may never find Memphis and Liberty in this post-Thanksgiving crowd.

When Hamilton slips something black from the duffle bag, my jaw drops. He slips on a pair of small, black, rectangular framed glasses and a Cardinals ball cap. *He doesn't need glasses. And couldn't he get in trouble if he's spotted in a Cardinals hat?*

"What?" He smiles at me.

"Since when do you need glasses?" I sputter in shock.

"I don't," he replies. "This is my travel disguise. No one would ever expect me to wear a Cardinals hat. I thought I'd use the glasses like Clark Kent does."

"Clark Kent didn't improve his looks by wearing the glasses. They made him look nerdy," I pant. "You look hot in glasses. I hope I don't get into a fight when women can't keep their eyes off of you."

His smile widens. "So, the glasses don't help my disguise?"

Oh, they help. They help make it harder for me to keep my hands out of his hair and off his face. My panties grow wetter the longer I gaze at him.

He chuckles. "I figured you'd like the hat." He places his thumb upon my lower lip. "Please, stop biting this. We need to meet Mom and catch a flight. If you keep biting your lip, I'll instruct the driver to drive a bit further and raise the divider. We'll miss our flight and worry my mom."

"We can't have that," I whisper.

"Here we are," the driver announces.

Hamilton opens the door and guides me out. Before he lets go of my hand, he asks, "Is it the hat or the glasses that have you so hot and bothered?"

I only shrug.

Hamilton accepts the two carry-on bags before tipping the driver. We hug Cameron goodbye and enter the airport.

"Mom plans to meet us at our terminal," Hamilton reminds me, understanding that I might be worried about finding Liberty in the mayhem.

Hamilton and I opted for carry-on bags to avoid the crowds and waits at the baggage terminals. He promised I'd have everything I need when we arrive in Las Vegas—I'm trusting him to know what he's talking about. He guides me through the masses, through the TSA Pre-Check, and to our terminal like a pro. I guess it helps to be over six feet tall and muscular to fight the crowds. He acts like a blocker on the football field, and I simply follow close behind.

"I see a stroller," Hamilton calls over his shoulder.

I follow his index finger. *There they are. What a relief.*

"You made it," Memphis greets. "I promised Libby she could get out of the stroller when you arrived."

"Hey, sugar." Hamilton immediately unbuckles Liberty and lifts her up.

"Need go potty," Liberty attempts to whisper, but we all hear her.

"Hamilton, do you mind watching all the stuff if I go with them?" Memphis asks, motioning to her carry-on and our backpack near the stroller. "I'll put my bag in this seat to save it for me."

"Have you checked in at the counter yet?" he asks before we leave.

"Yes. They will call me up before boarding," Memphis shares.

"I hope you get to take our flight." I verbalize my big fear. "I don't know what you'll do if it's full."

"It will all work out," Hamilton promises. The corner of his mouth twitches.

Hamilton

. . .

My girls return at the same time the flight staff announces we will begin boarding soon. I know Madison has worried about the four of us getting on the same flight. It's time I set her mind at ease.

"Mom, they called your name," I lie.

She smiles before taking her tickets up to the counter. I keep an eye on Madison as she watches my mom's interactions at the counter. I hate that I've caused her stress in trying to perpetuate my surprise.

My mom turns towards us, giving a thumbs up. I hear Madison release the breath she's been holding. Mom and I had this all planned out. We only pretended she had stand-by tickets.

"We're all set," Mom announces when she returns.

I pull the tickets from her hand then pull out our tickets to compare. "We're just across the aisle from you," I announce, adding excitement to my voice.

"Really?" Madison perks up.

She allows Liberty to stand on her own. "Stay with us, or we'll need to buckle you back in the stroller."

Liberty walks in the small area in front of our three seats, pointing to random items and chattering. The travelers around us seem to enjoy her banter, so I allow her to continue. The more energy she burns now, the better she will sleep during the flight.

"Those glasses…" Madison whispers huskily in my ear.

"You really like them that much?" I chuckle at her silliness.

"Plan on wearing them to bed tonight," she whispers. "And tomorrow night."

I shake my head.

"What was that Kenny Chesney song I used to tease you about?"

"*She Thinks My Tractor's Sexy*," I remind her.

"Now, she thinks your glasses are sexy," she twangs, still in a whisper.

I roll my eyes.

Madison

Memphis insists she will be fine helping Liberty settle in during the pre-boarding.

"They'll be fine." Hamilton pats my arm reassuringly.

"I just worry about the booster seat in the small seats. It won't be as roomy as the SUV to install," I explain.

"Honey," Hamilton leans forward to better face me. "we're in first class. There will be plenty of room for the booster, and Libby won't be able to kick or bump the seat in front of her. She'll nap. You'll see."

First class? Is he kidding? I love that he wants to treat us to a nice trip, but we don't *need* first class. I don't even want to know how much these tickets cost.

CHAPTER 35

Madison

I roll over and flop my arm out to find I'm alone. I crack one eye, searching the room for Hamilton; he's nowhere to be found. I raise myself on two elbows, quirking my ear to listen for sounds in the bathroom. Nothing. I grab my phone from the charger. It's 9:30 a.m. *Where could he be?* Maybe Liberty is awake.

I tie my hair in a messy ponytail, pull on a t-shirt and sleep shorts, and make me way out into the common area. I find Memphis and Liberty; still no Hamilton.

"Mornin'. Have you seen Hamilton?" I ask, wiping at the corner of my eyes after a big yawn.

"Good morning!" Memphis wears a huge smile. "He

went down to work out. Said he'd be a couple of hours, and I should let you sleep."

My nose leads me to the dining table. I spot the remnants of Liberty and Memphis' breakfast. *Bacon.*

"I'll order you some," Memphis offers. "Bacon, fruit, muffin. Anything else?"

"That sounds perfect." I place my hand on my belly as it growls in answer. "Make it a double order of bacon," I add.

Memphis nods before picking up the hotel phone to order room service. I plop on the sofa, tucking a throw pillow to my chest. Liberty plays with a toy car that flies across the ceramic tile floor with ease, causing her to giggle.

Two hours. Who works out for two hours while in Vegas? He's crazy, but I love him. If it's nine now, he should be back about eleven. By the time he cleans up, we will need to fetch some lunch for all of us.

I'm lazy for the rest of the morning. My breakfast of double bacon is divine, the sofa is comfy, and I have no desire to shower or even move for that matter.

At 10:45, Memphis suggests I shower and get dressed before Hamilton returns. It takes all of my strength, but I peel myself from the sofa cushions and slide my stocking feet across the tile toward our room.

The shower feels sublime. The water pelting my back and neck works out all of my kinks. I opted for a cooler temperature in the hopes that it would wake me up, and it does. I feel revived when I emerge, dressed and ready for the day. When I open my bedroom door, I freeze on the spot, raising my hands to the wood frame for support.

The room is full. Full of my friends and new family. *How can this be?*

"Surprise!" the group shouts, clapping and jumping up and down.

Still in the doorway, I scan the room, looking for Hamilton. I only find Memphis walking towards me.

"Hamilton planned everything," she explains. "He made arrangements to fly all of us out here weeks ago." She searches my face.

Tears well, and I'm finally able to leave the door frame. As I walk through the group, each woman greets me with a hug and excited words about my wedding tonight. *Wedding? I thought we were eloping.*

"You look like you need a stiff drink," Adrian states, thrusting a flute of orange liquid my way. "Mimosas. So, you're still eloping. Hamilton wanted your family and friends to celebrate with you."

I'm still confused. "Who's all here?" My voice croaks.

"The guys are spending the day in a suite with Hamilton. They're keeping him from seeing the bride on his wedding day. Memphis insisted on that tradition."

I look at Memphis then back to Adrian. I chug my drink then place the glass on a nearby end table.

"So, all of the guys came, too?"

"Yep," Adrian answers while refilling the glass I just abandoned.

Taylor walks up to me. "Are you nervous?"

"I wasn't until now," I confess.

"Oh please." Cameron approaches swatting at me. "It will still be the two of you with Elvis up front."

She acts like it's no big deal. Now, we will have an audience. That changes things a bit.

"Aunt Madison, can we see your wedding dress?" Taylor's daughter asks from across the room.

"Um..." I begin to walk in her direction. "We opted to not dress up. I'm not wearing a dress." At least I hope I'm not. *Surely Hamilton didn't change that without my input.*

"We brought our Cubs shirts," Taylor reminds her daughters. "That's what everyone is wearing to the wedding.

"I'm going to have a gown like Belle's in *Beauty and the Beast* when I get married," the other twin states.

"You better start a wedding fund in addition to a college fund," Cameron teases her older sister. "Sounds like the girls will want all the bells and whistles at their weddings."

"Tell me about it; their father is already dreading the day," Taylor teases.

"So, how long is everyone staying in Vegas?" My head is full of so many questions.

While waiting on our toenails to dry, Salem mentions she has a hilarious ER story to share.

"Now, I'm not sharing any names, so we aren't breaking any HIPPA laws," Salem starts.

"Athens is a small town. I'll figure it out," Adrian brags.

"Shut up, or she won't share!" Bethany draws closer, excited for gossip.

"Anyway..." Salem points her finger at Adrian to shut her up. "A guy came in with hives over his entire body. He even had hives you-know-where." She wiggles her eyebrows while avoiding words that might draw youngsters' attention.

Our group shares wide-eyed shock and giggles.

"While I asked questions, trying to understand the reason for his extreme allergy attack," Salem shares, "the guy tells me that they were trying to get pregnant, and his wife wanted to try to spice things up a bit. She slathered him in honey, massaged him a bit, then hoped to take her time licking it all from him, finishing in a very special spot." Salem blushes.

"So, he didn't know?" I ask. "I mean, honey is a common food."

"He claims he's never consumed honey," she states. "We gave him a shot of Benadryl and urged them to abstain until *all* redness and hives disappeared from his privates."

"No baby-making this month for them," Savannah blurts, causing wide-eyes from Taylor's twins across the room.

We burst into raucous laughter.

CHAPTER 36

Hamilton

My hands are shaking—I'm nervous. At any minute, the woman I love will walk through those doors. Today, I'll lock her into my life forever as my best friend, my wife, and the mother of my children.

I'm way too hot in this jacket, but I can't take it off and reveal the surprise beneath until Madison stands beside me. It's my final statement of love and support for her. She's my everything, and I plan to show her in every way possible.

My breath catches in my throat as the double doors open. I crane my neck in search of Madison in her gaggle of girls. The doors close quickly behind them, leaving me without a glimpse of her or Liberty. In scanning the room, my eyes lock with my mother's—she smiles and winks to let me know all is well. It does little to calm my nerves. I need to see Madison; I need to hold her hand.

Madison

Liberty and I stand alone in the large foyer. I nervously fluff her tutu that Aunt Amy purchased for her. She looks sweet in her little black and white striped umpire shirt, black tutu, and zebra-striped tights with black Mary Janes. Amy spared no expense in securing the perfect outfit for our wedding. We planned for Hamilton to wear a Cubs t-shirt and for me, a Cardinals t-shirt. Liberty, as our referee, is a perfect addition. I'm glad Amy took it upon herself to dress our daughter appropriately.

Well, it would have been a perfect picture for the three of us had I not decided to change things up at the last minute. Don't get me wrong; I'm still a humongous Cardinals fan, but I love Hamilton. At the altar, I plan to surprise him by unveiling my Cubs jersey.

When the ladies surprised me today, I learned they all brought Cubs attire. It would not bother me to be the only one sporting a Cardinals shirt, but I thought it might be nice to surprise Hamilton by showing my support of him and his team on our special day. I'm not even wearing my usual Cardinals tank underneath it to protect my skin.

The door opens a crack, and Trenton squeezes through.

"Did our nieces talk to you today?" he asks as he approaches.

I smile as I nod, remembering Taylor's daughters informing me they asked their uncle to walk me down the aisle.

"Well then," he extends his elbow, "shall we go get you married?"

I slip my arm under his elbow before prompting Liberty to walk in front of us to her daddy. Trenton opens the door, and I catch my first glance of Hamilton. As we step into the chapel filled with our closest family and friends, I only have eyes for my man. Subconsciously, I bite my lower lip as we slowly close the distance between us. I feel my temperature rise with his deep brown eyes upon me. My skin prickles as thoughts of what tonight will bring flood my thoughts. My cheeks flame, and my breath catches when Hamilton's tongue darts out to dampen his lips before his signature smirk shines. He's thinking about tonight, too.

Liberty hugs her father's leg as Trenton releases my arm, placing a kiss on my hot cheek.

"Let us begin," the Elvis impersonator states.

Hamilton raises his index finger, halting the magistrate. His fingers grasp the zipper of his jacket then slowly lower it down. I quickly follow suit with my own sweater, curious what he has under his. In unison, we remove them, letting them fall to the floor at our feet.

Laughter engulfs me as tears fill my eyes. We couldn't have planned this any better. Hamilton stands before me in a Cardinals t-shirt. He's shaking his head at me.

"I wanted to surprise you," I murmur.

Adrian, in the front row, heard my admission. "You mean the two of you didn't plan this?" A full belly laugh sounds as she slaps her thigh.

"We didn't plan this," Hamilton announces to the crowd.

"Great minds think alike," Memphis calls from her seat in the front amidst the laughter of our friends.

Taking Liberty's hands, Hamilton and I face Elvis to exchange our vows.

Before I know it, we are back at our suite, celebrating with our family and friends. Caterers bring us appetizers and beverages. With plates in hand, we mingle with our brood. I grab Hamilton's bicep to steady myself. Hamilton places his large hand over mine, looking down to access my reaction.

"What's wrong?" His eyes search mine for clues.

Unable to talk at the moment, I point toward his sister, Amy, across the room. She holds Liberty in her arms while chatting with the guy beside her. The guy. The we're-just-friends guy that she denies is her boyfriend.

Hamilton chuckles. "Yeah He's been with the guys all day. Mom texted me that no one is allowed to chat with Amy about it. I think Mom worries Amy will get mad and dump him if we do."

"Can you dump someone you're not dating? I mean she's adamant he's not her boyfriend," I tease.

"Be nice," he prompts. "They attended the World Series

together and now our wedding; I think it's safe to say they are a couple." He shrugs, quirking the corner of his mouth.

"I won't say a thing, but I think we should start a pool. The person that picks the month she officially admits that she has a boyfriend is the winner," I suggest.

"We are so totally doing that!" Hamilton leaves my side and approaches the guys from Athens who are standing near the alcohol in the corner.

CHAPTER 37

Madison

Upon returning to Chicago, our life does not slow down as I'd hoped. Fallon and Liberty submerge themselves in activities. They attend playgroup, tumbling, and swim lessons held in our building. I've observed a few times; Liberty seems to love playing with her peers. I'm settling into a new writing routine four days a week. Delta insists I leave one day a week open to run errands, go shopping, or just hang out with her. She ensures that I enjoy my new city and make new friends, and I love her for that.

I squeeze in a couple of hours to write this morning before my girls arrive. Our home will be crowded for the next 48 hours. My four friends, along with their two daughters, are driving up for a Christmas shopping trip. I don't look forward to shopping, but I do look forward to the time we will spend together.

"Lunch time," Miss Alba states, peeking her head through my closed door.

I save my document before shutting my laptop for the rest of the week.

Entering the kitchen, I find Fallon at the island and Liberty already in her highchair. Miss Alba sets out a bowl of fresh salad, sandwiches, and berries. We eat quietly in anticipation of guests arriving in the next hour.

Although I gave them the rest of the week off, Fallon insisted on playing with the three girls both days, allowing the grown-ups alone time to gossip, shop, or relax; Miss Alba insisted on cooking and keeping up with the dishes for us. I realize they will be paid for their time but am glad they want to ensure it's a great visit.

Liberty and I stand in our open door, anxiously watching the elevator. When it pings, Liberty hops up and down, clapping. I can't resist recording her; she's too darn adorable. With the swooshing sound of the doors opening, Liberty darts in its direction.

"Here, Mommy!" she squeals, still clapping.

"Well, hello Liberty," Adrian greets as she carries Bella into the hallway.

I'm not surprised to see a staff member wheeling a cart

loaded with luggage, diaper bags, strollers, and portable cribs. It's not easy traveling with little ones.

"I need alcohol," Savannah states near my ear before vanishing inside the condo.

I bet the six-hour ride with two little ones and a pregnant Salem taxed her patience. I'm a bit surprised she took the time off and agreed to make the trip.

"Got to pee." Salem waddles past me.

I instruct the man where to place the luggage in one guest room and thank him for his assistance. And just like that, the house is noisy, busy, crowded, and I wouldn't have it any other way.

Miss Alba hooks Savannah up with a delicious margarita. Once Adrian and Bethany get their girls settled in with Fallon and Liberty in her room, they seek Miss Alba's famous margaritas, too. Salem opts for water while rubbing her baby bump.

"So, how was the date?" I nudge Savannah as I plop down on the sectional next to her.

"Yes, finally," Adrian whines. "We've been asking for almost a week, and she has divulged nothing."

"I promised to share with all of you," Savannah defends. She makes an exaggerated effort to settle into a comfy position as we all wait. A wide smile slides upon her face before she begins.

"Start at the beginning, and don't leave anything out," Bethany demands, always one for gossip.

"It was an ugly sweater holiday party held at the principal's house. Lincoln found matching his-and-hers sweater vests for us to wear. They were hideous." She pauses to pull up the photos on her phone for us to see. As we pass the phone around, she continues.

"We stayed at the faculty party an hour. That was 45 minutes too long for me. Of course, every teacher shared stories with him about me. It was all good until the high school teachers started talking of my ditching, pranks, and poor attitude.

"The P.E. teacher spilled some rum punch on her chest, so I reached into my purse to hand her a moist towelette that I stuck in there the last time I had barbecue. I was in the middle of a conversation, so I didn't pay much attention when I handed it to her." Savannah shakes her head. "When the guests around us broke into whispers and laughter, I looked at my hand to see what was so funny. I grabbed a condom instead of a towelette."

"Oh my gosh! That is hilarious!" I snort.

"I bet half the teachers nearly fainted," Adrian adds. "Crusty old hags."

"My face flamed; I'm sure I was bright red," Savannah admits. "When we were at his place, we had a good laugh about it, but in the moment, it was horrifying."

"Um, can we get back to the sex?" Salem urges.

"Fine, we had sex," Savannah huffs.

"Well, it couldn't have been good if that's all you can say about it," Adrian states.

"What if I told you I stayed both Saturday and Sunday night at his place?" Savannah counters.

"Details. Now," Bethany demands.

"I'm not going to give you any specifics other than it was so good, I spent 24 hours at his place," Savannah shares.

She just told me all I need to know. My girl has found herself a guy. *Yay!*

While she continues, I notice the goofy grins on Savannah and Lincoln's face as they stand with an arm around each other's back for the photo. The sweater vests are hideous. Paired with red bell bottoms and a polyester shirt, the vests are too colorful, the design is too busy. She went all out for him–she likes him more than she's let on.

"We went back to his place where he made lasagna with garlic bread for us. We watched Netflix…"

"You watched Netflix and chilled?" Adrian blurts. "OMG!"

"No, we didn't," Savannah defends while blushing.

"Yes, you did," Bethany states. "I know for a fact you spent the night at his house."

Several of us gasp at this news.

"How the hell would you know that?" Savannah rises, hands on her hips.

"I stopped by at eight on my way to the grocery store," Bethany states, like she does this all the time.

"You nosey little…"

I cut Savannah off before this becomes a fight. "Enough!" I wave my hands in front of Savannah's face to get her attention. "Ignore her, and continue with your story," I urge. "I've been waiting to hear all about it. Please?"

Savannah throws herself back into the sofa cushions with a huff. "Anyway…" She throws a glare at Bethany. "We watched old sitcoms, making fun to the hairdos and clothes. He bought wine, but we ended up drinking beer all night." She chuckles. "We drank too much beer."

"Anyone need a refill?" I offer on my way to the kitchen.

Miss Alba assists me with filling the three margarita glasses.

"Yes, Bethany, I did end up staying all night," Savannah sighs. "I didn't plan it; in fact, I made myself promise before he picked me up that I wouldn't sleep with him."

"So, what if you slept with him?" Bethany chimes in again. "Was he good?"

———

When we return from our afternoon of shopping, the girls can't thank Fallon enough for keeping their daughters. While I struggled to find the perfect gift at the perfect price, they arrive back at my place with bundles of bags. I don't enjoy shopping, but I enjoyed their excitement in securing gifts for their families.

"I'm home," Hamilton calls as he enters.

"Daddy!" Liberty squeals, running to greet him.

He sweeps her up, kissing her until she can't stop giggling.

"Stop," she wails, squirming in his arms.

When she wiggles free of his grasp, she pulls him to the toys on the floor and points out Jami and Bella to him.

"Hamilton, are you ready for the estrogen invasion?" Adrian teases.

He greets the women one by one and assures us he can handle all of us.

During dinner, Salem shares photos of the work she's completed on the inside of my parents' farmhouse while sharing stories of Latham's work on the outside. I'm amazed how a coat of paint can change the appearance of the inside of my childhood home. She's lightened it up with her choice of colors and blinds instead of drapes. I like that it looks like a happy home once again. I'm glad their family will fill it with happy memories once again.

The rest of our visit passes much too fast. Before I know it, Liberty and I are waving goodbye to the Athens gang as they drive away. We promise to visit as we drive to Columbia for Christmas.

―――

Madison

Hamilton clocks my mood the moment he arrives home. "It's not easy to say goodbye, is it?" He brushes my hair over my shoulders, placing his palms on the back of my neck. He pulls me into his chest, holding my tight.

I don't need to admit I've laid on the sofa for the past hour, wallowing in my sadness. He knows me all too well.

"Let's put Liberty to bed early tonight," he suggests, steering me towards her bedroom.

She's tired from playing with her two guests; it should be

easy for her to fall asleep. I'm exhausted, but suddenly, my blood hums in anticipation of Hamilton's real intention for tucking Liberty into bed early.

An hour later, I melt into Hamilton's arms, my head upon his chest, and our warm comforter over us. Sated from our shower, my eyes are heavy and my muscles loose. The culmination of the busy day shopping coupled with the vigorous shower sex threatens to carry me off to sleep. Hamilton's fingertips lightly caress my arm, further encouraging the sandman carrying me away.

"When is your next shot?" he murmurs lazily near my ear.

I bolt upright, turning to face him where he still lays on his pillow. Sleep is no longer knocking on my eyelids as my mind flies. I visualize my calendar while staring at our headboard. I visited Dr. Anderson prior to Alma's fall. October… November…December…I snag my phone from the nightstand on my side of the bed. My thumbs fly over the screen through my iCal.

"Crap!"

Hamilton chuckles from his pillow. "I didn't mean to cause the cyclone that just occurred inside your head," he states.

"I messed up," I explain. "I need to request Liberty's and my medical records. I can't believe I didn't think of that while planning our move. We need to find a pediatrician we like before she needs her next immunizations, or, heaven forbid, she gets sick."

I widen my stare at the still very relaxed Hamilton in bed

beside me. "I have to schedule a new patient appointment and probably get a physical with my shot within the next two weeks."

"Okay," he smiles.

"Okay? Seriously? You don't understand," I inform the smirking man beneath me. "It takes a month or two to get a new patient appointment with good gynecologists."

Hamilton stretches his long arm; placing his hand on the back of my neck, he pulls me down beside him. "What if you don't get another shot?"

My eyes search for his meaning. My trembling hand covers my mouth. *He couldn't mean that, could he?* My eyes close as I take a deep, steadying breath.

"Ham..." My voice quakes with the revelation of his question.

"I know it seems too fast," he begins to explain. "I'm ready. We're ready. Liberty is nearly two; she'd be close to three by the time a baby would arrive."

He places one finger firmly against my lips when I begin to speak. "Amy and I are closer to four years apart. Don't get me wrong; I love my sister, but we were never into the same things. The age gap meant I was always the pesky little brother. I want our children to be close. Maybe they could even play on the same sports teams one day."

All of my arguments dissolve at his words. He's given this lots of thought. He's imagined himself with our children and, I'm sure, even envisioned coaching them.

"How..." I swallow, trying to calm my shaky voice. "How many...?" I find it hard to voice my question.

I witness Hamilton attempt not to laugh at me. His lips move from a smile to turn under his teeth and bite down.

"I know you wouldn't want Liberty to be an only child like you are," he correctly assumes. "There were two of us, and I always wanted a brother. I think three or four would be a good number."

Three or four? Could I endure four pregnancies? Envisioning it in my mind, I realize future pregnancies would be different than Liberty's with Hamilton by my side. *In a perfect world, it could be two of each, but what if it were four girls? Or one girl and three boys?* My eyes widen as wild, younger versions of Hamilton tear through my future house while Hamilton works.

"What's going on up here?" Hamilton taps one finger to my scrunched forehead.

"You see us with four kids?" I squeak.

"I can see it, yes. You're the one that does all the work for nine months, so I understand if you only want two." Hamilton's finger moves from my forehead to lightly brush my cheek.

"And you're ready now?" Before he can answer, I continue. "February means January, December, November." I tick them off on my fingers. "January means December, November, October."

Hamilton raises an eyebrow. "What are you doing?"

"I'm taking the month we might become pregnant and counting backwards three months."

"Why?" Now his brow is creased.

"If we get pregnant in January, I would deliver in October. If it happens in February, it would be November," I explain. "If we're really going to try to get pregnant, I want to deliver in the off-season, so you will be with me."

His face lights up. "So, we're doing this?"

"I'm just thinking out loud for now," I state. "If I don't get my shot in December, I'd have to see a doctor, but I assume we could try in January. Of course, trying doesn't mean we'll be successful. If we actively attempt to get pregnant in January through April, I could deliver before you had to report for spring training the next season."

Hamilton flips me onto the mattress, propping himself on his forearms above me. His eyes assess me, then his mouth smothers mine in a deep, all-consuming kiss that makes my toes curl and my body spring to life.

"It only took one night for Liberty." He dawns his sexy, crooked smile.

I swat his chest, but his proximity prevents the desired effect.

"We won't be that lucky next time," I muse. "But trying is also fun."

"Should we practice right now?" he whispers, his lips grazing mine.

I slide my hand between us in answer to his question.

CHAPTER 38

Madison

I place my left hand on Hamilton's bouncing knee.

He immediately stills, eyes finding mine, and whispers, "Sorry."

I knew he would be on edge when he struggled to fall asleep last night. I tried to assure him that she's happy, healthy, and we'll learn how to help her at this appointment —it's all positive and nothing to worry about.

"How long has she been back there?" Hamilton murmurs, squirming in his waiting room chair.

I look at my cell phone screen before answering. "Almost 45 minutes." I rub my hand up and down his back. "Taylor said they'd play, talk, and read. It takes time."

My words clearly don't soothe my anxious husband. He

rises from his chair, pacing along the back wall of the waiting room. A couple of the others in the room give me knowing smiles.

"Liberty's parents," a male nurse calls from the now open door.

Hamilton takes my hand in his as we follow the nurse down a short hallway. He squeezes my hand too tight. I squeeze his twice. He loosens his hold before moving his hand to the small of my back.

The nurse knocks three times on a closed door before he opens it and motions for us to enter. I quickly take a seat; Hamilton follows my lead.

"You have a dynamic young lady," Dr. Conway smiles and greets from across her large wooden desk. Her blonde hair is sleek in an intricate knot at the back of her head. A white doctor's coat covers her navy, silk blouse and matching pencil skirt. "I apologize for the wait. Liberty entertained us, and we lost track of time."

A proud smile slips upon my face. I made it my goal as a parent to raise a confident girl. I don't want her to sit timidly in class, downplaying her academic abilities. Liberty won't be a demure princess, waiting for her prince to rescue her, protect her, and make her happy.

"During our time in the toy area, she answered my questions easily and demonstrated her moxie," Dr. Conway smiles.

"I'm sorry to interrupt," Hamilton butts in.

I cringe. *Why can't he wait for the doctor?* I'm sure she'll answer all of his questions if he just has patience.

"Where is Liberty right now?" he demands.

The smile widens on the doctor's face. "She's in the playroom with two other children and a couple of my medical students."

Hamilton nods his acceptance.

"I'm going to share technical terminology as I explain my findings. You will hear words that might scare you, but please listen to my entire explanation before you jump to conclusions or ask questions." She looks towards Hamilton, hoping her last words sink in.

"Liberty has hyperlexia." Dr. Conway looks to both of us before continuing. "It's a fancy word for children that read much earlier than their peers. There are conflicting studies on children with hyperlexia. Some doctors believe all hyperlexic children fall on the autism spectrum. I'm among those that believe not all hyperlexia cases are autistic. Although some display 'autistic-like' traits and behaviors, they sometimes gradually fade as a child gets older," Dr. Conway pauses, allowing her diagnosis to settle in. "Are you familiar with the autism spectrum?"

Hamilton nods, and I answer, "I've read a lot about it in my teacher education courses, and we have a close friend with a son on the spectrum."

"Have you witnessed any 'autism-like' behaviors in her?" The doctor leans back in her large, burgundy, leather chair, steepling her hands in front of her.

Hamilton's worried eyes dart to mine. While staring at him, I search my memories. I shake my head when I look back to Dr. Conway.

"I want to be clear; I do not believe Liberty is on the spectrum," Dr. Conway smiles. "We may find some behaviors as we observe her more closely, but I feel these are not permanent behaviors. I'd like for both of you to keep a journal or notes on your cell phones. Note anything you feel is odd or not her normal behaviors. Also note if she is tired, hungry, scared, over-stimulated…any shifts in her environment. This will allow us to uncover trends, triggers, and situations that bring certain behaviors."

Placing her forearms on the desk between us, she continues, "Liberty is a delightful young lady. She didn't shy away from strangers or our strange office situation. While her ability to choose and speak words is advanced for her young age, they are normal for conversation. What I mean is, I don't find that she misuses words or struggles to express herself. She seems to understand the meaning of words and uses them correctly." The doctor smiles while shaking her head. "During our play time, she began asking my staff questions. She wanted to know why doctors wanted to play with her and if they liked Spiderman."

I pinch my lips between my teeth. That's our girl, always wanting to learn.

"We allowed her to choose the first book to read. Then, to ensure she hadn't memorized it as it had been read to her in the past, we chose two other books. She *can* read, and when asked questions about her reading, she seems to comprehend as she reads. This is important, because many children with hyperlexia can read most books placed in front of them, but they do not understand what they read."

"Checking for understanding," I whisper.

Hamilton leans forward, turning his head to mine in question.

"Yes," Dr. Conway confirms. "It's important that we check for understanding while Liberty reads. As she selects chapter books, we need to pause and check for understanding often."

"So..." I need to verify my understanding. "We should work with vocabulary words, context clues, and check for understanding, just like a teacher does for the appropriate level she is reading?"

"Yes," Dr. Conway affirms. "With your education and that of your nanny that Taylor mentioned, I feel confident. Liberty is lucky the adults in her life are equipped to nurture and challenge her. Hamilton, I'm sure this seems confusing, but it's easy."

"I…" He runs both hands through his long, dark waves. "I just need to know Liberty is okay."

I place my hand on his bouncing knee.

"Hamilton," Dr. Conway's soft voice soothes, "Liberty is a healthy girl on target in every area we observed today. Often hyperlexic children shy away from peers. They prefer interacting with adults over playing with children. Liberty quickly introduced herself to the two children in the playroom. She picked up toys and joined right in, even with adults still in the room. We also assessed her motor skills. Many times gifted or advanced children exhibit slower physical abilities than peers. Liberty did not display this. Physically, she is on track if not a bit more coordinated than her peers. Perhaps this is hereditary as her father is a talented athlete."

I find myself biting my lips again as the doctor's cheeks pink when Hamilton's crooked smile dazzles her. *My man is quite the charmer.*

"It's clear the two of you challenge her both physically and intellectually." Dr. Conway glances at the notes in front of her before continuing. "I don't like to label children, especially those under the age of seven. When you go home and look up hyperlexia on the internet, you will see the terms advanced, gifted, talented, savant, Mensa, and many others. You will read about IQ levels and their meanings. Labels tend to place children on one targeted path rather than allow them to just be kids. It's important to expose children to normal childhood activities, even if they show a propensity to excel in an area. In the past, some of my patient's families opted to begin testing the child immediately. Often, these children are then guided down one narrow path based on one facet of their abilities instead of allowing others to further develop. As Liberty enters kindergarten, it will be important to discuss her abilities with educators, but until then, I believe it is important that, while nurturing her talents, we continue to challenge her in a variety of subjects and activities. Well-rounded children become well-rounded adults that thrive in our society."

"So, we should continue to take her to playgroup, tumbling, and swimming lessons while we encourage her to read and ask her questions while doing so?" Hamilton inquires.

"Exactly," Dr. Conway states. "Remember to take notes should any difficulties arise so we might evaluate these situations, but otherwise, raise her like a normal little girl. Her diagnosis of Hyperlexia Type 3 doesn't need to disrupt her normal childhood."

"Would it be possible to get a copy of your notes and diagnosis to share with our nanny?" I ask, wanting Fallon to have everything. With her training, she will understand all of this even more than I do.

"If you'd like, you can sign a form allowing us to share all our records with her now and in the future," Dr. Conway offers. "It's my understanding she's working on her graduate degree in psychology."

I nod.

"I'll have my receptionist get the appropriate signatures." She jots a few notes on the pad in front of her.

"Fallon, our nanny, seemed very excited when I told her we had an appointment with you. Seems you come highly recommended," I share. You never know if Fallon might need Dr. Conway's help furthering her career, so I want to place a seed for future use.

"Taylor speaks highly of Fallon," she informs us. "You hit the nanny jackpot with that one. I would like for Fallon to join you on future office visits. She is an important part of Liberty's daily life and including her will also help Liberty."

As our appointment wraps up, a million thoughts fly through my mind. I want to rush home to scour the internet but know that will only further overwhelm me. I'm sure Hamilton has a million questions, too.

"Let's go find Liberty," the doctor suggests, rising from her office chair and motioning us towards the door.

She points out the observation window through which we see our daughter building a block tower with another girl. A boy sits nearby with a toy truck in his hands.

When we enter the playroom, Liberty immediately glances in our direction. "Mommy, Daddy watch!" She points to the tower of blocks. "Go!"

At her signal, she and the other girl scoot back from the tower as the boy rams his metal truck into its base. Blocks tumble to the carpet below as all three kids cheer. Hamilton and I join the other adults in the room in clapping.

"Libby, it's time to go," Hamilton calls to her.

"Bye," she waves to the children then to the adults. "This was fun."

Hamilton looks to me wide-eyed and surprised by her comment. While we stressed as parents over the doctor's analysis, our little girl had fun. She didn't find the doctor's questions or tasks stressful.

"Let's go home and have more fun with Daddy," I encourage as we each take her little hands in the hallway.

CHAPTER 39

Hamilton

"We're all loaded," I announce from the kitchen island when Liberty and Madison emerge from the restroom. "Are we ready?"

"I'm ready," Liberty states while Madison slips her winter coat over her arms.

"Are you sure you have the dogs' schedule straightened out?" Madison asks, pulling out her Notes app on her cell phone. She scrolls through her massive list for this trip to ensure we aren't forgetting anything.

"Yep. The guys know we are gone and plan to check in on them extra times to keep them from getting bored," I restate for the third time today. "Would you like a water for the road?" I ask as I pull one for me from the refrigerator door. When she nods, I grab her one.

"Okay, let's hit the road," I cheer, motioning for Liberty to lead the way to the elevator.

Now five hours into our nearly seven-hour drive, I long to stop and stretch my legs, but I don't want to wake a napping Liberty. We've stopped once to eat and use the restroom; it's my hope that we can make it the next hour and a half before we must stop again.

"Do you mind if I change the station?" I ask Madison.

She's typing away on her laptop, so I assume she won't mind if I turn it to country music. Singing along with my favorite songs will help to take my mind off of my squirming legs and tight back. I don't mind her pop music and rock stations, but for this last leg of the trip, I need to hear Luke Bryan, Blake Shelton, Luke Combs, Jason Aldean, and maybe a little Carrie Underwood. The first station I scan to is just what I'm looking for.

While Madison dives deeper into her writing, my mind sings along as we head down the interstate. They're expecting snow later tonight, but so far, Mother Nature gifts us with clear roads.

The music worked. I gently nudge Madison in the passenger seat, alerting her we have arrived. She places her closed laptop on the floorboard before stretching her arms above her head and her legs out in front of her. I force myself to keep my eyes on the city streets when all I want is to knead my hands into her muscles and help her relieve the tension.

"Sorry, I fell asleep," her raspy voice croaks before she takes a sip of her water. Looking out the front window, it dawns on her where we are. "We're here!"

She bounces in her seat like a red, rubber ball. Christmas is her favorite holiday and spending it with family is her new favorite tradition. I love that after so many years, she's surrounded by friends and family at all times.

"Liberty," she calls into the back seat while tugging on her little arm. "Liberty, we're here."

I see a bit of movement from her car seat in the rear-view mirror and the sound of clapping fills the air.

As soon as the SUV parks, Liberty announces she needs to potty at the top of her lungs. Maybe I should have stopped an hour ago. I hope she can make it past everyone inside before she has an accident.

"I'll carry her in real quick while you say hello to everyone," I offer. "Then, she can come back out and say her hellos."

Madison nods as we step from the vehicle. Cameron, Taylor, and Trenton swarm us to assist with unloading.

"Cameron, potty!" Liberty demands.

"I've got her," Cameron states, briskly crossing the porch with Liberty in hand.

I rub my hand down my face as I slowly shut the bedroom door behind me. Madison's sleepy eyes greet me from her former bed. I tug my t-shirt off over my head. When my eyes reconnect with hers, I find the laziness replaced with desire. I can't help myself. My shoulders straighten and my abdominals tighten. Subconsciously, my body reacts to her need, her want, and her invitation.

As I approach the bed, she extends her right hand. Fingers entwined with mine, she pulls me next to her as she slides to the other side of the bed.

"What a mess," she murmurs. "I've never seen so many presents in all my life."

"We went a little overboard," I confess.

"I think they all did," she laughs. "We'll need to set limits for next year."

It was worth it to see the excitement on Liberty's little face. Her eyes danced while inspecting each new gift-wrapped box in front of her. She delighted in the possibilities hidden in each. At first, she tried to neatly pull the paper from the gifts, then Trenton's sons demonstrated the fastest way to rip the paper from the boxes. She giggled and cheered as the scraps of paper piled up and new toys, books, and clothes stacked around her.

"She was fun to watch," Madison states, reading my mind.

"That she was. Mom and Amy seemed to have a good time, too," I add.

Madison nods, a wide smile slipping upon her lips. She's up to something—I squint my eyes at her.

"I have one more gift for you," Madison whispers.

"Oh, you do, do you?" I growl, positioning myself in a plank position over her.

She bobs her head up and down while biting her lower lip, eyes looking up at me through her lashes. My hands slip under the hem of her t-shirt, tickling the skin near her navel.

"As of tonight," she pauses her whisper, hoping for a dramatic effect, "we are officially baby-making."

Giggles escape from her as I swiftly free her from her sleep shorts and t-shirt. I'm a man on a mission.

The End

THE LOCALS SERIES CONCLUDES IN

**Tailgates & Twists of Fate,
The Locals #4.**

TRIVIA

1. Athens, Missouri is a fictitious town. There was once a township of Athens, but I could find no town.

1. The first and last names of *ALL* characters in this book are the names of towns in Missouri. (Except McGee & Indiana the dogs)

1. Haley Rhoades is my penname. I created it using the maiden names of my great-grandmother and great-great-grandmother on my father's side of our family.

ARE YOU SOCIAL?

Keep up on the latest news and new releases
from Haley Rhoades

Please consider leaving a quick review
by using the links at the end of
About the Author page of the eBook.

ABOUT THE AUTHOR

Haley Rhoades's writing is another bucket-list item coming to fruition, just like meeting Stephen Tyler and skydiving. As she continues to write romance and young adult books, she plans to complete her remaining bucket-list items, including ghost-hunting, storm-chasing, and bungee jumping. She is a Netflix-binging, Converse-wearing, avidly-reading, traveling geek.

A team player, Haley thrived as her spouse's career moved the family of four eight times to three states. One move occurred eleven days after a C-section. Now with two adult sons, Haley copes with her newly emptied nest by writing and spoiling Nala, her Pomsky. A fly on the wall might laugh as she talks aloud to her fur-baby all day long.

Haley's under five-foot, fun-size stature houses a full-size attitude. Her uber-competitiveness in all things entertains, frustrates, and challenges family and friends. Not one to shy away from a dare, she faces the consequences of a lost bet no matter the humiliation. Her fierce loyalty extends from family, to friends, to sports teams.

Haley's guilty pleasures are Lifetime and Hallmark movies. Her other loves include all things peanut butter, *Star*

Wars, mathematics, and travel. Past day jobs vary tremendously from an elementary special-education para-professional, to a YMCA sports director, to a retail store accounting department, and finally a high school mathematics teacher.

Haley resides with her husband and fur-baby in the Kansas City area. This Missouri-born girl enjoys the diversity the Midwest offers.

Reach out on Facebook, Twitter, Instagram, or her website…she would love to connect with her readers.

- amazon.com/author/haleyrhoades
- goodreads.com/HaleyRhoadesAuthor
- bookbub.com/authors/haley-rhoades
- facebook.com/Haley-Rhoades-1658656934155858
- twitter.com/HaleyRhoadesBks
- instagram.com/haleyrhoadesauthor
- pinterest.com/haleyrhoadesaut

Made in United States
North Haven, CT
16 April 2024